ELECTRIC DREAMS

ELECTRIC DREAMS

A novel

Goutham Rao

Lake Dallas, Texas

FIRST EDITION

This is a work of fiction, and is not intended to resemble anyone living or dead.

Requests for permission to reprint or reuse material from this work should be sent to:

Permissions
Madville Publishing
PO Box 358
Lake Dallas, TX 75065

Cover Design: Kimberly Davis
Author Photo:

ISBN: 978-1-963695-23-6 paperback
978-1-963695-24-3 ebook

Library of Congress Control Number: 2025932285

*To all those with creative passions
waiting to be unleashed.*

1. THE STRIKE

A steady rain fell. Simon heard a low-pitched hum outside. It sounded ominous, but Simon's colleague Anuja was unfazed. The thunder was so loud, it sounded like it was targeting Newell. Flashes of lightning appeared several times a minute. Some looked like they were striking near a small hill only blocks away. Then the lights went out.

"Oh, God. That happens a lot here unfortunately," Anuja said. "This doesn't happen too often in Boston, I imagine?"

"No, not too often. At least it's daytime. We should probably go now. No point sitting here. Hopefully, they have power up in one of the buildings up the hill," Simon said.

"I didn't even bring an umbrella. Is that one yours?" Anuja pointed to an old, long umbrella in the corner.

"No, I don't know who that belongs to. But I'll use it and bring the car around."

Anuja and Simon emerged onto the steps in front of the Jarvis Writing Center and stood under an awning as sheets of rain fell so hard it was sometimes difficult to see the other side of the street.

Simon opened the umbrella. "I'm going to go for it. See you in a couple of minutes."

Rather than run, Simon walked briskly, since the rain made it so hard to see and he was afraid of slipping and falling. The thunder and lightning continued. As he stepped out onto the street, both he and Anuja witnessed a lightning bolt strike a power line some distance away on top of a hill. Part of it exploded into a shower of silver sparks. Simon paused for only a few seconds to observe it. Next, that archetype of bad luck actually happened. The bolt of lightning didn't hit Simon. Based on Anuja's observation, it appeared to strike a light pole across the street, and a much smaller branch emanating from it hit the top of Simon's umbrella. There was an immediate loud pop.

Simon felt himself being thrust forward at an unbelievable pace. He looked downward to see himself moving across the street below him so fast that the median line was just a blur. He was airborne, and his feet tingled. He saw the laces on his shoes standing up. His black curly hair stood up. Even the hairs on his short, scruffy beard were erect. Then, with a huge thud, he was somewhere—he wasn't sure where, as he could see nothing. There was nothing but pitch darkness—no light and no sound at all. He thought his eyes were closed and that he just needed to pry them open. So he tried moving his right hand up to his face, but found he couldn't move at all. Both the intention and energy to move his arms were there, but they wouldn't budge. He turned his head from side to side, a bit panicked, as he wanted to see something. There was nothing but darkness.

Finally, after what felt like several minutes, he heard a high-pitched hum in his right ear, faint at first, then slowly, second by second, increasing in intensity. Soon, it was very loud, and then, unbearable. His right ear hurt and then the whole right side of his head hurt. He opened his mouth to scream, and he believed he did, but could not hear himself. The pain grew in intensity, and he could feel the bones of his face begin to vibrate. His teeth began to chatter. He thought he saw some light appear in the distance, but it faded away fast.

Simon was in agony and unable to move. It had to end soon, he thought. After all, doesn't all intense pain end soon, or at least get better?

Next came another intense popping sound and Simon lost consciousness. He fell into what felt like a conventional sleep. He even dreamed. The dream he had was about numbers going wrong. There were sequences of numbers in his dream: 147876, 356348. The trouble was that the numbers were wrong. He knew they were wrong, and others told him they were wrong. His boss Margaret Friedlander appeared in his dream, reminding him that the numbers were wrong and that he needed to fix them. It was a nonsensical, anxiety-filled dream of the type he had suffered many times before.

The numbers were followed by something he had never dreamt about. Music played in his dream. He heard a guitar and a piano. Something was off. There were notes out of sequence. Something was out of tune. Once again, he was responsible for the corrections. It wasn't clear who was making the music, but he saw his landlord Anna in his dream, upset that the music wasn't quite right. Next appeared his mother. She was young in the dream, wearing a flowery dress. She raised her slender right arm and pointed at Simon and then to a dark corner from which the music was coming. She said nothing, but Simon understood—she wanted him to fix the music somehow.

The music stopped and then Simon's father appeared in his dream. Simon was a grown man, but his father was young, just as he was when he died. Simon was playing catch with his father in their backyard, so small a yard that throwing the baseball hard or far wasn't possible. But Simon still had trouble catching the ball. His father would lob it. Simon's timing was always a little off, so that he either dropped the ball, caught it awkwardly in his glove, or missed it completely, which surprised him each time. Simon's father said nothing but was getting frustrated. This seemed to go on for some time, and at some point, Simon and his father weren't playing catch, not in the backyard, but in an expansive field at Newell. There they were separated by a considerable distance and the throwing improved a lot. Simon threw the ball hard and his father caught it each time. Within a few minutes, he was able to do the same. He could see even from a distance that his father was smiling.

Quite abruptly, playing catch ended, and Simon felt like he was accelerating above the ground, much like he was just after he was struck. The sensation of speed was intense. Air whizzed by his ear, which in the dream, no longer hurt. At some point, a building approached, and Simon feared a deadly collision. He could see that it was the large Newell Science and Engineering building. A gust of wind pushed him upwards. He could hear it against his feet. Within a few seconds, he was passing over the building and kept climbing higher and higher. He started to feel cold and wet. He could see only clouds, and he began to shiver. His feet and hands began to tingle. He wished to return to earth, and then he felt like he was waking up, only to return to the ground where he was being chastised by many people about faulty numbers.

The dream appeared to repeat itself, each time with small variations. The numbers were different. The music was different. In some iterations, he was floating above the clouds quite peacefully and felt warm instead of cold. The dream cycle continued so often that Simon, in his dream, began counting how many times the Science and Engineering building appeared, and how often he saw his mother and father.

2. NEWELL: THE ARRIVAL

Simon didn't choose to work at Newell. Compared to Boston, Newell, both the college and the town, he anticipated, would be dull and provincial. He was knowledgeable and conscientious in his old job, but his introverted personality left him stranded near the bottom rungs of both the social and academic ladders. He left Boston, not in disgrace, but in an inconsequential whimper— largely invisible. No party was thrown for him. Indeed, his departure was barely noticed. Even his own elderly mother was indifferent as to why he was leaving and where he was heading.

Simon's arrival was as inconspicuous as his departure. It was a cold, rainy December afternoon when he drove into town in his Volkswagen, a car he feared would break down at some point on the six-hundred-mile journey. He drove around surveying the town for nearly an hour. The main street by the college was quite charming, he concluded. The rest of the town looked a bit dilapidated, old houses crumbling after generations of transitory students. There were the expected coffee shops and boutiques, standard fixtures in any college town. He saw a few students gathered outside a taco joint, apparently so popular and full they were forced to wait outside for a table. He had seen enough after thirty minutes to say to himself, "Newell is a bit of a hole."

Simon drove along small side streets, hoping that one would lead him to a charming park or something else through which Newell could redeem itself. There were parks, of course, but he found none of them charming. Next would come his apartment, which he dreaded seeing. He found the place on the Internet. It was really just the basement of an old house, owned by an older Polish woman whose husband had recently passed away. She seemed decent enough on the phone, but Simon still worried that his rental would fall below acceptable standards. It wasn't a lack of cleanliness he feared, but rather, if the place would be freezing or boiling, dark, or simply so depressing it could never serve as a suitable retreat from the dreary town and college.

The apartment was located at number 33, on the unimaginatively named "C" street. The house looked to be in better shape than its neighbors. He rang the doorbell. He could hear footsteps approaching slowly. A pale, stout, stern looking woman in her sixties greeted him.

"Mrs. Dabrowski? Simon, the new tenant."

His new landlord took a good look at Simon, perhaps expecting someone younger.

"Okay, good, Anna Dabrowski. Hang on, I will get the keys."

Anna led Simon to a basement door under the front porch. The apartment had just two main rooms—a living area with a small kitchen and a bedroom, along with a bathroom equipped with a shower but no tub. It was furnished as Anna had promised but the furnishings were dismal, almost certainly discards from upstairs. Nothing looked to be less than thirty years old. There was a window in the bedroom. Other than that, the place was quite dark. All things considered, it was about what Simon expected.

"This looks fine," he told Anna. He had already paid a deposit for first and last month's rent of $1000.

"Good. These are your keys. One is for upstairs. Hope you can look out for my place when I'm gone."

Though never mentioned during their phone call or email communications, this seemed like a reasonable request.

"I can do that no problem."

"Good. Next rent is due January 1. The garage is for my car. There's only room for one. You'll have to park on the street."

Again, these conditions were acceptable to Simon. Anna went back to her place immediately.

Simon unloaded his car. Nearly half of it was full of books, most about writing. He planned to use them or recommend them to clients of the Jarvis Center. Simon had just one old suitcase full of clothes which he unpacked quickly and placed in a decent order in the old wood dresser in the bedroom. Apart from that were a couple of boxes, one with kitchen things, the other with miscellany—toothbrushes, some cleaners, a Bluetooth speaker among them. He unloaded this box a bit more carefully, unsure where to place the eclectic mix of items. Then he sat on the couch in the living area, a fine specimen from the 1970s with a musty odor and a few dark stains on the cushions, the origins of which he decided not to think too much about. No television came with the apartment, and Simon didn't own one. He grew restless after a few minutes and decided to explore the town.

3. BEGINNINGS

Simon grew up in New Bedford where his father Luis Galves worked as a bartender in an establishment that catered to a largely Portuguese clientele. Simon had no siblings. He had no pets. His father left for work shortly after Simon returned from school in the afternoons and worked Saturdays as well. He set aside some time Sunday afternoons to spend with his son, usually after church, where he heard many good Catholics were doing the same thing. Luis was not a natural family man and the expected one or two hours were uncomfortable for him. Simon's passion was baseball. He loved the Red Sox. Luis promised him he would take him to a game at some point, but whenever Simon brought it up, the response was always that the cost, the drive, the hassle was all too much "right now." Simon didn't attend a game until he was in college.

Simon had a few close friends when he was very young but was almost always under the watchful eye of his mother—an aloof Irish-born woman whose capacity for affection was quite limited. Luis's routine was to return from work around one a.m. and fall asleep on the couch with the television on. He snored loudly, sometimes alarmingly so, seeming to make the whole house shake. There were often lengthy pauses in the snoring, which even as a young boy, made Simon wonder what was going on downstairs.

One night when he was seven years old the snoring was especially loud—loud enough to wake Simon up. He followed its steady rhythm for a couple of minutes, hoping his father would stop and he could get back to sleeping. Instead, he heard a few loud gasps and then nothing at all. Simon fell asleep again, but for some reason awoke around five a.m. Perturbed by the unusual silence downstairs, he headed down to the couch where his father was cold and still. He ran up and retrieved his mother, who came down and felt Luis's forehead and right hand.

"He is dead," she said nonchalantly.

Simon had no experience with death and at his tender age, wasn't entirely clear about what she meant.

"So he can't move?"

"He's never going to move again, Simon. He's passed on to heaven." Helen remained unemotional, as if what had transpired was expected and routine. "We need to call the hospital."

"He was snoring, Mother. Then he stopped."

"You should have woken me up then, Simon."

Helen called a local ambulance service and a couple of unrushed paramedics arrived a few minutes later to confirm her finding. Simon watched them as they quickly zipped his father's body into a bag, loaded it onto a stretcher, and were gone. The empty couch still smelled of his father and he could see a few of his dark hairs on the pillow on which he laid his head.

The funeral was two days later. It was deliberately arranged by Helen as a very modest affair, as she couldn't afford much, and also seemed to want to get it over with as quickly as possible. A priest said a few kind words and shortly thereafter Luis was laid to rest in Sacred Heart Cemetery.

4. HELEN AND SIMON

So it became just Simon and Helen. Simon was more confused than mournful. He and his father had never been close. He wasn't sure how to digest the countless expressions of sympathies from teachers, classmates, and neighbors. Even clients of the bar would stop by, some with small toys, shake Simon's little hand and say, "Sorry for your loss," or even its Portuguese equivalent, "*Sinto muito por sua perda.*" The man who slept on the couch and spent a couple of reluctant hours with him on Sundays was gone, and Simon's mother was fully in control. She mourned, but mostly she worried, worried about being alone and worried about money. Her uncongenial disposition left her with no real friends. Her family in Ireland was distant both physically and emotionally. Instead, it was Simon who was forced to fill the void.

"It's just you and me now Simon. You're the man of the house," she said to skinny little Simon as he came downstairs for breakfast one morning in his Spider-Man pajamas. "It's a tough world out there. I will look out for you, Simon, and as you get older, you will look out for your mother. Do you understand?"

Simon just nodded, not understanding what dangers Helen was referring to and how he and his mother would protect each other. Nevertheless, with his father gone, he understood that he had entered into some sort of new pact with his mother.

Helen got a job cleaning nearby motels which kept her occupied in the mornings. She returned early in the afternoons to wait for her son to return from school. There would be no playing after school. She prepared for him a list of duties which she wrote each day and pinned to Simon's bedroom door. Some were unique to that day, others, reminders of what had to be carried out regularly.

Water the flowers in the backyard.

Check the mousetraps in the basement.

Go to the corner store for a pound of butter. The money is on the kitchen table.

Finish your homework.

Tidy up the dining table for dinner.

Around five o'clock, Simon was permitted to watch a little television. He usually chose cartoons. Then he retreated to his bedroom until seven, when dinner was served. Helen was a lousy cook. Dinner was something cheap with packaged and processed origins—Hamburger Helper, macaroni and cheese, or Chef Boyardee spaghetti with meatballs. She said almost nothing during dinner, and Simon learned to keep quiet as well. Afterward, he retreated to his bedroom to finish his homework. Lights were out at exactly nine p.m.

This continued for years, only the chores expanded in scope and complexity. When he was ten, Helen stopped paying an older boy to mow the front and back lawns. Instead, she instructed the teen to teach Simon how to start and stop the mower. He learned quickly.

By age eleven, Helen told him the bills were piling up and that it would be best if he earned a little extra money by mowing other people's lawns in addition to their own. She didn't tell Simon how to go about setting this up, only that he needed to get started as soon as possible. It was spring and grass was growing quickly. Simon went door to door, knocking on the doors of houses he knew had elderly occupants, for they might have more need of his services, but also may be more sympathetic to a scrawny kid offering to mow a lawn to help his mother. Within a day or so he had six clients, enough for about sixty dollars per week, a sizeable amount in those days. Helen demanded every penny.

Simon wasn't born with an awkward disposition. He grew into it. The never-ending chores kept him away from other children his age. There was always the persistent guilt of being away from his mother. From time to time, a neighborhood boy would invite him to play basketball. He would venture to the court, but within fifteen or twenty minutes, worry what his mother would think. "I've got to go back and check with my mother," he would say, knowing full well he wouldn't return to play.

The awkward boy became an even more awkward teen. There were no sports, musical instruments, or clubs for him. Apart from school, his duty was to help his mother.

He was allowed one indulgence. On Saturdays, his mother took him to the public library, where she read a Dublin newspaper. He was permitted, with his own card, to check out a few books. Simon became a fan of science fiction, especially the works of Ray Bradbury. He read *Fahrenheit 451*, of course, along with the *Martian Chronicles*. When he was thirteen, he discovered *Dandelion Wine*, an earlier and lesser-known Bradbury work, which had nothing to do with science fiction. It described a twelve-year-old boy growing up in a small town, a childhood which in many ways was a happier version of Simon's. Books became his escape from his lonely, unnatural life and he read voraciously. It was one of the few activities his mother didn't seem to object to.

Simon became more independent in high school. He started to push back on his mother's strong desire for control. "I've got too much homework. I will mow Mrs. Shea's lawn tomorrow," he would inform her.

His independent streak first caught Helen off guard. Then she became angry, which didn't seem to change Simon's attitude. What worked, as it often does in many mother-son relationships, is guilt.

"I guess your busy life is more important now than your own mother," she would say.

Simon could sense she was being manipulative but also sensed that she genuinely felt neglected when her wishes were not met. He would succumb if he could. If not, he would promise to do better by her.

Evenings at home were so dull, Simon decided to spend them at the public library—reading or doing his homework. This arrangement troubled Helen a great deal. It was Simon's duty, after all, to keep his mother company even if there were no chores to be done. Simon presented to her a cogent argument. She did little in the evenings except have dinner and watch television. He could easily prepare dinner for both of them after school, and take his share with him, as the library had a small room where eating was permitted. He presented this plan to her, not seeking her advice, but rather to rationalize a decision he had already made.

She was, as expected, unconvinced. "If your father were alive, he wouldn't let you run off wherever you like, you know?"

"That's not true. He was never here in the evenings," he replied.

She glared at him, knowing she was defeated.

5. MIA

Simon's interest in evenings at the library were not entirely academic. He was in the eleventh grade and a girl from the tenth grade whom he had, at least from a distance, grown fond of, also spent her evenings there. Her name was Mia, a cute Portuguese girl with black curly hair and big glasses. For a couple of months, Simon and Mia exchanged nothing more than glances and smiles. Then Simon worked out how to have a proper conversation. He even wrote it down.

Offer her a stick of gum.

Ask her if she has Mrs. Rodney for English—(He knew she had because he saw her emerging from Mrs. Rodney's classroom.)

Then ask her about her favorite subjects.

Then ask her about her favorite books.

Then tell her about my favorite books.

Mia was easy to approach. She could always be found in the same place, in a big wooden chair, legs stretched and propped on a window ledge. She also smiled a lot, which put Simon at ease.

He glanced at her and she smiled. Then he walked over.

"Want a stick of gum?"

"Thanks, but no, I'm good."

"Are you in Mrs. Rodney's class? I had her for English."

"Yeah, I am. Seriously cool lady."

"What are your favorite subjects at school?" Simon fired off his next question like he was doing an interview for a high school newspaper.

"Oh, English and history, yours?"

Simon was seriously thrown off. He stuck with his original plan.

"Well, what are your favorite books?"

"Well, I don't have, like, one favorite. I like *Trying Out*. It's a book about cheerleaders."

"Oh, okay. My favorite book is *Dandelion Wine* by Ray Bradbury."

"Okay, and what's your fave class?"

Simon became nervous but took a deep breath and thought for a moment. "Oh, English, of course. Yes, definitely."

"Cool. And what's your name by the way?"

"Simon, sorry, should have said that before."

"That's okay. I'm Mia. Thanks for coming over, okay?"

"Thank you. Well, I'm going to go back over there and finish my homework."

"Yes, sure. Stop by again whenever."

Simon saw Mia every weekday at the library. More awkward encounters followed. He was smitten but for the longest time never ventured past a discussion of books and teachers. On occasion he tried helping her with her homework. This meant sitting next to her, the closest he had been to a girl. She smelled nice, he thought to himself.

It was Mia who finally broke through the continued awkwardness. "Why do you come to the library every day? Too loud at home?"

"No, too quiet actually."

"I don't get it."

"Just me and my mom. It's boring there. She doesn't talk much."

"Okay. And what about your dad?"

"He died when I was seven."

"I'm so sorry to hear that."

Simon was uncomfortable with the focus on him. "You? Why do you come here every day?"

"Kind of the same. There's actually no one at home. My parents work late. I have a brother who is in college now. Do you have any siblings?"

"No, I don't. Just me and mom."

"Do you have a lot of friends?" Mia asked.

"Not really. Not at all, really."

"I used to have a lot, but too much drama with a lot of them. You know what I mean?

"I guess I know what you mean," Simon responded.

"It's harder to make new friends in high school," Mia said.

Simon started to feel more at ease with Mia and, at that moment, decided to offer a sincere complement.

"I'm surprised you say that. You're so nice and pretty. I thought everyone would want to be your friend."

Mia blushed and took some time to regain her composure. "Thank you, Simon. I think you're a nice guy, too. I won't call you pretty. So I'll just say you're 'cute.'"

Simon didn't know how to react. To that point in his life, he had never received a compliment like that. His mother had never told him she thought he was nice, only that he was late, or falling short in some other way. He was skeptical. "Oh, you don't have to say that. You don't have to say nice things about me."

"Why not? You can say nice things about me and I can't say nice things about you? That doesn't make sense. Did you mean what you said?"

"I did."

"So, like, we're both just saying what we feel then."

Simon said nothing. It was all a lot to digest. There were many more meaningful conversations in the weeks and months that followed. Simon and Mia began sitting together. Simon would share his dinner on occasion in the break room. Mia became his only close friend.

"I told my mom and dad about you. They want you to come over for dinner sometime."

"Really?"

"Yeah, really. I told them how you've helped me so much with my English class. They'd like to meet you."

While Simon was excited by the invitation, the necessary arrangements caused him some anxiety. Mia and her family dined late—after eight p.m. He normally returned home before that time, which is when his mother expected him. Dinner was set for Thursday evening, when Mia's father, an accountant, would be home relatively early. Simon would have to make a special arrangement.

"I'm going to be late tonight," he announced to his mother Thursday morning as he left for school.

"Why?"

"Got some work and other stuff going on," he responded.

Helen sighed and said, "Don't be too late though. Tomorrow is a school day."

Around seven that evening, Simon entered a household quite unlike his own. Mia's mother Theresa greeted him warmly. Her father Richard shook his hand.

"I hear you like science fiction," Richard said. "I loved it when I was your age. Not as much of it back then though."

Simon didn't know what to expect and Mia's family's friendliness made him very shy.

Mia helped him out.

"He's very shy, Mom," she whispered to her mother in the kitchen. "It will take him a while to open up."

13

"He seems very sweet," Theresa responded.

Dinner was far better than anything Simon could recall having—homemade lasagna, garlic bread, and a salad far fresher and tastier than the ones served in the high school cafeteria. Sensing he enjoyed the food, Theresa offered him seconds.

"Yes, please. It's really great," he responded.

"What time are you due home?" Theresa asked.

"I don't know. I guess about nine or ten."

"Mia's dad can give you a lift home if you like."

"I'd be happy to, Simon," Richard added.

"No, thanks. I'll walk. It's not that far."

"We've really enjoyed having you over for dinner," Theresa said.

"This was great, Mrs. Fernandes. Thank you so much."

Mia looked very pleased about how it all turned out. "I won't be at the library tomorrow."

"Oh, why not?"

"We're going to Boston airport to pick up my brother. He has a one-week break from college."

"Okay. I'll miss seeing you there."

"Maybe when we get back from the airport, we can go out for ice cream?" Mia asked.

Simon had never received an invitation like that. In fact, he couldn't recall the last time he went out for ice cream. It may have been with his dad on one of their Sunday afternoons together. He froze for a moment.

"What, you don't want to go?" Mia asked.

"I do, for sure," Simon said. Again, the necessary arrangements caused a bit of stress. "I think it would be better if we went some other time though. Might be very late when you get back."

Mia reflected for a moment and respected his concern. "Okay, I get what you mean. That weekend might be better."

"Yes, definitely," Simon said. The weekend would give Simon time to make some sort of arrangement with his mother.

Theresa was washing dishes nearby and heard the conversation.

"Simon, give us your phone number. If you two want to go out for ice cream, she can call you Saturday or Sunday."

Simon did exactly that, thanked his hosts multiple times, gave Mia a hug, and walked home. The lights were off when he got there. As quietly as possible he entered and headed up to his room, thinking he had just had the most wonderful evening of his life.

6. SATURDAY MORNING PHONE CALL

The phone seldom rang. When it did it was either a solicitor, or on rare occasions Helen's boss from the cleaning company calling to change her schedule. But Simon was expecting a call from Mia that morning. Unfortunately, he was upstairs, unable to intercept the call before his mother. He rushed down and stood quietly biting his lower lip as she answered. It was actually Theresa.

"Good morning, Mrs. Galves. This is Theresa, Mia's mother."

"Who?" Helen glanced over at Simon with a confused look. He extended his hand and whispered that he was willing to take the phone. Instead, Helen turned away and held the phone tightly to her ear.

"Mia. Simon's friend," Theresa clarified.

"I don't know a friend of Simon named Mia, sorry."

"Oh, okay. No problem. I have a son a few years older than Simon. Boys that age don't talk much. Just want to tell you how delighted we were to have Simon over for dinner the other night. He is a wonderful boy. You've done a great job."

"Have I really?" Helen sounded both confused and a bit angry at the same time.

"May I speak with Simon?"

"Of course."

Helen handed the phone to Simon, standing near the phone with her arms crossed, already disapproving of a situation she didn't fully understand. Rather than cowering before her, Simon glared at his mother, making it clear he was willing to accept whatever invitation was on offer. Theresa planned to take Mia and Simon out for ice cream that afternoon, after which, if Simon were able, they could also go to a movie by themselves. He thanked Theresa several times and hung up the phone hard, knowing that a combination of his mother's rage, self-pity, selfishness, and fear awaited him.

"Just like that. You're going to ignore your chores here just like that?"

"What chores, mother? Whatever it is, I'll do it now, okay?"

There weren't any chores to be done, and Helen came up with nothing. "When will you be back? In time for dinner?"

"I think so."

"What do you mean, you think so? You plan to be out all night?"

"Mother, how about in-between dinner and out all night?" Simon's clever response left Helen defeated. He retreated to his room, awaiting Theresa and Mia, who were due to pick him up at one p.m.

The afternoon would have been nothing special for most teens, but to Simon, it was the most fun he had ever had. Theresa left the pair to themselves. They watched the movie *La Bamba*, Mia's choice, and the first movie Simon had seen in a theater since his father took him to see *E.T.* when he was ten. Theresa dropped Simon off at home around seven, where he found his mother had heated up a frozen lasagna and was seated at the dining table waiting for him.

"How was your afternoon?"

"It was great, mother."

"That's so great to hear," Helen said, her tone cynical.

"What did you do this afternoon?"

"I took care of the house—laundry, sweeping, dusting, general cleaning." It was a very obvious attempt to make Simon feel guilty.

He shot back. "Why didn't you ask me to help you with all that this morning?"

"Oh Simon, you were just so excited to spend the day with your girlfriend. Why would I want to burden you with your chores?" She sounded more cynical than before.

"She's just my friend, not my girlfriend, and I didn't spend the whole day with her. I was here all morning and could have helped you out." Simon was unaccustomed to raising his voice, which had reached its adult tenor a couple of years earlier, but growing annoyed, he became louder. Helen looked downward, seeming not to wish to escalate the confrontation. She finished her dinner quickly and retreated to her bedroom to watch TV. Simon cleaned up.

7. DR. COATES

Helen had always suffered some sort of pain, something Luis heard much about during the ten years they were married. Whether the pain was physical, mental or both, neither he nor anyone else, Simon included, was sure. She visited Dr. Coates often. Her medicine cabinet was full of painkillers, antidepressants, and anxiolytics. The combination changed as often as the seasons. Simon was well aware of the pharmacopeia at home, though never sure of Helen's diagnoses. He dared not ask. So it was very unusual one afternoon after school, two months after he had gone to the movies with Mia, when Helen insisted he accompany her to Dr. Coates's office.

"Why do you want me to come?"

"So we can both hear his instructions. I want you to know what I've been through and what I'm still going through."

Simon did what he asked and found himself sitting in Dr. Coates's waiting room next to his solemn mother, her arms crossed. The waiting room was full of elderly patients.

"Helen Galves?" The nurse called her in. Simon stayed put, but Helen nodded at him, making it clear he should accompany her.

Dr. Coates was a genial physician, about seventy years old. He had never met Simon before and began the encounter with a friendly introduction and some questions. His warmth reminded Simon of Mia's father.

"You're seventeen?"

"Yes, sir."

"So, you must be getting to that point then, where you have to figure out what you want to do?"

"I am. I want to go to college."

"Good for you. Any place at the top of your list?"

Simon had always considered Harvard at the top of his list but wasn't yet sure if he would apply, nor what his chances of admission might be. It wasn't something he ever discussed with his mother.

Before he could respond, Helen interjected. "Simon's very

attached to New Bedford. He doesn't want to go far. Maybe U. Mass or Bridgewater State." By U. Mass, Helen meant the Dartmouth campus, just up the road from home.

"Is that so?" Dr. Coates asked.

Simon just shrugged his shoulders. He had no intention of discussing loftier plans than Bridgewater State in front of his mother, who would be affronted just as she had been when he had spent the better part of a day with Mia.

Dr. Coates went over Helen's medications, discussing adjustments based on her response and preferences. Simon did think it was strange that his thin, forty-year-old mother was taking so much stuff. The discussion took considerable time, as Dr. Coates and Helen went back and forth about what she had already tried, what was the best time to take her medications, and what she could expect with the adjusted dosages.

Dr. Coates, who had many other patients to see, seemed eager to draw the encounter to a close. "So, we're all set then. Good. I'll see you in a couple of months."

Helen looked disapprovingly at Dr. Coates. "Anything you'd like my son to know?"

Dr. Coates appeared to think for a moment. "Oh yes, sorry. Simon, your mother has a number of issues with anxiety. It's something that has to be looked after well. Do you understand?"

Simon nodded.

"Good. You love your mother very much, I would imagine?"

"I do, doctor."

"Good. You've grown into a young man now. And she's very vulnerable. Not easy to come to a new country as a teenager. Not easy to lose her husband. So, she can be in a fragile state at times."

Dr. Coates glanced at Helen from time to time as he spoke, and she nodded in agreement. It was hard for Simon to imagine his mother as being in some sort of fragile emotional state.

"Do you understand, Simon?"

"I think I do."

"Good. Helen tells me you're out about the town in the evenings. That you've got a girlfriend you spend time with in the evenings."

Simon turned a little red. He was furious that his mother

would share such details of his personal life with her doctor. He felt the need to clarify. "I'm not out on the town, doctor. I just go to do my homework in the library with my friend."

Dr. Coates looked confused and turned to Helen. "That sounds very innocent, Helen. I can tell Simon is a very nice young man."

"Thanks, doctor," Simon said.

"Nevertheless, it would be best for your mother's health if you stayed home in the evenings. She is prone to panic attacks. Do you know what those are?"

"No."

"They can be quite serious. It's like an attack of anxiety."

Simon was skeptical. He had never witnessed his mother have an attack of any kind.

"Do you understand, Simon?"

"You think I should stay home, doctor?"

"I think that would be best for your mother. She feels very strongly about it."

Simon felt cornered. He suspected this was another elaborate way to manipulate him, but Helen had the support of her reputable doctor, whose judgment young Simon was in no position to question. "Dr. Coates. If my mother has one of these attacks, what should I do?"

"You can try to calm her down. Hold her hand. Ask her to lie down and tell her things will be okay. It will pass. That's not why she wants you to stay home. She's afraid she will have an attack if you leave. Knowing you are in the house is a type of prevention."

Simon was unfamiliar with these matters and just nodded politely.

Helen looked toward her son. "Thank you, Simon. I knew you would understand."

Simon's evenings in the library ended. He saw Mia often at school, who was quite upset by the change in arrangements. As a compromise, he invited Mia to spend time at his house in the evenings to do homework in the living room. She came only once.

Helen was unaccustomed to visitors. Mia introduced herself to Helen, who shook her hand limply. The whole experience was awkward. Helen sat at the kitchen table, while the youngsters sat on the floor, their books sprawled out in front of them. Neither felt comfortable discussing anything besides homework, and even that they only whispered back and forth. Helen said nothing to Mia's father when he picked her up outside.

Week by week, Mia grew more distant. Always smiling and warm toward Simon, but with no real opportunity to socialize outside school, and being a year behind, she gravitated to other friends, leaving poor Simon feeling miserable, alone, and indignant towards his mother.

8. LIFE IN NEWELL

Simon set out to find the necessities. First, he found a laundromat, as his apartment didn't come with a washer or dryer. Anna was unlikely to allow him to use hers. Next, he saw a barber shop that looked like it provided simple, no-frills haircuts.

Simon inquired about dining options at Newell. He needed a place to obtain regular meals for lunch and dinner. The uninspired meals his mother had provided as a boy had a lasting impact on him. He never learned to cook anything decent, and as he grew up, what he could find to eat outside the home was almost always better than Helen's offerings. The student facilities were not available to him. Newell had an elegant faculty club. Despite not being a faculty member, he was permitted to join, but with an annual membership fee of $1600 plus the cost of meals, it wasn't a reasonable option. He purchased a meal plan for Brandy's Café, a nice clean on-campus casual restaurant open all day. For $350 a month, he could get three preset meals daily, as well as a pleasant place to pass the time when he wasn't working.

Finally, Simon searched for a pub. There were a number of raucous student bars in Newell, not what he preferred. There were a couple of rundown seedy bars on the edge of town. These were equally uninviting. Eventually, Simon found St. James Ale House, a respectable and unostentatious establishment he could walk to from his home.

The pub, like Brandy's Café, would serve as a refuge from work and his apartment, but also, he hoped, as a place where he could meet other people who worked, rather than studied, at Newell.

Simon took great pride in not wasting time. He had arrived in Newell on Saturday afternoon. By Monday afternoon, he had found all that he believed he needed and even opened a bank account in town.

His job at The Jarvis Writing Center began Tuesday at nine a.m. The Center was a resource for Newell's graduate students to help them refine and improve their writing. Simon's title was "consultant," which meant he would meet with individual students one-on-one, after taking a look at their work. Referrals were made to Jarvis by faculty members, once they realized their students had difficulty expressing themselves on paper.

Newell wasn't unique in having such a resource. The quality of writing among young Americans has deteriorated over the past twenty years, not helped by the near universal use of shortcuts for written communication such as texts and emojis. Simon lamented this phenomenon like many others and had witnessed the problem getting steadily more serious.

In his early years as a writing instructor, students struggled with grammar and usage. By the time he arrived at Newell, the problem was much worse—many students had no idea how to begin writing a dissertation or other papers. One might think students in the physical sciences and engineering were especially prone to poor writing, but Simon believed that the writing of humanities students was just as awful. The difference was that humanities students were less likely to recognize and acknowledge the poor quality of their own writing.

Simon wouldn't have a boss, per se. Jarvis was "managed" by a woman named Margaret Friedlander, some sort of university administrator, who also managed other centers. She was rarely at Jarvis in person.

Jarvis consisted of little more than one office and a single meeting table. There were three consultants in all, including Simon, but almost never more than one in the Center at a time. Instead, the majority of meetings with students took place elsewhere, such as at Brandy's Café. Students booked an hour at a time, and Simon was expected to follow a set routine.

First, he would provide constructive feedback about the work he had received by email (at least a week in advance). The idea was to uncover common errors in grammar, usage, or most often, just a complete lack of clarity. After discussing common errors and ways to correct them, Simon shared a couple of pages he had edited. His job was not to rewrite significant portions of the students' work, but to "help them fix it themselves," according to Ms. Friedlander. During each meeting, Simon asked each student to correct a few paragraphs on site, after which he would review the improved work and make further suggestions. Finally, Simon prescribed resources intended to help each student.

All this was fine in principle, but based on his experience in Boston, Simon knew that many students lacked basic skills. He had, over the years, created a set of well-defined templates to help, which he adjusted based on the students' topics, like the example below. His goal was to help students organize their thoughts. Corrections to spelling, grammar, and usage would come later:

> First, define water pollution (one sentence).
> Second, describe, using numbers, how common water pollution is based on the definition above.
> Next, discuss the consequences of water pollution in detail.
> Then, discuss what laws are in place to prevent water pollution.
> Finally, discuss the impact of those laws over time.

About half of Jarvis clients were Chinese graduate students, the majority of whom were enrolled in programs in engineering, or the physical or biological sciences. Simon had a fair bit of experience with such students in Boston and felt very sympathetic to their struggles in writing in English. What he found harder to understand is that many American-born students wrote just as poorly.

Simon's first client was a young man from Beijing named Xiao, working on a Master's thesis in mechanical engineering. Of course, the content was unfamiliar to Simon, but he didn't think Xiao's writing was all that bad. He even wondered why he had been referred. Xiao was gracious, deferential, and sat quietly during his hour with Simon, taking everything in, and writing copious notes, some in Chinese. Simon felt good about his first client.

"Must be a big change from Beijing to Newell," Simon said.

"Yes, this is very small," Xiao responded.

"I have to ask. Is Newell well known in China?"

"No. No one has heard about it."

"Okay. So, let me ask this. Why Newell?"

"Why not?" Xiao beamed.

Simon smiled as well, feeling that Xiao had more to say.

"Good music program," Xiao said. "I study music and engineering."

"I didn't know that. Great combination, Xiao."

9. SIMON FINDS HIS STRIDE

Simon's second client came in later that morning. She was a young lady from Florida named Tracy Steele. She was enrolled in a Master of Fine Arts program, a surprising referral to Jarvis, given that one objective of such programs is to teach writing skills.

Tracy was eager for help. Unlike Xiao, who was affable and funny, she was entirely serious. "Dr. Kolchin says there is something basically wrong. I have this flaw that I need to fix. She said you might be able to help me figure out what it is."

Simon had never heard a student describe the need for help in that way. She focused on Simon, hanging on his every word, waiting for him to reveal the fundamental problem with her writing and, most importantly, its implementable solution.

Tracy had sent him a piece a few days earlier. It was an exercise she had been working on. She was asked to describe an everyday experience in compositional detail. She chose the experience of renewing her driver's license in Orlando.

Simon could only get through the first few paragraphs when he mumbled to himself, "This is giving me a headache."

Tracy opened with "*I stood there silently in line, like trees in a forest.*"

A few years back in Boston, an opening like that by a graduate student would have made Simon annoyed, even angry. He might have put the student on the spot with a question like "Can you tell me what the hell this means?" But he was more mature by the time he got to Newell. Besides, he was a newcomer, and didn't want to develop a reputation for being uncongenial. He took a deep breath. "Okay, so like trees in a forest. You stood there silently, like trees in a forest. Can you tell me why you chose that analogy?"

Tracy paused to think. "I guess trees in a forest are silent, and I thought it sounded nice."

"It doesn't sound bad, Tracy. When you stand silently somewhere waiting, do you feel like you're a tree in a forest?"

"No," Tracy replied.

"How do you feel?"

"Bored, I think. Sometimes frustrated."

"Is that how you felt at the DMV in Florida?" Simon asked.

"I think so. It wasn't a pleasant experience, that's for sure."

"So it was boring and frustrating?" Simon asked, helping her to clarify her thoughts.

"Yes," Tracy replied.

"But by describing it like silent trees in a forest, you're not coming across with any boredom or frustration, are you?" Tracy's eyes lit up as Simon asked this.

"I suppose I'm not," Tracy said with a smile.

"We've only got through the first sentence, but I'd like you to sit at the table for a couple of minutes, and tell me how you'd re-write the opening, with the genuine feeling—a feeling the reader can understand. Can you do that?" Simon asked.

"I will try."

Tracy didn't expect to complete such an exercise. She was hoping Simon would explain a few basic rules she was violating and prescribe an easy solution. She struggled for more than a few minutes. Finally, she stood up and walked over to Simon's desk with a new handwritten opening sentence.

I stood there in line, both bored and frustrated, waiting for my turn.

Simon smiled. Tracy smiled back. "Young lady, I think we've had a breakthrough. This is excellent. Now why don't you head out and do the same thing with the rest of the piece and email it to me tomorrow or the day after."

Tracy left delighted with the positive feedback. She was a popular student in her program, and it took no time at all for her to relay her experience to her classmates. "Mr. Galves is awesome!" she told her boyfriend Tom, a fellow MFA student.

Tracy returned her composition to Simon, still with flowery, unnecessary language here and there, but overall improved. Within a week, Simon had between seven and ten appointments per day. In Boston, he was one among many writing instructors and largely worked in obscurity. At Newell, he was becoming a rising star and felt proud of the work he was doing. Even the other consultants sought his advice on how to help their own clients. It was certainly an auspicious beginning.

10. Bridgewater State

Simon continued to fulfill his duty to his mother in high school. Home by four, completing chores, having dinner, doing his homework, and off to bed. He never witnessed any of the crippling anxiety or attacks Dr. Coates spoke about, and never asked his mother about her symptoms. Early in his senior year, with talk of college circulating among his classmates, he began seriously pondering his own future.

A guidance counselor told him Harvard was unrealistic. His grades were generally excellent, but his introverted life would be a drawback, no matter how well he did on the SAT. A fellow student was a strong candidate for both Harvard and Princeton, but he was a soccer star and had written a college essay about his many travels throughout New England playing soccer.

"What would I write about?" Simon thought to himself. "Spending evenings at home sitting with my mother. I don't think the admissions committee would be too impressed."

Simon avoided discussing college with his mother. His plan was to go somewhere impressive, perhaps far away, on some sort of scholarship or with considerable financial aid, as Helen was badly off.

In the fall of his senior year, it was Helen who raised the issue with her son, breaking her habitual silence at dinner. "I suppose it's time for college applications, is it?"

"Yes, mother."

"The neighbor's daughter went to Bristol. I heard she's doing very well."

Bristol referred to Bristol Community College in New Bedford. He didn't know the neighbor in question very well, but had met the daughter, whom he guessed was in her late twenties. She was working as a nurse in Boston.

"True. Bristol's not a bad place."

"Where else were you thinking?"

"I have really good grades, mother. I think I'll do well on the SAT. So I think I can do better than Bristol."

Helen barely made it through high school and the SAT, the rankings of colleges, and the ambitions of teens like her son were all very unfamiliar. "What do you mean better?"

"I mean a place with a better reputation. A place with more opportunities, better teaching."

Helen shrugged her shoulders and glanced at Simon with disapproval. "You're saying Bristol is not good enough for you then? It was good enough for Katie, or whatever her name is. She also didn't have to pay for a dorm room since she stayed at home."

Staying at home was, of course, Helen's primary interest in promoting Bristol.

Simon grew more reluctant to expand the discussion about college. "I'll look into Bristol, mother. I'll look into other places, too."

"What other places?" she pressed him.

"Maybe Brown. Who knows? The guidance counselor thinks I have a good chance there. And it's close to home."

"I bet it's very expensive. We don't have the money."

"I'll get financial aid. It won't burden you at all."

"Tell me soon where you're thinking of applying. I'm your mother. I have the right to know." Helen seemed very annoyed.

"I'll let you know."

Over the next couple of months, Simon balanced his desire for an adventurous new life, far away from his mother, with his inescapable obligation to stay near her. His SAT scores were lower than he hoped for, and so Brown was out. Week by week, he resigned himself to remain close to home.

He was admitted to Bridgewater State, which offered him both a scholarship and some financial aid. The school was thirty miles from his home, and he thought for a while about living on campus. Knowing that might lead to his mother convulsing with panic, not to mention forever reminding him of his supposed selfishness, he came up with another solution.

"If I'm going to live at home, I'll need a car."

"Oh, you should definitely live at home. God knows what goes on in those dorms."

"They do offer some money, but not for a car. Will you help me out?"

"Help buy a car? Definitely not. We don't have that kind of money. You can take my car when you need it. I can take the bus to work."

It was an imperfect but acceptable solution to Simon. The thought of his mother traveling by bus to clean motels, especially in the winter, did trouble him somewhat, but he took some comfort in knowing she proposed it. A car of his own wasn't out of the question. Simon could have gotten a loan, and a job on the side at Bridgewater to help pay it off, if only Helen would help guarantee the loan. But she was no risk taker. Acquiring a large debt was not in her nature.

11. An Awkward Party

Simon's days at work were long but fulfilling. The big difference between being a writing instructor in Boston and a consultant at Newell was that his clients in Newell were much more appreciative of his help. He rarely engaged in any type of casual banter with his students as he did with his first client Xiao. He was never good at it, and he found it hard to relate to much younger people. Instead, he focused on being professional, kind, patient, and encouraging.

It helped that Newell was a much less formal place. Limited space at Jarvis meant he would sometimes meet students at coffee shops or in quiet rooms at the library. He offered to buy coffee for all his clients—a simple gesture, but one which distinguished him from the other consultants.

As well as things were going at work, Simon's private life remained in the doldrums. St. James Ale House was a less useful vehicle for meeting new people than he had hoped. Most came there in small groups, had a drink or two, and left.

Simon sat at the bar. He remembered his father engaging customers at a bar many times when he was a young boy. The Ale House bartenders, however, were either too busy or otherwise uninterested in engaging in much conversation. After sitting alone evening after evening, watching interesting parties enjoy food and drink after work, he felt very much left out, and figured he might as well save his money and head to his apartment.

The apartment only made him feel more depressed. It was too quiet. He could never hear anything from upstairs. He wondered if Anna ever went anywhere or did anything at all. After moving in, he rarely saw her, and she said little more than "Remember, rent due on the first."

Of course, Simon would read, and the quiet and solitude of his place was perfect for that. There came a time, though, when his eyes would hurt, and he was eager to do something with someone else.

"Simon needs a girlfriend," he mumbled to himself one evening. "Might not be so easy to find one around here. Simon needs friends, too."

He alleviated his loneliness to some extent by arranging client meetings in the evenings, which many students preferred. He met two history students, Dan and Alicia, together one Friday evening at a coffee shop around eight. Both very warm and engaging, they wrote pretty well and had requested a referral to Simon to improve further. Alicia, in particular, asked a number of excellent questions about usage and style. Simon found her enthusiasm invigorating.

"I just want to thank you for your help. This was great," Alicia said.

"Ditto for me, Mr. Galves. This was excellent," Dan said.

"I'm glad to be of help. You are both pretty good writers already. Just a bit of tweaking is what you need."

"Thanks. We won't take up any more of your time." Alicia folded her notebook computer and stood up.

"No worries. So, what are you both up to this evening?" Simon asked because he was curious about how graduate students in Newell spent their free time.

"There's a party at the Ross Club. Mostly just graduate students. Really low key. Hey, would you like to come, Mr. Galves?" Dan asked.

Simon was completely caught off guard.

"Ah, well, I don't know. Thank you so much for thinking of me."

"We would love to see you there, Mr. Galves," Alicia added.

"Maybe I could drop by for a while. What time does it start?"

"It's already started. We're headed straight there."

"Okay. I'll think it over. I'm headed home now."

Simon walked home, sat on his couch for a while, contemplating whether to go to the Ross Club or not.

"It might be awkward to be there," he mumbled to himself. "There may not be any faculty or staff there. On the other hand, I guess I don't have anything to lose. I'm not sleepy. I actually feel pretty energized. I will know Alicia and Dan at least. I should go." He set out to the Ross Club, realizing that his trip back to the apartment was a complete waste.

The Club was really an old Victorian house, of which there were many on or close to campus. He found the party on the main floor in what used to be an elegant dining room. There were about twenty people there. Not all appeared to be students.

"So glad you could make it!" Alicia said, noticing Simon right away.

"I'm just happy to see a familiar face."

"Help yourself to a drink and there are snacks over there in the corner."

"Thank you Alicia. I should pay for my share."

"Don't worry about it. It's put on by the History Graduate Students' Association. We always order way too much. Just enjoy yourself."

Simon walked around the room awkwardly for a minute or so. Everyone seemed engrossed in conversation, and he didn't want to interrupt. Instead, he went to a makeshift bar where a young man asked for his preference, wine or beer. He got a glass of Chardonnay and retreated to a corner where he could lean against a window.

There were a number of grey-haired people. He sat next to a

man who appeared to be there by himself. "Good evening. I'm Simon Galves, new to Newell."

"New to Newell. Has a nice ring to it, doesn't it? My name is Jeremy Casagrande. How do you like it here so far?"

"I like it. People have been really welcoming."

"What department are you with?"

"I'm with the Jarvis Center."

"I've heard of it. So, Department of English then?"

"It's a university-wide resource, so not in any department."

"Okay, but in what department is your appointment?"

"I don't have an appointment."

Professor Casagrande looked a bit confused. "I see. You're an administrator of some sort?"

"No, I'm a writing consultant." Professor Casagrande's probing had, by that point, left Simon feeling a bit insecure about his position. "How about you, Jeremy?"

"I'm the Norris Walter Professor of History here at Newell. Been here fifteen years. Did my PhD at Yale and then spent twelve years at Oberlin College in Ohio." Whether or not Professor Casagrande intended to intimidate Simon with his credentials, he certainly did.

"That's really impressive. I'm just a staff member. I wish I had an academic appointment."

"Do you have a PhD?"

"No, I don't."

"Well, it's a pleasure to meet you. I'm going to grab another drink. Welcome to Newell."

Professor Casagrande left Simon feeling so inadequate that he just walked about for a few minutes and then decided to head home.

Alicia saw him as he donned his coat. "You're leaving so soon?"

"Yes. I've got some things I need to take care of. Thank you so much for inviting me. It was very kind of you."

"Oh, it's great to have you. I'm glad you came. So sorry you can't stay."

Simon went home, changed into sweatpants, and read a couple of student compositions to be discussed in the week ahead.

12. ANGELA BETZ

Simon enrolled as an English major at Bridgewater State. Of course, it wasn't Harvard or Brown, but it was affordable and accessible. It would allow him to be more independent of his mother, while at the same time not abandoning her and thereby distressing her too much.

While she had agreed to let him to use her car to get to school, she complained about the arrangement. "It's freezing cold again, and it will be two buses this time," she would say on more than one occasion.

Eventually, Simon and Helen came up with a better arrangement. As his classes didn't start before nine, and she could start work whenever she wished, he would drive her to her first motel around eight a.m., before taking the highway up to Bridgewater. She could then take the bus to her second and, when work was especially plentiful, to her third motel. If there were other cleaners about, one might offer her a ride.

Simon grew not only more independent but also more social in college. At first, he fell in with a group of young men obsessed with video and fantasy games. It was a mutual interest in science fiction that first drew them together. Simon's new friends were kind and welcoming, but didn't take their studies seriously. It seemed all they did was play *Dungeons and Dragons* all day and sometimes well into the night, while drinking soda and eating Cheetos. At some point in his freshman year, Simon started to withdraw from them, feeling that they wasted too much time.

He was an excellent student and was accepted into the honors program in his sophomore year, which also served as the time frame for another positive development.

Like with Mia, Simon met Angela Betz, a musical theater student, in the library. She was from Worcester and lived in one of the dormitories. Unlike introverted, subdued Simon, Angela was bubbly and animated. At first, he felt a bit overwhelmed by her personality. She shared many personal details he would have felt uncomfortable asking about. He was perplexed as to why she did so. After a few conversations in the library, he began to realize that she liked him a lot, so he finally asked her out.

"Of course," she responded. "Why did it take you so long?"

Simon and Angela became a steady, happy couple. They were well matched at first—Angela's energy and what she called her "flightiness" with Simon's calm, cerebral demeanor, which Angela said kept her really grounded. About two weeks after meeting, they began a period of what could be described as physical experimentation.

Simon had no experience in such matters of any kind. First, he kissed her awkwardly, pressing her petite body against him uncomfortably as he did so. She taught him better ways. Soon after came late afternoons in her dorm room. They both stripped naked, and Simon began to feel an excitement he had never felt before.

His first time was a bumbling mess. He nevertheless enjoyed it, despite an underlying fear of hurting Angela in some way. Quite a bit more experienced, Angela helped him navigate. They began copulating daily in the afternoons after class, after which Simon would make the long drive home, feeling relaxed and satisfied.

Conversation with Helen remained limited, and he had no intention of telling her about Angela. Despite her past machinations, Simon did begin to feel sorry for his mother in college. She seemed tired. The lack of a car added at least a couple of hours to her workday.

One evening, when he was feeling especially content, Simon decided to challenge his mother about her current situation. "Why do you have to clean motels?"

"Because it's my job."

"Why can't you do something else? Like work in a restaurant."

"I don't have any experience working in a restaurant."

"It just seems like the traveling around is a lot to do. It's wearing you out."

"You took the car. If you didn't, I wouldn't be so worn out."

Simon anticipated such a response, and it didn't trouble him. "I think you should do something else. Maybe something in an office."

"Hard to get places in this town without a car. Even if I had one, I would have trouble in an office."

Simon didn't press her. It took a few minutes to realize why she chose to clean motels. It was solitary work she could finish with little interaction with anyone. She picked up a master key from the front desk, knocked on each door, and went about her work. Helen didn't like interacting with people, something almost any other job would require.

"If the car is a big issue, I'll get my own car. I can get a cheap car."

"How are you going to afford a car?"

"I'll get a job in Bridgewater."

"So, you'll be gone from home even more then?"

"Maybe. I can work around my classes. I can find something up there."

"I told you I don't want to guarantee a loan for you."

"I know. I will try to save up enough to buy it myself."

"But the insurance will cost a lot at your age."

"I'm already on your insurance. I can buy the car, and we can put it in your name. It should work out. Lots of commuter students at Bridgewater do the same thing."

Helen stared out a window and said nothing. Simon had learned that her silence meant she had reluctantly approved.

13. CHEVROLET CITATION

Jobs were plentiful in Bridgewater. Simon found a part-time job at Roche Bros. Supermarket. His job was to unload trucks as new inventory came in. As trucks arrived all day, he had very flexible hours. His manager insisted only that he accumulate twenty hours per week, for which would be paid roughly one hundred dollars. It wasn't much, but after six months, he earned enough to buy a 1980 Chevrolet Citation. A bit rusty on its underside and with more than 90,000 miles, it wasn't a great specimen of a car. It started and ran fine, however, and he encountered no problems on his daily sixty-mile commute. He kept his job to pay for gas, parking, and what he anticipated would be repairs from time to time.

The car gave him more independence. Helen had worried a great deal about the state of her own car. She insisted Simon clean it regularly, refrain from eating inside, and not get sidetracked on his trips back and forth to save on gas. With his own car, both Simon and Helen could worry less. He could also take Angela out on dates.

They even skipped class a few times and went to Providence for the whole day.

Helen's fatigue eased as she could get around more easily and make it home by two or three in the afternoon. Despite no change in Simon's class schedule, Helen was left with several more hours each day when she was alone in the house, and this became distressing.

"What time do your classes finish?"

"It depends on the day. Today I finished at one."

"But it's 7:15. You should have been home before two at the latest."

"Mother, I have to do more than just go to classes. I've got to go to the library to do research and work on assignments, for one thing."

"I see. Do you remember what Dr. Coates told you?"

"Of course. You might have a big attack of anxiety if I'm not here. Something like that."

"A panic attack."

Simon grew angry. If he had ever challenged his mother before, it was only briefly, after which she would back down and sulk. He went further. "I haven't seen you have any attacks at all, Mother."

"How would you know? You're not here much."

"Just saying, I've never seen you have an attack all these years."

"You think I just made it up? Dr. Coates told you about it." Helen didn't raise her voice but was clearly furious.

"I didn't say I think you're making it up. Are you having panic attacks now that you're home earlier? I thought that was a good thing. You got your car back."

"I didn't say I was having attacks. I just said that Dr. Coates recommended you stay here to prevent attacks. Why can't you gather your research from the library and come home and finish your work?"

"Because the research takes time. I need to go back and forth to the stacks. It's a complicated process."

"So, the library is all serious business, is it?"

"Yes, it's very serious."

"Just like when you were in high school." It was a deliberate jab, intended to remind Simon that he had met Mia in the library. Helen suspected something similar was going on at Bridgewater.

Simon's anger increased. "I'm a grown young man. I have my own car. I have my own future. If you'd like me to come home early to prevent your so-called 'attacks,' just say so. You don't need to question every detail about my life. I'm an honors student. You should be proud of my hard work, like other mothers."

Helen was stunned. She rose and went to her bedroom without saying a word.

Simon wasn't sure what to think. Helen hadn't laden him with guilt. He figured she left to process what he had just said. He calmed down after a few minutes and decided to try to understand things from her perspective. She was an odd woman, someone who found interaction with people distasteful, but for some reason, couldn't stand being alone. Of course, Simon could return home earlier, but that would mean giving up his late-afternoon adventures with Angela, something he felt he couldn't do. He couldn't understand what his mother gained from him being in the house, while she sat in silence, often in her own room. Was it just her knowing that he couldn't be doing anything she would disapprove of? Was it pure selfishness, keeping him close so that she always remained his top priority? Or was it a genuine fear that something terrible might happen, as Dr. Coates suggested, while she was alone? Was it a combination of all these things? Was there a mutually beneficial solution to her situation?

He had worked hard to buy a car, which he thought would make his mother's life better. Instead, she seemed more troubled than before.

14. FIONA THE BARTENDER

Spring came much earlier to Newell than it did to Boston and brought clear skies interrupted often by powerful thunderstorms. Buds began to appear on trees in March. In a short time, Simon had built an excellent reputation, but his personal life remained dreary.

He remained scarred by the evening at the Ross Club. He was neither a student nor a faculty member. He barely interacted with the other consultants. His clients were almost all delightful to deal with, but his interactions with them were professional, and given the uncomfortable short time he spent at Ross, he had no intention of accepting any future invitations to graduate student parties.

Sitting on his dingy couch one evening, he thought of buying a television, but decided that he wouldn't receive many over the air channels and might have to pay for some alternative he didn't feel he could afford in the long-term. He did have access to the Internet in the apartment through a discounted plan available for staff at Newell, and used it not only for work, but to watch the news and some mindless free TV programs, which he streamed just to keep him company.

He came up with an idea one Saturday morning, which he decided to present to Anna. He went to the front porch and rang her doorbell.

Anna responded promptly. She was in a bathrobe. "Yes, Simon, what can I do for you?"

"Sorry to bother you, Anna. Hope you weren't sleeping."

"I've been up since six. No bother. What's on your mind?"

"Just curious, Anna. The original ad I responded to didn't say anything about pets. Just wondering how you feel about that."

She looked at him sternly. "Well, that was a mistake on my part. I should have made that clear. No pets, sorry."

"Is there any flexibility about that, Anna? I don't mean a large dog, but how about a kitten?"

Anna looked very annoyed. "The answer is no pets. I don't have pets, and I don't allow pets in this house. Is that clear?"

"Al right. Thanks for clearing that up."

"Have a good day, Simon." Anna shut the door.

Simon went back downstairs. If Anna understood his social situation and why he wanted a pet, perhaps she would be more sympathetic. Then again, she didn't seem like a sympathetic person at all. He thought of taking the risk of acquiring a small kitten he could keep well hidden in his apartment, but then worried what would happen if Anna somehow discovered it while he was at work. He would be thrown out for sure.

He also thought of moving out, but the lease he signed required a penalty of three months' rent ($1500) for any early lease termination—an unaffordable sum. He was stuck then, pet-less, in the basement of a curmudgeonly Polish woman.

Quite desperate for company, Simon went back to the Ale House several more times. He sat at the bar in the same spot, arriving at seven pm each time. The usual small groups of well-dressed professionals were present, and he felt very much left out of their undoubtedly better lives as they enjoyed the evening. Finally, he had a candid conversation with a bartender, a middle-aged woman he had seen there several times.

"Looks like you're becoming a regular here."

"I guess I sort of am. I see the same people here sometimes."

"I meant at the bar. I don't have that many regulars. It's not a neighborhood bar. Mostly Newell folks who come and go. Are you at Newell?"

"Yeah, been there four months."

"How do you like it?"

"It has its charms."

"I guess that's a no." She chuckled. "I'm Fiona, by the way."

"Simon. Nice to meet you. Honestly, I'm still trying to settle in. Work has been going great. Just trying to find something outside of work."

"Bartenders are supposed to give advice, right?"

"They are. My father was a bartender."

"Good. So, my advice, and it's against my interests, but hanging out here every night is probably not the best 'something' you can find outside of work."

Simon smiled. "I think you're right. Just hoping to meet people."

"No one meets anyone here, Simon. It's not that kind of place. No one stays for much more than an hour. The owner likes it that way. They order their drinks, their food, and then new people come in. Almost everyone has something to do with Newell, which means they have money. He raises the prices every six months, and no one complains."

"You like working here?"

"I do. Tips are good. My husband's been out of work for over a year."

"What did he do?"

"Truck driver."

"Why is he out of work, then? I thought we were always short of truck drivers?"

"Getting personal, are you? Let's just say he had some issue with this stuff." Fiona raised a glass of beer she was about to serve another customer.

"Sorry, didn't mean to get personal."

"No problem. What about you? You married? Kids?" Fiona asked.

"No to both. On my own."

"That sucks. Newell is not a good place to be single, I would imagine."

"Doesn't seem like it," Simon replied.

"Why did you come here?"

"For the job. I was a writing instructor. Not like truck driving. There just aren't that many jobs in my field. I lived in Boston."

"Wow. Big change then from the big city! No wonder you're still discovering the charms of Newell."

"You got it."

"You must love music, right?"

"No more than other people. Why do you say that?"

"Because you're here, at Newell. They're obsessed with music here at Newell."

"I heard there is a good music program here."

"The absolute best," Fiona said. Coming from Boston, Simon couldn't imagine that, that was true. "You haven't seen a lot about concerts around town?"

"I've seen posters. I just haven't taken advantage of concerts."

"No rock and roll. Strictly classical. Not my thing. If you want to find something outside of work in Newell, that's the something everyone is into. You'll certainly meet lots of new people," Fiona said.

"I appreciate the advice. I knew sitting here at the bar would pay off one of these days."

Fiona smiled. She was very busy that evening, and Simon appreciated the time she spent speaking with him.

"Classical music, huh?" he thought. "Too bad it isn't drama or poetry."

15. A TENDER MOMENT

Simon continued to contemplate his near confrontation with his mother. She was subdued in the days that followed, barely speaking to him. Several times, instead of dining with her son, she left his meal covered up on the dining table and was upstairs watching television in her room by the time he returned home.

"At least I'm in the house in case she has one of those attacks," he thought.

One evening, he decided to discuss the matter further. He returned home around six and Helen hadn't yet eaten.

"What would you like me to do, mother? Come home earlier? Would that help you?"

Helen shrugged her shoulders at first. Then she responded, "You said you remember what Dr. Coates told you and what you agreed to do. The rest is up to you, I suppose. If you care for me, you will heed his advice."

"Okay." Simon tried to digest the passive-aggressiveness, guilt, and insincerity she had just thrown his way. He hadn't actually agreed to do anything that day with Dr. Coates—only that he understood his mother's situation, which he really didn't.

Helen continued. "It's called gratitude, Simon."

"What do you mean?"

"Gratitude for all I've done for you. For raising you, especially after your father was gone."

"I am grateful, mother." Simon decided to listen and not to challenge anything Helen said. "I will try and come home earlier from now on."

Helen said nothing.

In reality, by the end of his sophomore year, it became easier for Simon to return home earlier. He and Angela were growing more distant. Her "flightiness" was becoming a problem for him.

On several occasions, they had made plans, only to have her cancel them at the last minute for trivial reasons—"My stylist says she has an opening." This made things stressful for Simon, not only because he was steady and organized, but also because the schedule changes exacerbated his constant anxiety about not being home with his mother.

At times, after promising to be there, Angela wasn't in her dorm room when Simon came by. Worse still, her bubbly personality made it easy for her to flirt with all sorts of young men, especially fellow students in her classes.

Simon decided to take all these things in stride. "Am I in love with her?" he thought. "No, but she can be fun to be with sometimes," he concluded.

On one afternoon of Angela's unplanned unavailability, Simon returned home early and with a tinge of naked aggressiveness and frustration, emptied the cans and packages which would make up dinner for him and his mother, heated them up in the microwave, set two place settings, and announced, "Mother, dinner's ready."

Helen could tell her son was angry and remained quiet.

"It's 5:30 p.m., mother. Is this early enough for you? I just want to make sure you don't have an attack." He sounded harsh.

Helen was taken aback and said nothing.

Simon did not relent. "I figure you've been alone here for only a couple of hours, so the chances of you having an attack in that time are pretty low. I drove back here as fast as I could."

"I don't want you to drive as fast as you could. You could have had an accident."

"I drove fast, mother, because I was afraid you might have an attack. I'm sure you understand that." Simon was cynical and loud.

For the first time he could ever remember, his mother looked a little afraid. He took a deep breath and chose not to go any further.

Nevertheless, Helen put her fork down. "I'm not hungry." She rose and went upstairs.

Simon had lost his appetite as well. He cleaned up and went out for a walk to calm down. It worked well. He started to reflect on what had just happened. He had redirected his frustration with Angela toward his mother, trying to satisfy her, while knowing all the while that he was trying to make her seem foolish. That wasn't fair to Helen. Worse, he had frightened her with his demeanor, something he didn't mean to do. "I could have actually brought on an attack," he thought.

Simon returned home after about an hour. His mother came downstairs shortly thereafter. As he had thrown her original dinner in the trash, she grabbed a few shortbread biscuits from a cupboard, put them in a small bowl, and sat at the table to eat them. For a moment, Simon, who observed her, thought this was just a ploy to make him feel guilty. The message he thought she was trying to convey was that because of his rage, she had not had a proper dinner and was forced to eat junk food.

Then Helen did something unexpected. "Would you like some of these, Simon?"

She had never offered him anything like that. He thought for a moment about how to respond. A firm refusal would make it seem like he was still in a rage.

"Yes, I would, mother."

Helen returned to the cupboard and put three biscuits in another bowl, which she set in front of the chair next to her. Simon sat down and started to eat. Then came something not just unexpected, but rather shocking. Helen put her right hand on Simon's forearm. He could not recall any affectionate touch, even as a young boy. He stared at her.

"I hope you're not still so angry. You can come home when you like. I'll be okay."

Simon turned away, then back to his mother, and came to a realization. He had grown into a strapping young man, and there was Helen, a slight figure with graying hair. For whatever reason, she was truly vulnerable. He grabbed her hand in his, the first time he had ever done anything like that. "Thank you, mother."

16. A Love for Music

After speaking with Fiona, Newell's obsession with music became more noticeable to Simon. Not only were there the many posters announcing recitals and concerts, but he noticed that some students carried cases of musical instruments all over campus. Apart from a few mandatory classes in grade school and listening to the radio, Simon had no real experience with music. What he had heard of classical music he found a bit dull, and he imagined that the classical events taking place around town all the time would be both boring and lengthy.

Simon also noticed that many students, including many Jarvis clients, had discussions about music. Some of the compositions he reviewed were also about music. He recommended "Beethoven had a temper" in place of "Beethoven was a temperamental man," for instance. So, after a couple of weeks of spending lonely evenings in his miserable apartment, reading, worried about wasting time, and eagerly waiting for the next day to begin, he decided to attend his first Newell concert.

Massimo Chase was a contemporary guitarist from Syracuse, and the poster which caught Simon's attention was "An Evening with Massimo." The appeal was straightforward—a black-and-white photo of a bearded man with long hair hunched passionately over a guitar. "It can't be anything classical," Simon thought. For the paltry sum of seven dollars, Simon obtained a ticket from the Reinhart Auditorium Box Office, where a young lady assured him there was no need for assigned seats since so few tickets were being sold. This was somewhat worrying, as Simon wondered how good Massimo could be if he was coming all the way from Syracuse to play for a small audience.

The concert took place on a Friday evening, and as expected, the auditorium was less than half full. Mr. Chase emerged nearly twenty minutes after the expected start time, which, always troubled by the wasting of time, annoyed Simon from the start. There was nothing on stage but a folding chair and Massimo with his acoustic guitar.

"Sorry folks. I was running a bit late," Massimo said. He went on to provide a short biography, including how he took his first guitar lessons at age eight, and how he idolized Al Dimeola, whom Simon had never heard of. The music then began. Massimo played a series of short original compositions. During one, he sang a few verses. He didn't have a great voice and Simon concluded it was best for him to stick with just playing guitar.

Simon could tell that Massimo was an accomplished guitarist and composer, but he didn't especially like any of the music at first. The melodies seemed a bit disorganized, and sometimes seemed to end abruptly. He found a couple of them dull enough that he felt inclined to begin checking his email on his phone. He looked around to find the other thirty or so audience members to be quite engrossed in the music. Massimo played for over an hour, with only a short break for a glass of water.

"My last piece is not an original piece. It's an older piece by William Ackerman called 'Bricklayer's Beautiful Daughter.'"

Massimo began playing, and unlike his own compositions, the Ackerman piece sounded rhythmically perfect to Simon. It was also beautiful. After less than a minute, a warm feeling overcame him. As he listened to the simple, elegant melody, he started thinking about all sorts of things—his childhood in New Bedford, the death of his father, Mia Fernandes, his days at Bridgewater State, details of the many years that followed, even his mother sitting alone in her house. "I haven't lived a beautiful life," he thought. "But this song can make any life seem beautiful."

"Bricklayer's Beautiful Daughter" included a short refrain featuring lower notes, during which the warm feeling inside Simon intensified. During the second refrain, a few tears started streaking down both his cheeks. He wiped them away, hoping no one would notice.

The concert ended with Mr. Chase thanking his audience and letting them know he had to drive to Charlottesville that night. Simon sat still, stunned by the intensity of his own emotions. As people began to file out, Massimo rested his guitar on the chair and jumped down from the stage. He made his way to Simon, who was seated only three rows from the front.

"Powerful song, huh?" Massimo asked.

"What?" Simon was surprised that the performer would address him.

"The last one. 'Bricklayer's Beautiful Daughter.' It's a powerful piece."

Simon assumed that Massimo had observed him tearing up.

"It was nice. Very nice," he responded.

"Are you a musician?"

"No, not at all. In fact, this is the first concert I've been to in many years. I don't even know in how long."

"I'm surprised. You seem to react very emotionally to music."

Simon felt embarrassed. "I don't know. Just had a long day, and I'm tired. I really liked your concert, especially the last piece."

"Yes, wish I had written it! Anyway, I'm glad you enjoyed the concert. I've got to get on the road for the next gig tomorrow night. Enjoy your weekend."

Massimo left the stage, and a minute or two later, Simon observed him leaving out of the back of the auditorium. For some reason, he still felt like sitting there, trying to process what had happened—why had the music affected him so deeply and what did it mean?

A custodian entered the auditorium and called out, "Concert's all done. You okay, sir?"

"I'm fine." He stood up, put on his jacket, and headed home.

17. MUSIC AND SENTIMENTALITY

Simon sat on his dingy couch in near darkness, still trying to process the experience of the concert. He had told Massimo he was tired. In reality, the concert left him feeling quite energized, and he didn't feel like going to bed. He decided to process his feelings by writing them down as a short composition.

Despite being a skilled writing instructor, Simon had never been much of a writer. His collective creative works consisted of a few poems and a short story he wrote while an MFA student. He attributed this lack of productivity to simply not having much to write about. He believed his life had, at least to that point, been too dull to share and his experiences too mundane to generate prose or poetry creative enough to interest other people. The task he set for himself, however, was quite different. He turned on a lamp, sat at his desk, pulled out a notepad and pencil from his briefcase, and began, with the warmth and emotion of the evening still within him.

That song in particular reminded me so much of New England, my home. Not just New England, but New England at a particular time of year—autumn. Not just autumn, but late autumn, when only a few leaves remain on the trees, and we are due for a light dusting of snow any day. It took me back to my college days. It took me back to the days when almost anything seemed possible. My frigid single mother, my isolation, my poverty were only slight handicaps to overcome. I felt all this, especially on the trip to Dartmouth. I felt it out on the field, as it got a little colder. It snowed that night in early December.

The trip Simon referred to was to Dartmouth College in December 1991. The English students' association at Bridgewater was part of a coalition of similar organizations which organized an annual conference in different locations. The conference included various students' readings, a few faculty readings, and even some sports events. Simon attended only once in his sophomore year, when Dartmouth hosted. Angela didn't accompany him.

The students traveled by chartered bus and stayed in dorm rooms that had just become empty for the Christmas holidays. It was a very nice trip for Simon and one of the few opportunities he had to get away. The beauty of Dartmouth was breathtaking. One afternoon, when all the events had concluded, on a field near Shattuck Observatory, a couple of Dartmouth students he had met at the conference invited Simon to toss a football back and forth. The trio did this for almost half an hour. The throwing and catching achieved a nice rhythm. There was no conversation, only an occasional "nice catch," "nice throw," or "oops, sorry about that one." It had been a cool, rainy day. No one else was outside. After a few minutes, a few wet snowflakes began falling. The young men, by that point, having some fun but getting a bit bored, decided to wrap things up.

From a not-too-distant open window, Simon heard music. It was a guitar. He couldn't tell if it was a recording, or someone was actually playing. After he wrote, *It snowed that night in early December,* he began to understand why "Bricklayer's Beautiful Daughter" had moved him so much: He had heard it before. It took him back to a more innocent, hopeful time in his life, and to a brief point, when he felt he was part of something, even something simple, such as a trio of young men throwing around a football.

Simon left a space on his page and wrote one last sentence.

Music is all sentimentality disguised as rationality and complexity.

He wrote that instinctively, unsure what it meant. It was either

45

very profound or entirely foolish. If only he had someone to share it with.

Saturday evening, he returned to the Ale House, hoping Fiona would be there so he could thank her for steering him towards concerts. He was in luck. Not only was she there, but the Ale House was quiet, as unseasonably cold weather kept many folks at home.

"You're back again? Didn't I tell you not to waste your time here?" Fiona smiled.

"You're a wise woman, Fiona. I just wanted to thank you."

"Wise? My husband says I'm sexy, but he never called me wise."

"I went to a guitar concert last night."

"Terrific. Did you enjoy it?"

"Tremendously. It was the best thing I've done since coming to Newell."

"Thank you for thanking me. Even though I wasn't playing guitar at the concert."

"Are you a musical person?"

"Not at all. Been working here for four years. Music is pretty much all a lot of folks talk about. I never got into it. Never had the chance really."

"Never had the chance? What do you mean?"

"To take lessons. Even to appreciate classical music. Got married right after high school. Then raised my two kids. I suppose I could take lessons now. How about you? You ever think about that? Newell is full of music teachers."

"No. Not yet anyway. Same story for me, I guess. We didn't have much growing up. It was just me and my mother. I focused on working and going to college."

"Nice to talk to someone who understands what that is like. At least you made something of yourself. You're an educated man. I'm just a bartender."

"Like I said, I think you're a wise woman, Fiona. I know what you mean, though. If you can afford $50,000 a year tuition here at Newell, you probably don't know what it's like to grow up with very little."

"Spoiled brats!" Fiona replied.

"Actually, all the young folks I've met are just really nice."

"I know. Just kidding. So, what's next for you? Are you going to subscribe to a classical series? Don't get me wrong, I think you're a super nice man, but I don't want to see you here too often, okay? Well, at least not by yourself."

"Sounds like a challenge, Fiona. I'll only come back here with someone."

"Good deal. Your second beer is on the house. Fiona's treat."

18. DINNER WITH MOM

Simon hoped the tender moment he shared with his mother after he returned home angry that evening in college would have some lasting effects. Helen returned to her usual cold demeanor, but didn't harass Simon about the time he returned to the house.

His relationship with Angela continued to crumble. The end came when, together with a classmate and his girlfriend, Simon and Angela were invited to go camping in western Massachusetts. He had even told his mother he would be away.

Not unexpectedly, for frivolous reasons, Angela backed out. "I am, like, so far behind in the anthropology class. Sorry, maybe next time." She said that just a couple of hours before their planned departure, when Simon called just to find out when to pick her up.

At first, Simon was stunned, and told her, "That's fine." He called up his friend to let him know the situation, who insisted he still come along.

Being a third wheel to a young couple on a camping trip didn't appeal to him much, so he also backed out. What could have been a lovely weekend away was lost.

He became furious and called Angela back. "I want to say what you did was just awful, Angela."

"I told you I can't spare the time right now. I don't want to fail the course."

"You agreed to go along. I told Steve we were coming. I even told my mother I would be away for the weekend, and I've told you many times how prickly she can be."

There was a long pause before Angela responded. "Maybe you should take your mother camping then." She hung up.

Both Simon and Angela understood at that point that the relationship was over.

He returned home, keenly aware that he shouldn't again redirect his anger with Angela toward his mother. "Camping trip is canceled, mother."

"Is that so? Poor weather expected?"

"It will be a beautiful weekend. It's just canceled. Too hard to make all the arrangements."

"It will be a nice weekend here. Can you repaint the back porch stairs? A few spots where the stairs are unsteady, too."

"Certainly."

Simon actually felt good about the breakup. Angela had been an unreliable partner since the beginning of their relationship, and tolerating her many excuses and changes of mind had always been stressful.

He also felt good about spending Saturday repairing stair treads and repainting the stairs. It was a bright, clear spring day. The work was cathartic. He hammered aggressively, but carefully. He jumped on the stairs to check his work so they wouldn't budge. He painted meticulously, covering his work as he went along so that bugs or leaves didn't ruin it. He wanted to impress his mother with the quality of his work, but also to reassure himself that he was an assiduous, responsible young man who could do better than a flippant college girl who didn't understand commitment.

Late in the afternoon, when the paint had dried and his mother began to ponder what to have for dinner, he called her out. "Mother, I'm done. I'd like you to come out and see."

Helen came out back and provided a half-smile, whereby she pushed the edges of her lips into dimples on either side of her face and then nodded, a gesture Simon had learned over the years meant she approved.

"Go ahead, walk on it."

"Are you sure the paint's dry?"

"Definitely."

Helen walked down and up the stairs slowly. She inspected the bottom of her slippers to make sure they weren't covered with paint. "Feels very steady, Simon."

Then Simon, with much more aggression and his greater

weight, demonstrated the solidity of his work. He jumped on each step and noted how none budged, not even a bit. He did this going up and down. Helen nodded approvingly again.

"So, no camping for you then?"

"No, canceled as I said."

"So, what will do you do this weekend?"

Simon was perplexed by the question. He assumed Helen had a list of tasks for him to complete and that painting the back porch stairs was the only one she had disclosed to that point. Sometimes, Simon thought, she made up tasks which were unnecessary— "Clean the gutters," she would say, when Simon knew the gutters were already clean.

"What will I do? I'm not going camping. Don't you have other tasks for me, mother?"

"I don't."

Helen had never indicated that Simon had met her expectations by keeping up with his chores. He was always behind, and there were always new things to do. He was so bewildered he thought it might be a trick. She might have a list of expectations she would throw at him late Sunday, as he prepared for the week ahead, and then complain that he had wasted the weekend.

"You really don't have anything else you want me to do around the house?"

"You've done really well with the steps. If you're not going camping, you should do something else enjoyable, like go up to Boston."

Helen sounded sincere, but Simon wanted still more clarity. "You don't mind me being away for the weekend when I don't have to be? What about what Dr. Coates said?"

They hadn't discussed Dr. Coates for some time, and Helen seemed surprised Simon brought him up. "I just think it must be disappointing if you planned to have an enjoyable weekend and it's suddenly canceled. I think you should still be able to enjoy something."

Simon could have pointed out that Helen had never before made any such suggestion and probed her for what might have changed her attitude. He chose a different approach. "That's very generous of you, mother. It's really too late to go up to Boston. I would have to stay overnight, and it will be expensive. How about you and I go out to dinner in town?"

Helen said nothing for a long moment. Never had she and Simon dined out. In fact, Simon had never known his mother to have been to a restaurant of any kind. He reinforced his offer. "A nice dinner someplace close. I'll drive, and I'll pay. It won't be anything fancy."

"I don't want anything fancy, Simon," Helen finally responded, making it clear that she was accepting the offer.

Simon and Helen went to the modest and crowded Pa Raffa Italian restaurant. Helen was very quiet. A friendly waitress seated them and gave them two plastic-coated menus.

"What are you planning on getting, mother?"

"Oh, I don't know. So many items. Just something small. What do you think I might like?"

Simon hadn't dined at Pa Raffa's either. He ordered a large serving of lasagna along with a couple of Caesar salads and two glasses of root beer. He realized his mother was so out of her element, even the idea of ordering off of a menu might be too much to expect from her.

They ate in near silence. Helen ate very little. Instead, she looked around at the boisterous patrons, talking, laughing, a few even singing.

"When's the last time you ate in a place like this, mother?"

"I don't know. A long time Simon. So different from eating at home."

"It certainly is. Have you been to a restaurant at all?" Simon asked gently, not trying to embarrass his mother.

"Some of the motels have restaurants and allow us to eat our lunch there sometimes. Sometimes the owners are very kind and will give us a meal, too. Not very often, though. So, I guess I've been to restaurants if that counts." Helen half-smiled again.

At that moment, his anger toward Angela had dissipated and, finishing the stairs having given Simon a sense of accomplishment, he also felt warmly toward his mother. He held her hand and stroked it once again.

She seemed to appreciate it. "Thank you for bringing me here, Simon."

19. THE SPRING STORM

As the Spring semester at Newell drew to a close, there was a mad rush of referrals to and appointments at Jarvis as students tried to complete their papers and theses on time. All three consultants stayed busy. On a few days, Simon met with ten clients. The work required in advance of these meetings was considerable, keeping him busy well into the evenings. Simon never compromised on the quality of his work. Each student received the same attention as his first two clients, Xiao and Tracy. Nevertheless, it was very hard to keep track of things.

On a muggy, warm April morning, he began his first meeting at eleven. It was with a chemistry student named Patrick, who, he was told in advance, wrote everything in bullet form, without using any actual paragraphs. Patrick had sent some of his work a few days earlier. It began with a few poorly organized paragraphs. Then it appeared that he gave up and reverted to his habitual bullet form writing. Simon was planning to meet with Patrick at Brandy's Café, but realized around nine, that he had printed out Patrick's paper at Jarvis and left the printed copy on which he made handwritten notes at the Center itself.

"Damn it," he thought. "This is the sort of thing that happens when you have too many clients."

Simon wasn't inclined to walk to Jarvis, as time was scarce and it looked like rain was on the way. Instead, he drove to the Center and parked at a meter a block away.

He found the Center to be occupied. Inside was one of the other consultants, Anuja Sharma, meeting with a young woman. They looked like they were engaged in an intense discussion.

Anuja and Simon had only met a few times, due to the space constraints at Jarvis, but he had heard much about her from graduate students and even others in the broader Newell community. In short, Anuja was impressive and impeccable. Her husband was a respected professor of engineering at Newell. Once her two sons entered high school, Anuja, who had an undergraduate degree in English literature from Columbia, went back to school and obtained an MFA at Newell. She had been at Jarvis for more than two years.

Simon had witnessed Anuja's work, as they shared some

clients, and he deeply respected her. He gathered the feeling was mutual, as she sometimes CC'd Simon on emails to students with messages such as, "Will be away next week, but do meet with Mr. Galves. He is impeccable."

Simon didn't wish to interrupt, but he could see his papers on a filing cabinet behind Anuja, which she must have placed there while she did her work. He stood outside the windowed door for a moment until she noticed him.

"Hi, Simon. So great to see you. We're almost done. Do you need the room?"

"Actually, I just need the stack of papers behind you, if you don't mind."

"Sure. Do you have a few minutes? If you can stick around, just want to get caught up with you. Thinking we need a fourth consultant. This is crazy this semester."

"I have a client at ten at the café, but I'll stick around."

Anuja finished and the young client stuffed a notebook into her backpack, smiled, and left. "How are you getting on here at Newell, my friend?"

Simon took the client's place at the meeting table. "Overall, it's been a good experience. Crazy busy, huh?"

"Glad to hear it's not just me. Can you believe these referrals?"

"I've even been getting referrals from the MFA program," Simon said.

"MFA? That makes no sense. I'm concerned some of these professors are dumping problems on us that they should be solving. You get that feeling? I saw eight clients yesterday. Of course, my husband sent a few himself."

"I haven't gotten any from Raj," Simon responded.

"They all come to me, and he wonders why I'm late for dinner! You have any time for lunch, Simon?"

"You know, that would be great. I'll be at Brandy's anyway. Are you done with clients?"

"I started at 7:30, my friend. That young lady was the third today. I've got three more late this afternoon."

"I have four. The rest are in the evening."

The skies darkened over Newell, and Simon could hear the wind pick up outside. The lights flickered inside the center.

"Looks like a storm, Simon. Raj dropped me off here. I don't have a car with me."

"No problem. I brought mine. I'll give you a lift wherever you need to go."

"How about we go up to the Café? I've got plenty to do while you meet with your client, and we can have lunch afterwards."

"Excellent."

The gust outside increased. Traffic signs bent in the wind. A light rain began.

"Quite different weather than in Boston, I know."

"Quite."

"Wait till the storm comes."

20. AWAKE

The dream cycle in which Simon flew over the Science and Engineering Building ended abruptly as one occasion Simon was headed straight for one of the building's tall spires. In his dream, he put his hands over his face and woke up breathing hard, his hands feeling sweaty.

"Oh, hello there. Looks like you're awake! That's wonderful," the nurse said as she changed an IV bag at Simon's bedside. "Don't try sitting up or anything just yet. Relax for now."

"Am I dead?" Simon's voice was faint and throaty.

"No Mr. Galves. You're not dead. You're a very lucky man I would say. You're at Newell Mercy Hospital. Quite a lot you've been through."

"What happened?" Simon sounded more energetic.

"Gosh. Not sure where to begin. You'd best talk to the doctor for more details. I know you were struck by lightning during the storm the other day. You have burns on your right forearm and your left foot. That's what the bandages are for. You were unconscious, and there was some swelling of the brain. So Dr. Mattei decided to sedate you, induce a coma."

"I've been in a coma?"

"Yes, until just now. He gave you something to bring you out of it. It's Sunday evening. The storm was Friday morning. Before I forget, I'm going to call that woman."

"What woman?"

"A woman who asked me to call her when you woke up. A friend of yours I believe."

"Okay. When can I leave?"

"Dr. Mattei will be in in a couple of hours and will make the decision. I can tell you you're not going anywhere today, that's for sure." The nurse completed her work and left. A few minutes later, Anuja arrived.

"Hello my consultant-brother! Nice to hear you're awake."

"What the hell happened, Anuja? Nurse said I was struck by lightning."

"I saw it. Hit that umbrella. Saw you literally fly across the street and hit the pavement on the other side. I called 911 right away. A student walking by helped me put out the fire on your left shoe."

"My shoe was on fire?"

"It was. Even in the rain. We took it off." Anuja stayed for the better part of an hour, reassuring Simon that many practical matters had been taken care of. He grew more and more alert with each passing minute. She made sure he was placed on a short-term medical leave, canceled his scheduled appointments, and distributed ongoing work with the other consultant in the best manner she could. Not long after she left, Dr. Mattei arrived. He was a short, balding man of about sixty with thick-rimmed glasses and a heavy accent which Simon thought sounded Italian.

"You are a lucky soul, my friend," Dr. Mattei said as he smiled. "How do you feel? Any pain?"

"My foot hurts a bit. Other than that no."

"Let me tell you what happened. You came in by ambulance unconscious. We did the usual scans. Part of your brain was swelling. We treated it and put you into a coma for a couple of days. You have second-degree burns on your right forearm and on your left foot. Your brain is back to its normal size already. Basically, you're doing quite well given what happened."

"When can I leave here doctor?"

"A couple of days. We don't think there's any injury to your brain. But we really won't know. Rest for now. Tomorrow, I'll get physical therapy to come and help you get up and walk."

"Are you sure I was really struck by lightning?"

"Your friend saw it, Mr. Galves. Rare things happen rarely, but they do happen. You're lucky to be alive. You have a family?"

"I'm here in Newell by myself. Only family is my mother in Massachusetts."

"Anyone you can stay with for a while when you get out?"

"No. Not really."

"We could send you to a rehabilitation hospital. Other alternative is just to have someone to check in on you from time to time for the next couple of weeks."

"My landlord lives upstairs. Maybe she can do that."

"Good. I'm an internist and I don't know much about lightning strikes. You're my first patient who has been hit. The burns should heal up quite nicely. We did consult a neurologist who said that there could be lasting effects on you. She just doesn't know what they might be. We'll arrange a follow-up appointment with her sometime in the next month. She may want to do more scans or other tests."

Simon bore a subdued look. "You're saying I won't be the same again?"

"I'm saying I don't know. I reviewed some papers on survivors of lightning strikes, Simon. No one is the same again. It's good that you're conscious and able to talk to me, I'm guessing, pretty much the way you did before. The brain is a wonderful thing in so many ways." Dr. Mattei again encouraged Simon to rest and left.

Simon felt lucky and unlucky at the same time. *Lightning probably strikes one person in Newell in a decade, and it had to be the new guy in town*, he thought. On the other hand, he felt a little groggy but otherwise well. He could see and hear perfectly well. Dr. Mattei made it sound like the burns were not too serious. He could get back to work soon. In his own mind, he downplayed the need for someone to check in on him. He could always call 911 if he needed help, he thought, or Anuja.

Simon watched television for about an hour in his hospital room, the first time he had watched television in over a year. Then he fell into a normal, comfortable sleep.

21. Up and About

The full extent of the damage became clear to Simon the next day. He peeled away the bandages slightly on his right forearm to reveal a significant burn with multiple blisters. An incision had been made through the center of it to relieve pressure from the swelling tissue underneath. He didn't try to take a peek at his foot.

A physical therapist arrived shortly after breakfast. She helped him sit up, which made him lightheaded. She placed slippers on his feet. "Please go slowly, Mr. Galves. Don't assume you'll be able to walk normally."

He stood up slowly and carefully, and his bandaged left foot immediately began to hurt as it bore weight. The young lady held onto his left elbow and encouraged him to take a few careful steps to the edge of his hospital room. His legs felt rubbery at first, but he gradually grew steadier as he took a few steps around the room.

"How do you feel?" the physical therapist asked him.

"A bit like I can't feel my feet."

They entered the hallway, and within a couple of minutes, Simon felt comfortable walking on his own, however slow and tentative. He made a few trips up and down the hallway.

"That's probably enough for this morning. I'll be back in the afternoon," said the physical therapist.

Simon wasn't satisfied. The fact that he was walking much more slowly and with such great caution troubled him immensely. He wanted to keep walking, hoping that the physical therapist would return in the afternoon convinced that he had recovered his gait completely. Instead, a few minutes after she left, Simon fell hard against the wall of the hallway, and then backward striking his head.

Two nurses and an orderly rushed to his aide. He didn't understand why he fell. He may have simply slipped. The back of his head throbbed. He was taken back to his room in a wheelchair and encouraged to stay in bed the rest of the morning. He felt humiliated, but apart from the headache, he was fine physically.

Simon remained in the hospital two additional days, his

walking improving steadily, though never completely returned to normal. He was eager to leave on a bright, sunny Thursday morning.

"We'll get you an appointment with the neurologist in a couple of weeks. Anything comes up in the meantime, you can call your primary care physician," Dr. Mattei said.

"I don't have one."

"Oh okay. You can call me through the hospital office then. I'm happy to help. Take things slow, Simon. No jogging in the park. Don't drive any long distances, just when you absolutely need to. Expect things to be different, maybe very different. There really isn't anyone you are close to here in Newell?"

"Woman I work with at the Jarvis Center. That's about it."

Simon was discharged. His first priority was retrieving his car which had been towed to a garage. He got an Uber ride there. He explained to the lady in the garage office what had happened. She was both uninterested and unsympathetic.

"$300. We take cash or credit card. No checks."

Simon drove home slowly, aware of all the cautions he had received from Dr. Mattei. His hospital discharge papers included a lengthy list of symptoms to watch for—double vision, paralysis of one or more limbs, loss of vision or hearing. It frightened him a bit. He had no trouble driving and parked at his usual spot on C street. He took a shower and changed into fresh clothes. Then he paid a visit to Anna.

She stood in the doorway. She had never invited him in.

He said, "Good morning, Anna. I just want to let you know I was in hospital for the past few days."

Without much change in expression, Anna said, "Okay. Something happened to your arm? I can see the bandage."

"You could say that. I was electrocuted—struck by lightning."

Anna remained expressionless. Then she looked at Simon sternly, as if to say, "What does this have to do with me?"

Simon continued, "So, I've been through quite a lot. I'm supposed to have someone check in on me once in a while. I'll be off of work for the next two weeks. Just wondering if you wouldn't mind giving me a call once in a while, just in case something happens." Simon felt extremely uncomfortable asking Anna for anything. She had never been the slightest bit friendly.

"Call you? On your cell phone?"

"Yes, maybe every second day. I really don't have anyone here in Newell. No one to stay with for the next couple of weeks."

"Yes, I can call you. I might forget once in a while, but I'll call you and see how you're doing. Do you need anything now?" Simon was surprised by the offer.

"I'm okay. I really appreciate it, Anna. I hope it's not too inconvenient."

"No, it's fine. You've been a good tenant. I don't mind doing that at all."

"Thank you Anna and have a nice day."

Simon went back downstairs to his apartment. He had expected Anna to respond harshly to his request, so her agreeing to help was a bit surprising. He sat on his couch thinking about the unusual dream he had had shortly after he was struck. The details were still fresh. He could recall the numbers, the musical notes, flying above the field at Newell—all of it was remarkably clear. What did it all mean?

He did feel different. He even knew he looked different. While not quite Moses descending from Mount Sinai, he felt his skin was different. He looked in the mirror to find that his hair was slightly greyer. Mostly he moved and spoke much more slowly. Even in his short conversation with Anna, he felt the words were coming into his head quickly, but exited his mouth at an unusually slow pace, to the point he feared she would get annoyed because he wasn't getting to the point. His gait was supposedly normal when he was discharged, according to Dr. Mattei and the physical therapist, but he certainly didn't think so. He walked slowly, he felt, because he had to plan each step, or at least plan a few steps at a time. He walked gingerly, perhaps fearful of falling again. He could only hope that things got better day by day.

22. A SLOW RECOVERY

The boredom was intense in the days that followed. He called Anuja a couple of times, who assured him everything was under control at Jarvis. The third consultant, a young man named Brian, whom Simon didn't hear from after his accident, had taken on a heavy burden of appointments but was doing fine. Anuja, as expected, was doing a superb job with her increased workload.

"Raj and I would like to have you over for dinner when you feel up to it."

"That sounds really nice, Anuja. I'll let you know how I feel." The boredom itself would have been enough for Simon to respond to such an invitation with enthusiasm, but he found that he was remarkably fatigued. Even walking around his apartment required an unusual degree of effort—not just physical, but he felt like he had to plan his mini-excursions—almost as if he needed to decide first how to walk from point A to point B before actually doing it. Anna did call as she promised. Her first call came on a Saturday afternoon.

"Simon. This is Anna calling from upstairs. You asked me to call you every couple of days to check on you." She sounded very uncomfortable speaking to Simon on the phone. She waited for him to respond, as she had no idea what was expected of her beyond calling.

"Thank you for calling, Anna. I'm doing fine. Thanks for checking in."

"Very good. I'll call again on Monday."

Simon had a few student compositions in his apartment. He tried reading them but found he couldn't concentrate. He could see the words on each page, and he could read them just fine, but for some reason, he didn't have enough focus to analyze what he was reading, even after reading the same passages several times. It was incredibly frustrating. He called the neurologist's office and left a message asking if his appointment could be moved up. He was eager to learn what she thought about his prognosis. If his current state persisted, he believed, he would be a permanently disabled forty-seven year old, a depressing prospect.

Simon ventured outside, still very tentatively. He made it to a corner store where he bought a newspaper. He got very tired on the return journey and had to lie down for half an hour before doing anything. Though he had driven once since the accident, he believed it would be unwise to drive again. His concern was not being able to react quickly enough to a pedestrian caught in the middle of a street or a car in front of him that braked suddenly. He did little that Saturday evening. He ordered a pizza that he thought didn't taste especially good. Even getting up to greet and pay the delivery man wore him out.

Alone, tired, and fearful of the future, Simon engaged in a number of morbid thoughts.

Is this the future? Living like an old man in an old woman's basement? What could I possibly enjoy? I liked the concert. Will I be able to go to a concert again? If I did go, would I enjoy it? Would the music even make me happy? Not sure life is worth living like this at all. Wish I could see the neurologist now. If she doesn't think things will get better, life will not be worth living. Sad thing is, I don't even have the strength to end it.

The morbid thoughts gradually dissipated as Simon found he could read his newspaper reasonably well, probably because it required much less attention than reviewing and editing student compositions. It was a local paper. On page 3, a small story in two paragraphs read:

Man struck by lightning during electrical storm leaves hospital

The story summarized the incidents of the previous week, and included a section about how Anuja and an undergraduate student came to Simon's aide. How the reporter knew he was discharged, Simon wasn't sure. Simon was not mentioned by name.

At least I made the news. My fifteen minutes of fame, I guess, he thought.

As the boring Saturday evening continued, Simon decided to call his mother. He hadn't spoken to her since before he had arrived at Newell. The infrequent pattern had been established not long after he graduated from college. It just seemed natural to both Simon and Helen.

Helen was seventy. She still lived in the same small house but had told Simon a few months earlier that she was thinking about moving into a seniors' apartment building at some point. She was careful to insist, "If I move, it's to a regular apartment—not assisted living. I don't need assistance."

Simon's motivations for calling were certainly not to solicit sympathy. He thought Helen deserved to know what had happened in case things took a turn for the worse, and Simon could no longer take care of himself and might have to rely on her to help handle his affairs. He also regularly sent her money, usually relatively small sums of two to three hundred dollars every two to three months. That, of course, would have to stop if he was no longer able to earn a living.

"Good evening, Mother."

"Yes, Simon. Wasn't expecting your call."

"I don't want to trouble you for too long. Are you doing okay?"

"I'm perfectly fine," Helen replied.

"I had an accident. I wanted to tell you about it. I was struck by lightning last week."

"Are you joking or serious?"

"I'm perfectly serious. Just my luck, I suppose. Newell's otherwise been a good place for me."

"How are you now?"

"I have a couple of burns and my head's not quite right. It's hard to explain."

There was a long silence before Helen spoke.

"Is there something I can do for you?"

"Not at the moment. I'm getting steadily better, especially with my walking. I thought it would be best for you to know, in case things get worse. I may not be able to work or send you money."

"Well, I have Social Security, and some money saved. I should be okay. Thank you for letting me know about your situation." Simon could sense that Helen wanted to end the call.

"You're welcome, mother. I'm going to rest now. I'll call you again if something changes."

"Very good. Enjoy your weekend."

What kind of mother have I been cursed with? Simon thought, though her reaction was consistent with his experience throughout his life. *Her son calls to say he has had a terrible accident, and things may get worse, and she tells him to enjoy his weekend!* Simon wished he hadn't called. Fatigued beyond anything he'd experienced before, he fell asleep on the couch in his regular clothes, hoping things would improve the next day.

23. MUSIC REDISCOVERED

A vicious headache woke Simon up around five a.m. It started as a throbbing in the back of his head which gradually got more intense to the point it could be described as more of a pounding. He hadn't experienced anything like it before. He was advised to be cautious about taking medication. He took just two acetaminophen tablets which had no impact at all. Around five-thirty he got out of bed. The headache got suddenly worse when he tried to stand. The pounding became more frequent. So, he lay back down again, but in his bed, rather than on the couch, hoping it would pass. No such luck. The headache actually got worse.

Simon's eyes then started to hurt, and he felt quite suddenly nauseated. He went into the bathroom and threw up in the toilet. He felt immediately better. Even his headache started to subside. He lay back down, and by about nine a.m., he felt well enough to get up and have a bowl of cereal for breakfast. He did worry, of course, that the crippling headache was an ominous sign of worse things to come. He thought about going to the emergency room, but eventually decided to wait to see if the pain returned.

Simon tried again later that morning to return to his work. He had much more success. He was able to focus quite well on the student compositions and made his usual detailed notes. This gave him a great deal of satisfaction. His work that morning was more of an experiment. He knew Anuja had probably distributed those same compositions between her and Brian already, who were also planning to meet with the students who wrote them. He wanted to prove to himself that he was still capable of functioning. He finished feeling good about himself.

It was a sunny, warm, mid-May morning in Newell. Undergraduates had largely disappeared from both the campus and the town. He decided to take a walk. His walking had advanced a great deal. While his gait was still not quite normal, he no longer had to plan every step. He walked around his neighborhood a few times. Almost no one was out. By noon, it was quite muggy, and he decided to return home. Having accomplished two things which made him feel more confident about restoring himself, he decided then to take a drive. It was a quiet Sunday, he thought, and he would be able to navigate the town without encountering too many hazards.

Simon drove to Jarvis, but didn't go inside. He drove to a supermarket to buy a few necessities. He felt quite famished by three p.m. and bought a calzone from a local pizza shop which he ate inside at a counter. These simple things had a great impact on his spirit. Despondency gave way to optimism in a short time. He even considered returning to work the next day despite his doctor advising against it.

In addition to completing simple tasks he originally feared would be hard to accomplish, the terrible fatigue he had experienced soon after his discharge from the hospital had largely resolved. He estimated he had walked at least three miles Sunday afternoon and felt perfectly fine. Even the previous day, he would have had to rest after short excursions around his apartment. He returned home around five and found himself bored again. The Ale House was closed on Sundays. Nothing was going on at Newell as most activities were suspended for summer. Even Brandy's Café was closed. He ate a pre-made macaroni salad he had bought at the supermarket for dinner.

Given his peculiar and isolated upbringing, Simon never developed any real hobbies beyond reading for pleasure. But at some point, he, quite naturally, associated reading any prose with his job, and reading became less pleasurable overall. He was so dreadfully bored he thought that if Anna called, he would try to engage her in a longer conversation. Then he thought, *Fat chance.*

Simon returned to campus that evening hoping something interesting would be going on. He walked by the Jarvis Center. All the lights were off. Newell was beautiful and quiet. A gentle breeze tempered the humidity of the evening. Flowers were in bloom all over campus. Every garden, every spot of green was immaculately maintained. As dusk approached, the unmistakable fragrance of Japanese honeysuckle was everywhere. *Such a naturally beautiful place. But so unnatural to be here completely alone*, he thought.

Simon ventured past several elegant stone buildings without

encountering a soul. In the distance he saw a light emanating from the Newell Music Studies Building. Curious about what might be going on, he walked toward it. The light was coming from a ground floor room. A window was open. As he got closer, he heard piano music. At first, he thought it was someone's stereo, but soon, the clarity of the music made it evident that someone very skillful was playing. Like the campus itself, he thought the music was beautiful.

He sat on the steps of the music building for a few minutes just listening. He felt at peace. The optimism that he had started to experience earlier in the day continued to build. *I can still enjoy beautiful music*, he thought. The pianist inside stopped playing for a minute or so before continuing. He heard a slight cough which made it obvious the pianist was a woman. She played a few more classical songs before stopping completely. Simon could hear her gathering her things. He remained in place. The sun had set completely, and a few stars began to appear on the horizon. He heard the door of the music building open.

24 JENNA

An attractive woman in a light orange cotton summer dress and white shawl emerged.

"Hello. Beautiful evening, isn't it?" she said.

"It certainly is," Simon responded.

"I didn't think anyone was around. Hope my playing wasn't bothering you."

"Oh no, I thought it was beautiful. Absolutely beautiful. I was enjoying it. That's why I sat here."

"That's so kind of you to say. Odd, isn't it? A couple of weeks ago there would be students all over the place, kids playing Ultimate Frisbee and flag football. It feels so empty. Are you done with grading yet?"

"Grading?"

"Submitting grades for the Spring semester. They're due this Tuesday. I'm nearly done with mine."

"Oh, I see. I'm not a faculty member. I work at the Jarvis Center."

"Oh, the writing center, right?"

"Yes. We don't grade anything. Just help graduate students with their writing."

"Very important work for sure. You don't help undergraduates?"

"No, we wait until they've written badly for four years before helping them," Simon said, as he smiled.

"I'm Jenna. Jenna Cobb."

"Simon Galves. It's a real pleasure, Jenna. I take it you're a faculty member?"

"Yes, Associate Professor in Music Studies."

"That's terrific."

"It's been really great meeting you. I'm headed home. My piano is being repaired which is why I've been coming here to practice. Feel free to stop by in the evenings, Simon. I could use the company. You don't have to sit outside on the steps."

"Thank you so much. I was going to hang out here a little longer, but would you like me to walk with you somewhere?"

"Oh, that's very kind of you. My car is really close, just behind the building actually. I have to tell you Newell is perfectly safe. You must have come from a big city."

"Boston."

"I'm from Oakland, California. Staying safe is a big deal there too. Have a wonderful evening. Hope to see you again."

"You too, Jenna."

As he sat on the stone steps staring at the stars and the shadows of the tall oak trees that lined a pathway in front of the music building, Simon started to feel that his initial impressions of Newell were flawed. Parts of the town may have been unappealing, but the college was beautiful. The majority of people he had met had been absolutely wonderful. His landlord may have seemed unfriendly, but at least she called to check up on him. The music professor he had just met, he thought, seemed beautiful both on the inside and out. Yes, he had suffered a terrible accident, but he knew he was on the road to recovery. He also believed the accident had changed his outlook in important ways. A rough and isolated upbringing had taught him to expect almost nothing from anyone. In Newell, the kindness of people he scarcely knew touched him deeply.

Simon made his way home slowly, enjoying the breeze, the

peace, and the stars. He settled in for a good night's sleep. Kindness touched him the next morning—to an almost embarrassing degree. A delivery man rang his bell around ten a.m. and left a huge gift basket full of coffee, chocolates, fruit, and sundry other edibles. Attached was a note, "To a great colleague and friend. A few things to tide you over until you return, Anuja and Raj Sharma." Their generosity was something he had never experienced before.

I don't deserve this, he thought. Then he thought about Anuja and young Brian, and how they must be overloaded. The workload at Jarvis, fueled entirely by graduate students, doesn't slow down in the summer. Simon imagined them both with as many as 10 meetings a day, staying up late working on compositions. The best way he could repay Anuja's kindness, he thought, was to get back to work.

"Anuja?"

"Yes."

"It's Simon. Just wanted to thank you so much for the care package. That was really kind of you and Raj. I don't deserve anything like that."

"You're very welcome, Simon. You do deserve it. You've been a great colleague even though we hardly get to see each other."

"I want to get back to work. I feel quite well. Please steer all new business my way for a week or so."

Having witnessed what had happened only a week earlier, Anuja was very skeptical. "I thought the doctor wanted you off for at least two weeks. You were struck by lightning after all."

"I feel like I need to get back to work."

"How about we compromise? For the next week, you can take on let's say five new clients. If you feel well after that, you can get back to a full load."

Anuja sounded perfectly reasonable to Simon. "That's a good starting point. I just worry about you and Brian taking on so much."

"Don't worry about us. We'll be fine. We'd rather you take the time to recover completely and be able to take on a full load, than come back early and be in a tough situation."

"You're a smart lady, Anuja."

"Can you tell that to my boys? They need to hear that," she said, chuckling.

For the first time since the accident, Simon started to feel quite well both mentally and physically. Not only was he no longer fatigued, but he also felt quite energetic. Neither walking nor driving was a problem. Anna called again, and he told her politely that he was doing quite well, and that calling was no longer necessary. She seemed relieved as her second call was as uncomfortable for her as the first.

Another glorious spring evening in Newell, and Simon headed out for a long walk and a little classical music.

25 A REVOLTING ENCOUNTER

Simon had never met any member of Helen's family, neither those who lived in Ireland nor any of the cousins in New England. She had made no mention of them at any point, until April 1993, shortly before Simon was due to graduate from Bridgewater with an Honor's degree in English. It was an evening like any other, with mother and son sitting silently at the dinner table.

"My mother's ill, Simon."

"Sorry to hear that. How bad is it?"

"I don't know. She has cancer. I don't know much about what's going on. She called me this morning and told me."

"What are you going to do?"

"She wants me to come and see her. Then my brother got on the phone and made the point again. The family wants me to come see her. I want to go to Ireland this summer, probably just for a few weeks."

Simon wasn't sure how to react. He had never even spoken to his grandmother on the phone, nor the uncle in question. He knew Helen had four siblings, all in Ireland. She was the eldest. "I think that's understandable. Especially if it's pretty serious. You should go."

While always reticent, there was a change in Helen's demeanor. Simon sensed a tinge of sadness in her voice. He knew she hadn't told him everything, and that his grandmother's situation must have been quite dire. She said nothing else. When she would go and how she would afford it were uncertain.

While graduates in business, science, and engineering scooped up jobs, often before even graduating, Simon's situation as an honor's English graduate was less sanguine. His fellow English graduates mostly found jobs that had nothing to do with English or literature. Many went on to advanced degrees, which Simon thought he would pursue eventually. There was the thorny question of where to seek work. Jobs were certainly plentiful in Boston but relatively scarce in New Bedford. Simon never had any discussion with Helen about moving out of the house and given the ebbs and flows of her anxiety and their relationship, he had no idea how she might feel about it. He applied broadly, but mostly to jobs in New Bedford, eventually landing a position as a substitute teacher in a network of local schools.

Simon's work schedule was irregular. He was poorly paid. Expectations were low. His main job was simply to provide some basic supervision to children while their regular teacher was away. Lesson plans and assignments for such circumstances had already been formulated. Simon's duty was to make sure the children sat still and carried on their work, being available for help if and when needed. In between assignments, he found himself at home often with little to do, waiting for the school commissioner's office to call. Within a couple of weeks, he decided he couldn't stay in the job.

Though he was never far away, Helen actually grew even more distant at first in the months after Simon's graduation.

Among the motels assigned to Helen on a regular basis was Ford's Quality Lodge, which catered to mostly traveling businesspeople. Helen's other motels were much shabbier, one could say almost seedy. As an attractive woman of forty-two, her wiry frame, big, sad, blue eyes, and angular face attracted much unwanted attention from unsavory types who insisted on remaining in their rooms while she cleaned. "How about you and I hook up and then you clean up afterwards?" she heard on one occasion from a grotesque older man in town to make a court appearance for a speeding ticket. She had been openly propositioned in that way at the shabby motels many times. She took it in stride. Mostly she ignored the comments. Sometimes she responded, "No thank you."

Ford's Quality Lodge had always been a refuge from such indignities until that spring. The business clientele was rarely present in their rooms when she cleaned. Most were downstairs enjoying the free breakfast or out and about for meetings quite early. Almost all were men and almost all were polite and respectful. She came across the same men many times, as they had regular clients they visited often in town. The respectful decorum of the place, from Helen's vantage, changed profoundly one May morning.

"Good morning. Glad it's you. You always do such a nice job with a room," said a gentleman in dress pants, shirts and tie, lying on one of the two beds in his room, watching local news on TV.

"Thank you."

"My name's Steve. I'm in town about once a week. Come from Hartford."

"I'm Helen." Few guests engaged her in conversation, and she was rather indifferent to Steve's friendliness. She continued with her work. Steve said making the bed he was lying on was unnecessary.

"So, I guess you're a regular here huh?" Helen didn't know what he meant and didn't reply.

"I mean you're here at the Lodge a lot as a maid."

"I work here every week."

"Good place to get away from the husband huh?" Helen said nothing but was starting to sense what Steve was getting at.

"Have a nice day, Steve. It was a pleasure meeting you."

"Wait, wait a second. Just thinking about things. Guessing you don't make much as a cleaner. You could use some extra I would imagine."

Helen remained quiet. Steve was ogling her intensely. By that point she could easily tell what he wanted.

"Gosh, this job sure keeps you in shape. Your waist is so tiny."

Helen had already gathered her supplies and was ready to leave. She didn't feel threatened, but the conversation made her more and more uncomfortable.

"We could come to some sort of arrangement perhaps?"

Helen had been propositioned crudely in the past. Steve was

more circumspect. She stood by the door, ready to leave any second. "What type of arrangement?"

"I think I could make your cleaning here more worthwhile every week. Do you understand?"

Helen didn't reply.

"A hundred dollars. Probably as much as you make the whole week."

In 1993, a hundred dollars was a large sum for an impoverished woman who needed to buy an airline ticket to Dublin. She stood there silently, thinking that she would either leave immediately or actually ask Steve precisely what he had in mind. She put her supplies down after a few moments as they were getting awkward to hold. Steve approached, and with no discretion, began removing his clothes. Steve's politeness was replaced with naked crudeness as he grabbed her forcefully, kissed her, pulled down her underwear, directed her to the bed forcefully, and insisted she be on top of him until he was fully satisfied. She could have run out, but Steve was aggressive and authoritative. Refusing to acquiesce may have enraged him. He dressed himself quickly, pulled out five twenty-dollar bills from his wallet, and placed them next to her cleaning bucket.

"You can go now," he said coldly. "Same time next week, okay?" Helen didn't reply. She didn't pick up the money. Instead, Steve grabbed the bills and stuffed them into a pocket on the front of her dress and then stroked her bottom. She grabbed her supplies and left.

She felt guilty and disgusting. Instead of going on to the next room she needed to clean she went instead to an already cleaned room and lay on the bed, immensely distressed, eventually sobbing. At first, she tried to rationalize what had happened—She desperately needed the money; Steve, at least at first, seemed respectable, especially compared to the crude men from the seedy motels, whom she had steadfastly refused. She didn't believe that he would be so crude. Then the guilt set in deeper—She could have simply refused him and left immediately; she could have worked additional hours to earn more and not given Steve any consideration; she could even have asked Simon to help her with her planned trip. It took hours for her to pull herself together enough to finish her work. She decided immediately there would be no more liaisons with Steve.

The following week she saw him briefly again in the same room. He fully expected the arrangement to continue. He seemed even more overtly aggressive. She feared what might happen if she turned him down bluntly.

"I can't today. I'm on my period. I just can't."

"Well, that's that I guess," Steve sounded very frustrated.

The following week she was able to avoid Steve's room completely. She asked another cleaner to take care of it, while she feared what Steve's reaction might be. She had good reason to be worried.

Early that afternoon, Helen was still at work, but Simon was at home with nothing to do. It was easy, even in those days before the Internet, for Steve to find out where they lived. Helen wore a badge at the motels with her name, Helen Galves in bold letters. She was the only Galves in close proximity to the Lodge.

"Good afternoon, young man. Is Helen home?" Steve asked politely standing in the front doorway.

"No, she's at work."

"And you are?"

"Her son."

"I'm a friend. Just wanted to see if she might be interested in taking a drive in the countryside, perhaps to get some coffee. I will make it worth her while," Steve said.

While Steve was very polite, this all sounded bizarre to Simon. Helen didn't have any friends, certainly not middle-aged men who were prepared to offer her a drive in the country.

"I can let her know you stopped by."

"You do that." Steve left a business card for Simon and drove off.

26. LOVE AND FORGIVENESS

Helen returned home around three p.m. She acknowledged Simon by nodding and then went to her room to change into more comfortable house clothes. She came back down a few minutes later and poured herself a glass of water.

"A gentleman stopped by for you mother."

"Oh, was it the gentleman who reads the water meter?"

"No. Someone named Steve. He was dressed in business clothes and said he wanted to take you for a drive." Already pale, Helen suddenly grew paler and froze completely. She dropped her glass which landed on the floor, spilling the water, but somehow not breaking.

"Are you okay, Mother? You look terrified all of a sudden." Helen was indeed terrified—fearful of a strange, aggressive man pursuing her obsessively, reliving what had happened two weeks earlier, and also about trying to explain all this to her twenty-two year old son. Simon quickly picked up the glass and wiped up the water with a towel. Helen remained frozen. He gently took her by the arm and led her to the couch where she sat down. Her breathing became shallow.

"Mother, are you having an attack? Please answer me!" Helen stared at the wall saying nothing.

"Mother, are you having a panic attack? Your breathing is fast. Should I call Dr. Coates?"

After a lengthy pause, Helen spoke. "Dr. Coates is retired, Simon. A new doctor has taken over."

"Should I call him or her? Should I call 911? Let me know what you'd like me to do?"

"Forgive me," Helen whispered.

"What?" Simon asked as he put his right hand on her shoulder, partly to comfort her, but partly because he feared she might fall over.

"Forgive me," Helen repeated. Simon was perplexed.

"You want the good Lord to forgive you, Mother, for what?" Simon had never known his mother to be religious, but still thought that's whom she was speaking to.

"Forgive me, Simon," she said.

Helen's breathing returned to normal. He let her rest for a couple of minutes, but still completely confused, pressed her for answers.

"Mother, who is that man? Why was he here?"

"I met him at the Lodge, one of the hotels I clean."

"Is he your boyfriend?"

"No."

"Why does he want to take you out for a drive then?"

"He wants to have his way with me, Simon." Simon was shocked. His hands were trembling.

"I'm calling the police, Mother, now!"

"Don't do that, Simon."

"Don't do that? Are you serious? A strange man wants to rape you, and you don't want me to do anything?"

"He doesn't want to rape me. He wants me to pleasure him for money."

"He propositioned you? Still, something the police I'm sure would be interested in hearing about. Damn idiot even left his business card. He won't be hard to find!"

Simon got up and walked over to the phone.

"Simon, please don't call anyone. I will take care of it. Please don't call."

"Why not? He's a disgusting pig."

"Because I've already done it with him once."

"What? No, you didn't."

"Yes, I did, Simon. I turned him down after that and I think he's being persistent. He gave me a hundred dollars."

The woman who had protested his innocent evenings with sweet Mia in high school and who had insisted he return home after class in college to stay out of trouble, had given in to a gross, out of town motel patron. It was too much for Simon. He slipped his shoes on, went outside, slammed the door shut, and took a brisk walk. He returned thirty minutes later, much calmer, but no less angry. Helen was still seated on the couch, still frozen.

"Why did you do this, Mother? Why did you do something so disgusting? Aren't you ashamed?" Simon wouldn't normally be so direct with his mother, but filled with disgust, he spoke instinctively.

"I asked you to forgive me, Simon."

"It's not about forgiving you, Mother. You know, I have hoped many times that you would find someone to love and who would love you too. A nice man from the neighborhood. There are certainly quite a few. Instead, you did that. Tell me why!"

"He was insistent and very forceful. I need the money to go to Ireland." Helen continued to stare straight ahead without looking at her son. "He promised me $100 each time, once a week. Had I chosen to do it for a few months, I would have enough money and stop."

"But he wouldn't want it to stop, would he? I know something about being a full-blooded male."

"I don't want to hear about your exploits, Simon."

"I don't want to tell you about them. So, what happens now?"

"I'm not going to be with him again. Ever. I will just work more to get enough money for a ticket."

"The Irish won't give you any money?"

"No, they won't."

"I will put in some hours at the supermarket. I'll pay for the ticket."

Helen finally looked at Simon. His face was red.

"I'm so sorry, Simon. I've brought so much shame into this house. I'm so sorry." For the first time in his life, Simon saw his mother cry. Not just a few tears, but full-blown sobs. She put her head down against the side of the couch. Simon sat next to her and put her head on his lap. He put his arm around her back. She shuddered occasionally as she cried, and Simon could feel just how frail her ribcage was. She said, "I'm so sorry," at least a dozen times. It was difficult for Simon to imagine that the woman he was comforting was the mother he knew.

"Mother. I forgive you. I love you." It was the first time Simon had expressed his love since Dr. Coates had asked him specifically if he loved his mother. "Why don't you go upstairs and get some rest? We'll deal with this situation tomorrow."

Helen rose silently and did just that. She wasn't embarrassed by her tears, nor did she return immediately to her cold demeanor. She gave Simon one of her half smiles before ascending the stairs.

Simon waited until she was upstairs with her door closed before taking action he had already planned. He called Steve's number and left a voicemail telling him sternly that his mother didn't wish to see him again, and that any future unwanted contact would result in a call to the police. He then called the New Bedford police anyway, who told him there wasn't much they could do unless Helen had clearly not been a willing participant. Frustrated by their response, he called the Lodge and spoke to a manager.

Simon told her Steve had been harassing his mother. The manager responded that as Helen worked for a private company that was contracted to clean motels, Simon ought to take up the issue with them. She also added that she hadn't heard any complaints about Steve or other guests. Thwarted to a great extent in his efforts to protect his mother, Simon just hoped both he and Helen had seen the last of Steve.

27. CLAIR DE LUNE

Feeling quite energetic, Simon walked briskly across the Newell campus. It was as eerily quiet as it had been a day earlier. A couple of deer darted across the main commons. He could see the Music Building in the distance, with the same light on. As he got closer, he heard the piano once again, but not mellifluous sounds, but rather jerky notes that sounded a bit like someone pounding the piano keys with a hammer. He made his way to the building swiftly. He didn't wish to interrupt, but Jenna had made it clear he was welcome inside.

Simon found Jenna seated next to a young woman, almost certainly a college student, whom she was instructing.

"Good evening, Simon."

"Sorry I didn't mean to interrupt. I didn't know you had a student."

"Don't worry about it please. This is Chelsea. She's actually an English major here for a private lesson. We're actually wrapping up. You're free to stay."

Chelsea smiled but said nothing. She looked to be a little frustrated with her own progress. Jenna was getting her to divide the piece into parts, mastering each one before moving on. She appeared to be a little stuck. Simon took a seat in a corner of the large room. He didn't want to appear too attentive, for fear of making Chelsea self-conscious. He found a college newspaper and began perusing it.

"Not bad. Tell you what. Let's work on that page for this week. Sound good?" Jenna asked.

"Yes Dr. C. Sounds fine," Chelsea responded.

Chelsea gathered her things and left. Simon had only been there a few minutes and wasn't sure if he should have stayed or left as well.

"Simon, are you next?" Jenna asked.

"Sorry?"

"Just kidding. I meant next for a lesson."

"I might break the piano. You must be awfully busy giving private lessons on top of your job," Simon said.

"The summer is slow at Newell. I don't teach, so I have spare time. How about you? Are you busy in the summer?"

"Jarvis is very busy in the summer since we only help graduate students. But I had an accident, so I'm off for a couple of weeks."

"Sorry to hear that. Are you doing okay now?"

"I feel much better."

"What happened?"

"You're probably not going to believe this, but I was struck by lightning."

"Oh God. I read about that a couple of weeks ago. Had no idea it was you. It was on campus, right?" she asked.

"Yes, during the big storm."

"I guess you're lucky to be alive."

"Yes, that's what they tell me. A couple of burns that are healing well. I also get nasty headaches. I had trouble walking and concentrating, but that's getting a lot better."

"I'm pleased to hear that."

"I don't want to interrupt you, Jenna. I just came to hear some beautiful music. I don't want to get you sidetracked."

"Oh, don't worry. Chelsea was working on 'Clair de Lune' by Debussy. Have you heard of it?"

"No sorry."

"It's a beautiful piece. It sounds simple. But it's actually very difficult to play well."

"I wish I knew more about classical music. I have no background in it at all."

"It's a curious piece—kind of a bridge between classical and modern music. Early twentieth century. Would you like to hear it?"

"Of course."

Jenna stretched out all her fingers and then began to play. The first few notes were subtle, almost imperceptible, a prelude to a beautiful melody. She swayed back and forth gently as she played. The melody was slow and clear. It was the most beautiful music Simon had ever heard. The flowing harmony of 16th notes reminded Simon of water falling. A warm feeling overcame him, much as it had when he heard Massimo playing. This feeling was more intense. Instinctively, he closed his eyes and put his head back against the wall behind his chair. He could see numbers again, numbers which made no sense—18712, 32457, and on and on. These were followed by strings of musical notes arranged in various combinations he didn't understand. He opened his eyes shortly before Jenna finished. She turned around.

"What did you think?"

"That is so beautiful, Jenna. Most beautiful thing I've ever heard."

"And you said you have no background in classical music. So glad you're able to enjoy it. Are you okay? You look a little worn out all of a sudden. I can imagine you're still experiencing effects from the accident."

"I'm okay. The music really affected me, that's all. I think I just need to sit here for a while."

"Oh, that's fine. I'm going to go. Flying to see the family in California tomorrow for a few days. Would you mind just locking the main door and turning off the light on your way out?"

"Sure, I can do that. No problem." Simon remained seated in some sort of half-meditation, his eyes neither fully closed nor fully open. He worried Jenna may have thought of him as being odd, so he added, "It was really nice to hear you play, Jenna. Have a wonderful trip. I am feeling a bit tired all of a sudden. Just need a few minutes to regain my energy."

"I understand. I'll see you again next week I hope?"

"Definitely."

28. STRIKING THE KEYS FOR THE FIRST TIME

Simon remained seated after Jenna left. He had trouble processing how he felt. Clearly the music had moved him. He told Jenna he felt tired, but after a few moments realized that the feeling which overcame him was not fatigue but a feeling of peace. He feared that moving about might disrupt it. He closed his eyes once again, and within a few seconds, the bizarre sequences of numbers and notes appeared. He could see them more clearly. They intruded into the darkness and disappeared immediately as he opened his eyes. He stared at the piano for a few seconds, a beautiful baby grand Steinway, illuminated in all its majesty by a chandelier above. How fluidly Jenna had played, he thought. He was drawn to the piano, perhaps it was its beauty or how it dominated the room, or just the strong desire to touch the keys, hoping something pleasant might be heard. Then he thought he had no skill to play anything worth listening to. The piano continued to draw him, not in some hallucinatory or even metaphysical way. It just seemed like the obvious place he ought to sit was on the bench, with his fingers gently over the keys.

He walked up and sat down, trying to sit as straight as possible which he had seen Jenna do. He struck a few keys. The ones under the "S" and "T" seemed most accessible and he struck them a few times. He had never learned to read music, but Jenna had left an old copy of "Clair de Lune" on top of the piano. It wasn't the copy Chelsea was using. Instead, it was probably something that belonged to the music building that Jenna was using. Simon didn't feel like going home but wasn't sure what to do.

He pulled out his phone and found a series of videos online which explained the history, structure, and organization of a piano, including the notes which corresponded to all the keys. He watched over an hour's worth, while still seated at the piano, experimenting with what he was learning by playing a few notes now and then. He worried a bit that some custodian would ask him to leave at some point, but no one appeared. He then watched another video about piano chords, including how they were structured. It was a lot of very complex information to take in, but the videos grabbed Simon's attention like nothing ever had before. He had never taken as much interest in any work of literature, nor any usage or grammar manual. In fact, he seemed a bit surprised by the intensity of his own interest. It was nearly eleven p.m. when he thought to himself, *Now, let's try to put this together.*

He found a simple piece of sheet music for beginners on top of the piano. He played the melody with his right hand as written, then added the chords with his left hand. The piece was called "The Long March." He decided it must have been a piece instructors used to help beginners get oriented. He didn't like the piece but played it a few more times, more proficiently each time. While he understood the notes, he didn't understand the rhythm or time signature, and knew these must have been critical to playing the piece expertly. But satisfied enough with his progress, he went home, humming "Clair de Lune" all the way.

The next morning, he got up very early and went to Humphrey's Books in downtown Newell where he bought a copy of Nicolas Carter's *Music Theory: From Beginner to Expert*. In the quiet solitude of his apartment, he set out reading it voraciously. He had a pizza delivered which he nibbled on all day. He felt he had never absorbed information so easily and with so much fervor. He couldn't stop. In fact, he went back to earlier sections of the book several times to reinforce his knowledge. It was two a.m. the next day when he stopped reading. His eyes hurt. His head hurt. But he felt absolutely wonderful about what he had accomplished.

The following morning, more energized than ever before, Simon set out to apply his newfound knowledge to his piano playing. He didn't own a piano and knew this would be a bit tricky. He went to the reception area of the Music Building.

"May I help you, sir?" A young man asked.

"I'm a staff member here at Newell. How would I access a piano here to play on my own?"

"You're not Music Department faculty?"

"No."

"Are you enrolled in any classes?"

"No, I'm not."

"Then I'm afraid I can't help you," the young man said quite politely. Simon was not deterred. He needed a piano. Why? Not just to continue learning. He wanted to impress himself by mastering "Clair de Lune." He wanted to impress Jenna. It was easy to locate several used pianos on Craigslist. Simon drove around looking at a few, each seemingly in worse shape than the last. An older woman had listed an apartment sized upright only a mile from his apartment.

"It's in good shape. I just don't play and have no desire to learn," she said. "The piano belonged to my grandson who played it when he came over. He's moved away now."

Simon didn't know how to gauge the quality of a piano. The piano was a Hobart Cable and looked to be at least fifty years old. He tried all of the keys which seemed to work, and peered inside as well to make sure there wasn't anything obviously broken. The woman seemed sincere enough.

"How much are you asking for it?"

"How about a hundred dollars?"

"Sounds good."

"It will cost you more than that to move it to your place," she pointed out.

Simon gave the lady a hundred dollars cash and the same day arranged to have the piano moved to his apartment, making it clear to the movers that navigating the stairs down to the basement apartment would be treacherous. A few hours and two-hundred and fifty dollars later, the piano was successfully relocated. Simon was ecstatic. He didn't mention anything about it to Anna. She can object to a pet, he thought, but who would possibly object to a piano, especially if he played it quietly?

29. Music and Meditation

Not unexpectedly, the piano was very much out of tune, and even Simon, with his lack of experience could tell it didn't sound quite right. It also lacked the rich sound of the Music Department Steinway, not to mention the beauty of that glorious piano. But it was what he had, and he began experimenting with it enthusiastically. He reviewed some of the scales and key signatures in his theory book and played a few scales, correctly, but not as fluidly as he would have liked. He kept playing them over and over again, until they sounded much better, even if a bit out of tune. The piano came with an old piano bench with a storage compartment. Inside it he found an old book of sheet music for pieces by Johannes Brahms.

He started by studying "Canon in F Minor," a relatively simple piece. He looked over the key signature, tapped out the rhythm with his index finger on top of the piano, and placed his hands in the correct position to start the piece without playing. He followed the notes with his mind. He could almost hear the contours and rhythm of the piece. Even the dynamics of the notes became slowly apparent to him.

Next, Simon closed his eyes, feeling it would help him think about the piece more deeply. He took deep breaths. After a minute or so, the odd sequences of numbers and notes he had encountered before appeared. They annoyed him at first, seeming to disturb his peace. But by this point he understood what the notes actually meant. He could see them very clearly. They comprised the "Canon in F Minor." The numbers were more mysterious, and he didn't think too much about them. He continued to take deep breaths. He was in a sort of meditation. He had emptied his mind of all thoughts, but the numbers and notes kept intruding. After a few minutes, faintly, but clearly, he could hear "Canon in F Minor" in his right ear, at a pace which corresponded precisely to the appearance of the notes in front of him. He was alarmed by this phenomenon at first, but let it continue until the piece concluded. He opened his eyes and began to play.

He didn't play the piece perfectly well, but to his inexperienced ears, it sounded pretty good overall. He played it thirty additional times that day. By the end his fingers were sore. He recorded the last repetition on his phone and replayed it a number of times that evening. Then he compared it to a version uploaded to YouTube by a professional pianist. He felt his playing was a little choppier and his rhythm not quite as precise, but he felt that he had done quite well. He tried a couple of additional Brahms pieces, seeking to perfect each in the same way. It was past midnight when he decided to quit for the day.

The next day he saw Anna briefly while she was watering flowers in front of the house. She acknowledged Simon with a nod.

"How are you feeling, Simon? All recovered?"

"Pretty much. I should be back at work next week."

"Was that your music I heard last night? I wasn't sure if it was coming from the basement or from the house next door."

"It was me, Anna. Piano. I bought a piano."

"I see. Must have been difficult to get it down those stairs."

"It was. I had some professional movers do it. They didn't cause any damage to the door or the floors."

"That's good to hear. Well, I hope you enjoy it. I actually like piano music."

Simon felt good about receiving what was essentially a blessing from his landlord. That same day he was able to hire a piano tuner, who, though unimpressed with the quality and state of his piano, was able to tune it satisfactorily. It sounded so much better. He did little else besides play piano that day or the next. It had a powerful hold on him. He would read a student composition, but after a few minutes would be drawn to the piano. Part of the motivation was to continue to learn, but mostly he believed it helped him relax. The pull was so powerful that he believed he couldn't live without playing. "What on earth has happened to me?" he thought. "Was this what I was meant to do all along?"

He continued his obsession by tackling "Clair de Lune," this time with much more background knowledge. He played the piece very slowly at first, then slightly faster each time. He played it more than a hundred times in two days, to the point that he felt it wasn't bad, though not nearly as beautiful as Jenna's rendition. He found a video online of the great Chinese pianist Lang Lang playing "Clair de Lune" on a barge floating down the Seine. Lang Lang is not only a rare talent, but his passion is reflected by his body language and facial expressions in a way that makes it seem like he is enjoying himself immensely. *To be that carefree, relaxed*, Simon thought, *is something that will take a lot of practice.*

He got a phone call from Anuja one evening while he was playing.

"Hello, Simon. Just checking in. How are you feeling?"

"Thanks so much for calling. I'm doing quite well. Eager to get back to work. I'm sure you and Brian have been swamped."

"It hasn't been too bad. I know we talked about having you over for dinner. You may not be quite up to that. But how about just for tea this afternoon. It will be just Raj and me. The boys are off doing their own thing today."

Simon hesitated to reply for a moment. Of course, he

appreciated the invitation but was worried about tearing himself away from the piano for a couple of hours.

"Okay, that sounds very nice."

"Great, how about around two?"

"Perfect."

Anuja and Raj lived in an elegant Victorian styled home close to campus that they had renovated extensively over the course of many years. They had a beautiful garden. Tea, along with rich Indian sweets, was served in the living room, overlooking the front yard. The Music Building could be seen in the distance. Raj was an affable gentleman, about fifty-five.

"So sorry to hear about the accident. I heard you're still having aftereffects," Raj said.

"Thanks. I'm doing much better. Grateful to Anuja for getting me help quickly."

"Besides that, do you like Newell?"

"Yes, I do. I'm settling in quite nicely."

"He's a star consultant," Anuja added.

"Thanks, Anuja. I've heard nothing but great things about you too," Simon said.

"We've been here twenty-five years now. I think it's a decent place, especially if you're into music. Do you like classical music?" Raj asked.

Simon wasn't sure how to reply. It would take some time to explain his incredible transformation.

"I started playing the piano, Raj."

"Wonderful, taking lessons?"

"No, learning on my own."

"Our younger son took lessons for a long time. So many great teachers in town, but he's pretty much given it up now," Anuja said.

"That's an understatement. He hasn't touched the piano for a couple of years," Raj said.

"I bought a piano last week."

"That's too bad. We would have given you ours. It's just sitting there," Raj added.

"I think it's a decent one too," Anuja added.

"Mine is a bit beat up actually."

"Take a look. It's upstairs. It's yours if you want it," Raj said.

Having not played for a few hours, Raj's offer was tempting. Simon went upstairs with Raj and Anuja to find an old Baldwin upright piano that looked extremely heavy.

"May I?" he asked.

"Sure," Anuja responded.

Simon stretched his fingers in the way he had seen Jenna do it. Then, with no sheet music in front of him, purely from memory, he played "Clair de Lune," with perfect rhythm. Anuja and Raj were stunned.

"So why did you say you started playing the piano, Simon? You meant started playing since you came to Newell," Anuja said.

"I can't explain it well. Honestly, I never played ever before. Had no background in music at all. Just can't stop learning and playing."

"That was absolutely beautiful. You have an incredible gift," Anuja said.

"I agree. If you want to get rid of your rundown piano, you're free to take this one. I know it won't be easy to move. Just think about it. You can clearly make better use of it than we can," Raj said.

"I appreciate the offer. Moving pianos is a real ordeal I've learned. I'll think it over."

Simon made his way home shortly afterwards so that he could get back to playing as soon as possible.

30. Crippling Headache

Over the next couple of days Simon ate little, slept little, played voraciously, and when not playing, listened to classical music as much as he could on his phone or computer. For a man who had never touched a musical instrument, it was a sudden and unfathomable obsession. He went to bed around three a.m. one night, having done nothing apart from piano that entire day. He got up at six, eager not to waste time and get back to piano. But he started to experience a pounding headache.

Like his other headaches, this one started insidiously, in the back of the head. It was a gentle, regular pounding at first. As it got more intense, he could feel the muscles in his neck tighten. About an hour later, the headache was becoming unbearable. He could hear an annoying, high-pitched hum in his right ear. He lay down and closed his eyes hoping it would pass, but it only got worse. He got up to take some acetaminophen. Just standing up intensified the headache tremendously. After swallowing the pills, he lay back down immediately. His breathing became shallower. For a few moments, he thought of calling someone, even 911, but the idea of moving in any direction to use the phone and the anticipated likely worsening of pain kept him in place. A fit of successive, painful throbs came on around nine. He felt suddenly nauseated and threw up in the toilet. He lay back down with his eyes closed. Gradually, over the next few hours, the headache subsided. By noon, he was able to get up and function. He didn't head straight to the piano. The severity of his headache was alarming enough for him to consider more immediate medical attention than what had been arranged by Dr. Mattei.

Dr. Mattei had arranged for a follow-up with neurologist Carmen Delarosa who worked in a small group practice in the center of Newell. Simon called that morning to explain that he was suffering severe headaches and if there was any way to be seen earlier than originally planned. At first, the receptionist suggested he go to the emergency room, but Simon told her he felt that wouldn't be all that helpful since he felt quite fine at the moment. Dr. Delarosa was able to squeeze him in later that afternoon.

Dr. Delarosa was a pleasant woman in her mid-sixties, originally from Colombia, who had practiced in Newell since 1986. She had a wealth of experience and was one of only four neurologists in town.

"I got the notes from the hospital. I even read about what happened in the newspaper. It's great to have the chance to look after you. How are you feeling?"

"I've had bad headaches. Horrible actually, including this morning. They only get better after I throw up. I feel fine now. I'm really scared of having another one."

Dr. Delarosa obtained a thorough history of Simon's case since he was discharged, including asking about symptoms like double vision, loss of touch sensation, and difficulty walking. He provided lots of detail, even discussing his experience day by day. She examined him thoroughly, finding nothing abnormal.

"We can get an MRI. It might show what's happening."

"I had scans after the accident."

"Yes, you had a CT scan. We might get more detail from the MRI. Also, something may have changed. I don't find anything wrong on my physical examination. Does that sound like a reasonable starting point for you? We can discuss the results by phone next week if you like. In the meantime, I'm going to give you some migraine medication for the headache. I realize it may not be migraines, but the medication may help. You take two tablets as soon as you feel a headache coming on. You can repeat the dose two hours later if you still have pain."

"That all sounds reasonable, Dr. Delarosa. There is just one other thing I didn't mention. Since the accident, I started playing piano."

"That's very nice."

"Thank you. The thing is. I never had any interest in playing before. It's become an obsession. I think about piano music all the time. I listen to it. I practice it. I read about it. I even see notes and numbers in front of me when I close my eyes and meditate for a few minutes."

Dr. Delarosa looked at Simon skeptically. For a few moments she felt that the gentleman who had been so articulate, polite, and reasonable was suddenly talking nonsense.

"You see notes when you meditate? Is that what you said?"

"Exactly. Yesterday, I played piano for thirteen hours."

"Are you serious? I know you're off work but still, why so much?"

"I am drawn to it. I can't stop. I actually feel terrible when I'm away from a piano."

"This is all very interesting. How's your mood been? Would you say you're depressed at all, or anxious?"

"I am anxious about what might be going on inside my head. Not just the piano but the headaches too. But I don't think it's anxiety that's driving me to play. It's like a force, like it's a very hot day and someone offers you a cold drink. It's irresistible. I can't stop."

Dr. Delarosa thought deeply for a few moments. "There is a phenomenon, Simon, where a very small number of people who are struck by lightning develop new interests or even new abilities. I don't have any expertise in that. That might be what's going on. Mind you, it's extremely rare. Most people struck by lightning are either killed or disabled in some way. I think you're very lucky."

"Everyone tells me that. I've got a new hobby at least."

"Sounds like more than a hobby, and there's nothing wrong with that. You must be getting pretty good at playing?"

"I think I'm doing well. I'll keep you updated."

31. Remarkable Progress

Simon returned immediately to his piano, playing a few simple classical pieces intensely. He turned his attention to "Clair de Lune" in the evening, working through it slowly, line by line. This continued the next day as well, until he felt it sounded decent, albeit a bit too slow. He listened to several versions available on the Internet and tried his best to mimic the style and pace. Although he was inexplicably drawn to the piano, there was, in the back of his mind, a clearer purpose. He wanted to impress Jenna and was looking forward to her return. While just about everyone he had met at Newell had been decent and warm, Jenna seemed especially convivial. He knew the day she would be returning from Oakland and set out across campus to find her at the Music Building. He wasn't disappointed. He found her finishing her lesson with Chelsea.

"Simon, how are you, my friend?"

"Doing quite well. How was your trip?"

"Very good. We need just a few more minutes."

Chelsea smiled at Simon without saying anything. With Jenna at her side she started to play "Clair de Lune." She struggled through several parts. There were a few incorrect notes, which grated on Simon as he had learned the piece so meticulously. She stopped halfway through, seeming to lose track of where she was on the sheet music in front of her. Nevertheless, she finished, and Jenna complimented her on her progress. Chelsea gathered her things, smiled and left.

"She's a really good student."

"Yes, seems like a nice young lady too. So, you had a nice time visiting family?"

"Yes, I did. How was your week, Simon?"

"It was pretty interesting. I've taken up the piano."

"Wow, that's wonderful."

"I even bought a piano and have been playing nonstop."

"I didn't know you were so interested."

Simon wanted to show Jenna the progress he had made of course. The beautiful Steinway in front of him was also irresistible.

"May I?"

"Of course."

Simon exchanged places so that Jenna was seated close to the piano and had a good view of the keyboard. He stretched his fingers and set out playing "Clair de Lune." His performance was nearly flawless, the dynamics of a few notes not being quite right. He closed his eyes several times as he played, and even swayed a little with the contour of the music. Once he finished, he turned around and looked at Jenna who had a shocked look on her face.

"You have a strange sense of humor, Simon."

"What do you mean?"

"You're obviously an accomplished pianist who has been playing for years. Why the story about not knowing anything?"

"I swear, Jenna, I just started. I've been playing 10-15 hours a day for the past week, studying a music theory book, listening over and over again to classical piano music. I've been going nonstop."

"Why?"

"I don't know why. I can't stop. I never had this obsession before the accident. I really have no idea what's happened to me."

"But how is it possible that you've learned so much in a week? I've never heard of such a thing no matter how much work someone puts into it."

"I can't explain it. I'm not trying to deceive you in any way. I want to express my gratitude to you for turning this on within me. It's become a major purpose for me."

"You never took lessons as a kid, right?"

"Never."

Jenna sat there looking neither impressed nor unimpressed but confused. "Play something else."

Simon played a few Brahms pieces he had memorized. These, once again, were nearly perfect.

"That was wonderful. I don't know what to make of it." Jenna quietly gathered her things and prepared to leave.

"Goodnight, Simon."

"Wait, will you be here again tomorrow?"

"I don't have any students here tomorrow, but I might come to practice. What kind of piano do you have at home?"

"A piece of crap."

"I'll text you the code for the front door. You can come and practice here any time you like. Have a nice evening." Jenna departed leaving Simon imagining that at best he had bewildered her, and at worst, offended her, as he feared she still believed he was vastly underreporting his piano experience. He continued to play for another couple of hours, enjoying the Steinway's mellifluous tones, so superior to the instrument he owned. Then he went home, played a bit more, and fell asleep.

32. A New Job for Helen

Her vulnerability and questionable judgment having been on full display, Simon's relationship with his mother changed fundamentally after he learned about Steve. Fortunately, neither he nor Helen heard anything from the man. Helen was able to avoid cleaning his room. Simon was able to secure twenty hours a week at the supermarket, which in addition to his irregular hours as a substitute teacher made for a grueling schedule. Helen continued as usual, returning home in the early afternoons. She didn't know his schedule and never pressed him for it. She wallowed in firmly rooted shame. For several days, she could barely make eye contact with Simon. He would ask her daily, "You didn't run into that guy again, did you?" She would respond, "no" firmly and then resume her silence. Simon believed her of course, but wondered, what else she might have been up to all those years that he might have found distasteful. Within a short time, no longer did Helen seem wary about Simon's whereabouts. Instead, it was Simon who worried about his mother and who felt a duty to protect her.

Simon could not easily wipe away what had happened with Steve from his conscience. He was in no way religious, nor prudish, but continued to experience a low-grade visceral repugnance the moment he thought about what had happened, which was many times a day. He blamed the licentious Steve, of course. His seeming politeness was all an act, he figured, designed to disguise his vulgar intent. He also remained angry with his mother. How many times had she done something like that? he wondered. He also thought about how much guilt *he* had felt over the years, for merely trying to enjoy himself now and then away from her company. And after that, she sold herself to a traveling salesman for a hundred dollars. He believed she no longer had any business questioning his behavior or judgment. Nor would she dare try.

Simon put all these intense feelings aside and decided to break through the habitual silence at home to have a proper conversation with his mother about her future. The trigger was a job posting he saw at one of the elementary schools where he was working, looking for a cafeteria worker. The hours were very reasonable and at $5.50 an hour, the pay significantly better than what Helen was making. It was, of course, a more social position than cleaning motel rooms. But she was unlikely to be propositioned, and Simon believed the more regular socialization might do her good. He spoke to a secretary at the school who told him his mother would need to apply through the school board and also go through a brief interview.

"I came across a job at the school I think would be very good for you."

"Cleaning?"

"No, working in a cafeteria and serving food to children. I suppose there would be some cleaning afterwards."

"Why would it be good for me?"

"The hours are regular. The pay is better. Many decent people around."

"What about the children? Would I have to look after them? I don't think I could do that well."

"I don't think that's a big part of the job. Just preparing and serving food. They have lunch monitors who look after the children while they're eating. I would really like you to apply." Helen shrugged her shoulders, which Simon interpreted as some interest in the idea. Only a couple of months earlier suggesting a job for his mother was unthinkable, and she may have reacted with hostility. "Don't you think it's better for you to work in a school where you won't run into someone like Steve?"

Helen paused before replying. "That's true. I still fear running into him, Simon."

The next day Simon brought home a simple one-page application which asked for some basic details and references, and he helped his mother fill it out. She listed a couple of cleaners she knew well as references. He took the application to the school board's employment office the next day where a polite woman named Joanna said she could review it on the spot.

"Thanks for recommending your mother, Mr. Galves. It's hard to find good people for these types of jobs."

"You're welcome. I think she'll do very well."

"Normally we would carry out an interview, but instead, can you tell me a bit about your mother? She has no experience working in a school, right?"

"No, her only experience is cleaning motels."

"No discipline problems, drugs, alcohol issues to be aware of?"

"None, whatsoever."

"What's her personality like?" Simon didn't expect the question and thought for several seconds.

"She's very quiet."

"That's actually good to hear."

"She's reliable, conscientious, I would say."

"Does she like working with children?"

"She doesn't have any real experience working with children, but I'm confident she will learn quickly."

"Her date of birth is February 12, 1943, correct?"

"Yes. She has no physical limitations?"

"No."

"I'll tell you what. She sounds like a decent fit. Ask her to show up this coming Monday at eight a.m. at the school for an orientation with the cafeteria manager. We will try her out for a week and keep her if it works out. Does that sound reasonable?"

"Thank you." Simon was very pleased. The hazards of Helen working in isolation cleaning motels could soon be forgotten, he hoped.

"Mother," he said as he came in that evening, "wonderful news, you got the job!"

"Just like that. I thought there was an interview?"

"I vouched for you. They will try you out for a week beginning on Monday." Helen seemed indifferent to the news. Simon didn't expect her to be excited but was hoping for some type of positive reaction.

"I will have to let my boss know today, then, that I'm quitting."

"You should do that. I think this will be very good for you. You will be much safer working in the school. I can even come and see you sometimes. I'm really happy you're doing this."

"I didn't do anything. You did all this for me. You decided what I should do," Helen said, somewhat irritated. Simon took a deep breath.

"You're right. I did this. If it doesn't work out you can blame me then, okay?"

Helen didn't reply.

33. First Date

Simon began to feel that his piano obsession was having detrimental effects. He had confused, perhaps even frightened, Jenna. He also knew the date he planned to resume his work at Jarvis was fast approaching, and that there would be no way he could devote entire days and part of each night to playing piano. The morning before he was due back at work, Simon played for just an hour. "Fur Elise" was a popular and relatively simple Beethoven piece. He decided once he was able to play it to his own satisfaction, it would be time for a short break. Later that morning he began to experience a headache. It began as his previous ones, insidiously in the back of his head. He took the migraine medication as instructed, but the pounding continued to intensify. Within an hour he felt completely disabled and had to lie down.

A few minutes after lying down and closing his eyes, with his head still throbbing terribly, Simon began to see numbers and musical notes again. Instead of the parade of images he had seen before, this time, the notes and numbers looked quite distant and got closer gradually. As they did, he struggled to make them out, feeling like he was squinting under his eyelids. As they became clearly discernible, the numbers and notes did not stop advancing upon him. It was a menacing sensation which made him shudder. Each set of notes and numbers would eventually dominate his entire field of view, and instinctively he put his right arm over his eyes to protect himself. All this with the additional agony of a headache that only got worse.

After an hour, he struggled to make his way to the bathroom and took another tablet of migraine medication. It proved as completely useless as the first dose. Finally, after an additional hour, the pounding, now more severe than ever was accompanied by the intense sensation of nausea of the type he had experienced before. He vomited, and a few minutes later his headache began to subside. It was early afternoon. He felt exhausted and lay in bed for two more hours before, with some trepidation, emerging from his darkened bedroom to try to make the day more productive than it had been.

Simon pondered many practical matters. A disabling headache of the type he had just endured would put an end to any workday, leaving many clients unhappy, not to mention his fellow consultants. Never one to complain, Simon also felt a strong need to share what he was going through with someone. Jenna was the right person. If she understood that his newfound musical obsession, and possibly talent, came with a significant drawback, perhaps she would be sympathetic and more understanding of the whole picture of what had happened.

That evening Simon made his way to campus, stopping for a slice of pizza on the way. Eerily quiet as usual, he looked hopefully for the familiar light in the Music Building, where he expected Jenna to be either teaching or practicing. He found her in the usual place. She was seated at the piano, but rather than playing, she was reading from a notebook.

"Hi, Jenna," he said quietly, not knowing what to expect from her.

"Hi, Simon. How has your playing been going?"

"Trying to be a bit less obsessive about it. Just working on 'Fur Elise,' that's all."

"Great, let's hear it."

Simon played the piece slowly and carefully. Jenna smiled.

"It's good. But I have to tell you, it's a bit choppy at points. Sometimes, you speed up here and there, like you're rushing to finish. I think you could be a great pianist with a little refinement."

Simon was delighted to receive her feedback. "Wow, thanks. That's really helpful. I want to become more refined."

"You play beautifully, Simon. But you can't be a truly great pianist until you have a real emotional connection with the music. It's not about playing the notes, or just following the rhythm. It's hard to explain. You ever hear about pianists 'interpreting' a piece?"

"Yes, I've heard that."

"What do you think it means? After all, a single piece has all the same notes no matter who plays it."

"I thought it meant trying to figure out what the composer expected to hear. Trying to interpret the rhythm and dynamics because I find sometimes, they can be ambiguous."

"That's what most people think. I actually believe 'interpreting' is trying to figure out what the composer wants the audience to feel, not just hear—or trying to figure out what the composer felt as he wrote the piece."

"That's fascinating," Simon responded.

"Did you have dinner?"

"I had a slice of pizza on the way here."

"I'm famished. Would you like to get another bite to eat?"

"I'd love to and I know just the place, too," Simon said.

The compactness of Newell meant that St. James Ale House was only a short walk away. Simon walked in and spotted Fiona at the bar who immediately gave him a thumbs-up when she noticed he was with Jenna. A waitress seated them at a corner table. The place was relatively quiet as it usually is in the summer.

"I've never been here, believe it or not." Jenna said.

"How long have you been in Newell?"

"Nine years."

"Wow," he said. "A good pub is one of the first things I look for."

"I like it. It's very homey."

"It is. Thanks for coming out with me," Simon said.

"No, thank you. It was my idea, remember. So what's Simon all about?"

"Not sure how to answer that question but I'll give it a try. I grew up in Massachusetts. Studied English at Bridgewater State. I did an MFA at Boston College a few years later and stayed on there for quite a number of years as a writing instructor. They downsized a lot of things there last year, and so I came to Newell."

"Sounds a bit like my story. Grew up in Oakland, all my education was at UC Davis. Came here nine years ago."

"Why Newell?"

"Well, that's a long story. Have you heard of a music professor named Albert Foster?"

"No."

"Very well-known jazz pianist. I came here with him."

"I see. You were his trainee of some sort?" Simon asked.

"I was at one point, yes. But I was with him." She turned to look at him. "You understand?"

"Ah, takes me a while to clue in."

"That's okay. To make things simple, it didn't work out. How about you? Married, kids?"

"No to both. Never married."

"What's your excuse?" she asked.

"No excuse really. Committed introvert, I would say. I was pretty sheltered growing up. Still have a lot of trouble connecting with people." Simon looked down. His candid confession left him feeling embarrassed.

"That's okay. Lots of good, lonely people in the world. People are lonely for different reasons," Jenna said.

"You've never been married?"

"No. Sure wasted many years on the great professor Foster. You know, it's a bit harder for people like me. Many of us are not married."

"I know."

"You know?"

"I mean I've heard that. You know on the radio. Oprah Winfrey, stuff like that."

"You're an Oprah fan?" Jenna sounded surprised.

"Not really. My mother used to watch a lot of TV."

"Does *she* play piano?"

Simon chuckled. "No, she doesn't. There is no musical talent in my family."

34. DeValles Elementary School

Helen began her new job at John B. DeValles Elementary School with a sense of dread. Simon wasn't working that day, but he knew her first day might be difficult for her, so he offered to drop her off and pick her up to make things a little easier. Helen was silent as expected on the drive over, but Simon could tell she was very nervous. At one point, her right hand was trembling.

"It's always hard to start a new job in a new place," Simon said, in an effort to calm her down.

"I know. Just not sure I can deal with all those kids," Helen replied.

"There is a whole team there in the cafeteria. They will help you out."

Helen said nothing. She got out quickly at the school, arriving well before the seven a.m. start time. Simon picked her up promptly outside at two p.m.

"How did it go today?"

"Fine. I'd like to go home now." That was the extent of Helen's initial communication to Simon about the new job. She drove herself the rest of the week. At the end of the week, Simon asked her again.

"The trial week is done. How do you think it all worked out?"

"They won't be keeping me on."

"Why not? What happened?"

"Nothing happened. They just told me it wasn't working out, and not to come in on Monday. I called Harold as soon as I came back who told me I can get my old job back cleaning motels."

"Mother, did you say something to someone that was a problem?"

Helen looked offended. "I didn't say anything that was a problem, Simon." Simon was livid. He believed his hard-working mother had been unfairly dismissed because she was taciturn and serious. He could imagine the other cafeteria workers joking, telling stories about their weekends, engaging the children in playful ways. His mother couldn't do those things, but surely, she could serve food and clean a kitchen.

That Monday he called the school board to speak with Joanna. She told him only that Helen hadn't worked out well, and encouraged him to speak with the cafeteria manager, a woman named Audrey Silva. He wasted no time and drove straight to the school, where he found Ms. Silva, a woman roughly his mother's age, seated at a table inside a small office next to the cafeteria.

"I want to talk to you about Helen Galves."

"She doesn't work here anymore."

"I know. I'm her son. I helped get her the job." Simon sounded very frustrated, but not angry. "Ms. Silva, can you tell me why she was let go?"

"She was given a one-week trial period. That's pretty common for people who have no experience in a school. At the end of the week, we had to make a decision. I asked everyone if we ought to keep Helen, and no one thought we should." Simon felt immediately hurt. His mother was a pitiful figure after all, and the indignity of no one sticking up for her, whether she was fully aware of it or not, was hard to bear.

"Did she do something inappropriate?"

"Like what?"

"I don't know. Say something to someone, maybe one of the kids, that made them upset?"

"Your mother barely acknowledged any of the children. She barely interacted with the other staff. So no, she didn't do anything to upset anybody like that."

"I know she's very quiet."

"Quiet? She seemed like she was terrified the whole time. The big problem is that your mother didn't ask questions when she didn't know where something was. She would just try to find it on her own. She did anything she could to avoid people, especially me. I can't have someone like that on my team. I'm sure she's a fine lady, but this is not the place for her. She probably needs something where she can finish her work on her own."

Simon felt increasingly hurt by Ms. Silva's candid comments. There was a long pause before he responded.

"Is there something she can do at the school, that doesn't require her to interact so much?"

"I don't know. I'm just the cafeteria manager."

"I think my mother works hard. She can do a good job. I thought this job was a good change for her. She would be around people. Make friends. I guess I was wrong."

"What did she do before?"

"Cleaned motels. She wants to go back to it now."

Joanna smiled and invited Simon to sit down on a chair on the other side of the table. "I feel badly for you. I do think she works hard. She hustles, that's for sure. But think about my position. What am I supposed to do if no one wants to work with her? If people say she's not friendly? We thought it would be just the first day and by the end of the week, she'd feel a lot more comfortable with us, but it didn't get better."

"She's very quiet, like I said. Not used to being around a lot of people."

"I appreciate you coming in. I also think she should be very proud to have a son who sticks up for her the way you do. Great that you're trying to help your mother. But sorry, this isn't her place."

Simon thanked Ms. Silva and left. Her assessment of Helen was painful not because it was surprising, but because it reinforced what he already believed about his mother. He had hoped it could have been different, that though she had been so cold to him for so many years, in the right environment, she may have blossomed and experienced joy, as well as stayed safe. Instead, he regretted ever engaging her in the opportunity. He thought perhaps her only destiny was to clean motel rooms, quietly, with no radio or television, alone whenever possible, and trying to preserve her self-respect in the presence of guests whenever not possible. It was a destiny of poverty and isolation, but one whose familiarity, Simon believed, provided her with comfort.

35. SPRING ROMANCE

"Thanks for a lovely evening, Simon," Jenna said.

"No, thank you. It's wonderful to spend time with someone, especially after everything that's happened," Simon said.

"My car's right here."

"So, I'd like to give you a hug," Simon said.

"Of course."

Simon gave Jenna a tepid hug, one that one might provide to a professional female colleague after not seeing her for a while. "So, will you be around at the Music Building tomorrow?"

"Yes, I will. My own piano won't be ready for some time. I would enjoy working with you, too."

"Really? I'm a hack." Simon looked down at his shoes.

"You're something special. I've never met someone so determined, and you really have a gift. The way you play 'Clair De Lune' would take most people many years."

Simon felt embarrassed by Jenna's flattery. So, he returned the attention to her. "You're a great pianist, and I'm sure you're a great teacher. I appreciate you wanting to work with me. I can pay, of course."

"No, you're not going to pay anything. Don't even think about it. It's not going to work that way. You're eligible for continuing education credits as a staff member. It's free anyway. Just sign up for piano, and I will receive credit for teaching you."

"Still, very generous of you, Jenna." Under the dim lights of the parking lot, with crickets chirping in the warm, late spring air, Simon thought Jenna looked lovely. "May I kiss you?"

"You may."

Simon kissed her gently on the lips.

"I must say, you are a true gentleman. Are you sure you're not from the South?" she said.

"That's funny. No, I grew up near Boston. Quite the opposite. It's pretty brash up there, if you know what I mean. Besides, a lowly staff member has to be careful kissing an associate professor, I would think."

"You're funny. Goodnight, Simon."

Exhilarated by a delightful evening and a meaningful new connection, Simon made his way home slowly. The campus was truly beautiful, the near stillness interrupted only by an occasional breeze rustling through the majestic oak trees which lined the Newell Oval. Simon felt no fatigue. His head didn't hurt. Even the incessant urge to play piano had been tempered to a significant degree by the joy he felt from his evening with Jenna. When he arrived back at the apartment, Anna was outside watering plants she had placed on the front porch under which was Simon's separate entrance.

"Good evening, Anna."

"Good evening, Simon. I know you didn't feel I needed to check in with you, but how are you feeling?"

"I'm doing really quite well. I hope my piano playing isn't bothering you."

"I can't really hear much of it, so no. Are you going back to work?"

"Yes, planning for tomorrow."

"Good. So, you'll be able to pay the rent June 1st?"

"Yes, I will, don't worry."

"I don't mean to badger you about it. It's just that I rely on that money now that my husband is gone. I hope you understand that." It was the most candidly Anna had ever spoken to Simon.

"I do understand, and I won't let you down."

The piano beckoned Simon later that night. He resisted for a little while. Instead of a prolonged, obsessive session lasting hours, he played a few familiar pieces for about thirty minutes and settled into bed quite early. Around four a.m., the familiar and unwelcome throbbing in the back of his head returned. He knew exactly what to expect but it didn't make it any easier to bear. He took the migraine medication as soon as possible, but just as before, the headache intensified. He couldn't fall back asleep. The pain just kept getting worse. It seemed to him that it had a life of its own, taunting him, punishing him, trying to knock him down after he had had a wonderful evening. *These headaches are really determined to finish me off somehow*, he thought.

He remained in bed with his eyes closed and waited for the musical notes and numbers to appear. They did in short order with the same menacing pattern he had experienced before - distant at first, then closing in slowly, threatening to run into him, forcing him to instinctively cover his eyes with his arm. The pain got worse and worse, to the point he felt, "something's got to break." After a few, intense, violent throbs during which he writhed on the bed, came the intense feeling of nausea. He vomited immediately expecting relief, which came shortly afterward. By seven a.m., he was headache free.

36. A Medical Referral

Simon was anxious as he made his way to Dr. Delarosa's office for his follow-up appointment. His passion for piano may have been an unexpected benefit of the lightning strike, but he feared the headaches were a sign of something gravely wrong.

"I reviewed the scan this morning. It shows your brain looks perfectly normal."

"I guess that's good news. Thank you Dr. Delarosa."

"More importantly, how have you been feeling?"

"I still get severe headaches every day or two. They're really bad. The medication you prescribed doesn't seem to have any effect."

"I'm sorry to hear that, Simon. The headaches leave you unable to function at all?"

"Yes, for about two hours at a time. They follow a familiar pattern. Throbbing in the back of head that gets worse and worse. I need to lie down. Then I start to see numbers and musical notes. Eventually the throbbing gets to a point that it makes me throw up and I feel better."

"Back up a few seconds and talk to me again about the music notes and numbers. What exactly do you see?"

"I see them when my eyes are closed. They are very clear sequences of numbers and notes. Now that I'm more familiar with music I know what the notes mean, but the numbers are a mystery."

"What happens if you open your eyes?"

"I don't open my eyes when my headache is really bad. Because I feel like the pain will get worse. I just close my eyes as an instinct. But I imagine the numbers and notes would disappear if I opened my eyes. They are surrounded by darkness."

"But you're awake when you see them?"

"Oh yes, definitely awake. I can hear a car going by on the street, or the bell sound on my phone when I receive an email. I'm definitely conscious."

"Okay. We can try other medications for your headaches, including a medication that might help prevent them from coming on. But the other things going on are very unusual."

"I realize that. I'm still obsessed with playing the piano. I've been making very good progress. I even have a new teacher."

"That's wonderful. Yours is an unusual situation. Have you heard of Dr. Mark Brenner, the neurologist? He's written some popular books."

"No."

"He studies people who've had trauma to their brains and then go on to develop a new, unusual talent. He's studied somewhere around fifty people. I should connect you to him. He's in Ann Arbor, Michigan, though. Would you be willing to make the trip?"

"If you think he can help me."

"I don't know him personally, and I don't know if he can help you. But he can probably tell you more about what happened and what to expect. He may even have some solution for the headaches if none of the usual medications work. He's a bit unorthodox from my understanding. He has even started a small peer support group of people like you."

Simon replied, "I would appreciate you connecting me with Dr. Brenner. Thank you."

"You're welcome. I wish I could do more for you."

Knowing that there was no obvious brain damage, Simon left Dr. Delarosa's office feeling more hopeful. He was due to return to work that afternoon and had three meetings scheduled, all at Jarvis, whose space Anuja and Brian had kindly given up so that Simon wouldn't have to travel so much as he eased back into work.

Simon's meetings went very well. It felt terrific to get back into the swing of things. Two of the students needed highly specific help organizing their compositions. The third was a Chinese student looking mainly for guidance on a long-term strategy to improve her English writing. Late that afternoon he received a call on his cell phone.

"Mr. Galves, this is Jean calling from Dr. Mark Brenner's office. He would like to speak to you for a few minutes. Would now be okay?"

"Yes, certainly."

"Simon, Mark Brenner here. I got a call from Dr. Delarosa about what happened. First of all, let me express my sympathy for all you've been through. May I ask how you're doing now?"

"Thank you, doctor," Simon said. "Today, I'm doing quite well since I found out my scan was normal."

"Your MRI. Yes, well, that's not unusual after a lightning strike. But sometimes there are changes that are hard to detect," Doctor Brenner said, a note of caution in his voice.

"You're saying there may still be damage?"

"Yes, possibly. More importantly, tell me how you feel."

"I get awful headaches every couple of days. Migraine medicine doesn't seem to help. I have also developed a really intense, new interest in playing the piano."

"That's what Dr. Delarosa told me. You had no musical background before?"

"None whatsoever."

"And how are you progressing with piano?"

"I think I'm making rapid progress because I play for many hours a day. I also have a new teacher."

"Wonderful, Simon. I would like you to come up to Ann Arbor for a couple of days, so that I might interview you at depth. Most importantly, you'll meet other people just like you. We will, of course, pay for everything."

"Thank you, Dr. Brenner. How are some of the others doing? Do they have headaches? Are they able to live normally?"

"We can talk more when you come up. To be perfectly honest, no one is back to their usual self. That having been said, most of the people I study are able to carry on with a life that is meaningful to them."

Simon thought Dr. Brenner's response was cryptic and not necessarily encouraging. Jean made the arrangements for his visit to Ann Arbor at the end of the phone call.

37. JENNA AND SIMON FIND THEIR RHYTHM

In the weeks that followed, Simon engaged in a slow, halting courtship of Jenna Cobb. Their piano lessons naturally assumed an informal tone, so much so that Jenna never bothered to seek any credit from Newell for providing them. Simon would arrive as she finished up a private lesson or was otherwise occupied playing. He would then play a few pieces for her and she would offer constructive feedback. The essence of her guidance was this: Simon played all the notes and followed the rhythm perfectly. In order to interpret each piece, he needed to relax both his fingers and his mind and try to follow what he believed was the underlying emotion of the composer. It made more and more sense with each lesson. Simon could tell a significant difference between Jenna's versions of the same pieces and his. She was much more fluid and relaxed—she enjoyed herself much more.

After their time at the piano together, there would be dinner and drinks, almost always at the Ale House, where Fiona continued to express her approval for the new life Simon was carefully building. Simon made it clear that his place "wasn't a place anyone ought to be unless you had to live there." Instead, they would go to Jenna's immaculately maintained townhome at the edge of Newell. Any significant intimacy began only several weeks later, after several faltering starts in which Simon offered only a kiss goodnight. It wasn't just his shy, introverted nature that held him back. It was an intense fear of coming on too strong too quickly and thereby spoiling a relationship he truly valued. Jenna was gentle, prim, dignified, but she made the first move, advising Simon that it was fine for him to move forward, as she slowly removed her clothes. Once the ice had been broken, things came much more naturally to Simon. What had been an unfortunate life soon seemed very blissful. The headaches persisted and the new medications were as useless as the old ones. But he learned to cope with them and knowing that someone cared for him more with each passing day gave him the strength to do so.

"My dad is coming to visit next week," Jenna said one day.

"Wonderful. Just for fun or for business?" Simon asked.

"No business, silly. He's been retired for a long time. He would like to meet you."

Simon appeared a bit nervous. "May I ask why?"

"He heard I was dating a nice guy. Isn't that a good reason?" Jenna said.

"I guess so."

"Nothing high pressured. We can all go to the Ale House one night. My mom is not coming with him. She's visiting her sister in Seattle at the same time."

"That sounds fine. I'm leaving for Ann Arbor on Wednesday."

"Great, we can go Tuesday night. He gets here Tuesday. Funny how little we know about each other's families."

"True."

"It would be nice to meet your mother someday, Simon."

"I don't know about that. She's a bit different. Hard for me to explain. It might not go like you would expect it to."

"Oh, okay. You mean, she won't like the fact that I'm Black."

"Ah, no, I doubt she'd care. Maybe she would I really don't know. And you know what, I actually wouldn't mind if she was bothered by it."

"You wouldn't mind if she was bothered? Why would you say that?"

"It's hard to explain my mother. We've had a tough relationship. Lots of tough times. Some good times too. It sounds immature but sometimes I feel like I should dare her to disapprove."

"Oh God. That does sound complicated. Well, I don't want to get between you and your mother."

"You won't. I actually don't think race would be the issue. Just make sure you tell her you're not Catholic!"

"She sounds old-fashioned."

"No, she's been fashioned as a unique human specimen. There isn't anyone else out there like her, I can tell you that."

Jenna, her father Harold, and Simon had dinner that Tuesday at the Ale House.

"Looks like you brought your future father-in-law," Fiona whispered in Simon's ear as the three walked in. Harold Cobb was pretty much what Simon had expected. An extremely affable, warm gentleman around seventy who beamed with pride every time he looked at his daughter. He also took an instant liking to Simon. "I can tell you're the strong, silent type," he commented, to which Simon just smiled.

"I've been trying to convince Jenna to move back to California now for years, but she really likes it here."

"The place will grow on you," Simon said.

"Jenna tells me you went through something horrible. Struck by lightning."

"Yes, in May."

"Now I've heard a lot of stories about this. Are you religious, Simon?"

"Not at all."

"Did you see anything strange after you were struck?" Simon felt Harold was getting at something very specific.

"Such as?"

"I don't know. A warm white light. Floating above your own body. Floating up into the clouds but eventually coming back down."

The Ale House was a bit crowded and loud. Simon hadn't shared the experience immediately after being struck with Jenna. He feared she might think he was crazy. He didn't feel like sharing too many details in front of her father. The floating into the clouds was something he did experience.

"I just developed an intense interest in playing the piano."

"Well, you've definitely found the right woman. I just thought you might be able to give us a glimpse of the life beyond, you know what I mean?"

"I think I know what you mean. I don't know how long I was unconscious right after the lightning strike. It was odd. I wasn't sure if I was alive or dead, or what would happen next," Simon offered.

38. GLIMPSES OF THE PAST

"I need a passport," Helen said quietly during one of her near-silent dinners with Simon.

"Did you ever have one?"

"An Irish one. Need an American one."

"You could go up to Boston with your papers."

Helen sighed. It took a moment for Simon to realize that she was actually, in her own circuitous way, asking for his help. He had already purchased an airline ticket for a hefty six-hundred dollars. "How can I help you with the passport, Mother?"

Helen looked a bit embarrassed. "I know there are a lot of forms, and I need a picture. Not sure where to get all that done."

"We still have a few months. Actually, we can do all that here in New Bedford. We could even mail your application in. Sure, I'll help."

Helen seemed reassured. "Thank you, Simon." She rose immediately. The house had a very small, unfinished basement where the water heater and furnace were located. She went down and retrieved an old metal chest, about two feet across and one foot wide and with two metal fasteners as locks. Simon hadn't recalled ever seeing it.

"What's this?"

"There are a lot of papers and things there I might need for my passport application. If you have the time, you could look through it and find out what might be useful." Helen presented this task to Simon not as one of the many chores she had assigned to him over the years, but as something he might actually find interesting.

"I'm happy to, Mother," he said.

Helen went upstairs to watch television.

Simon snapped open the case from which a musty odor emanated. There were numerous papers and many things which seemed completely useless. Simon found a few expired credit cards, for example, including some that belonged to his father. He also found a photo album he had never seen before.

The album had a thick, red vinyl cover that was worn out in spots, revealing some decaying cardboard underneath. Simon at first assumed it was another useless, discarded item until he discovered the treasure inside.

Many of the pictures were in black and white. The album began with pictures of Helen's family. The first was a picture of the family in their Sunday best. Helen was a slender teenager with a blank look on her face. Her three younger brothers all appeared to be under ten years of age and all looked like they were chuckling as they enjoyed the moment. Her father was holding her sister, no more than three or four in his arms. He looked like a kind and gentle man, Simon thought, as he was smiling broadly. Helen's mother looked very much like Helen—rail thin, stern, almost cross. Below the picture was a handwritten description, "Moran Family, Dublin, Sunday, 24 February 1957." Below the picture was one of Helen's parents alone taken in the same place on the same day—her father smiling, her mother with her arms crossed, looking even more stern.

The first two pictures were followed by pictures and descriptions of people Simon was unsure he had any connection to. About halfway through the book was a picture of his father. Luis was seated on the front steps of the house. Simon thought the house hadn't changed much. Many pictures were undated, but Simon guessed based on his father's very youthful appearance that the picture had been taken around 1970. Simon's father was smiling. He was leaning back against the top step with his hands to his side. He looked relaxed and happy. Simon remembered little about what his father was like, but the picture immediately gave him a warm feeling. "This was my dad," he thought, "and I'm sure he loved me."

The first pictures of Simon followed. He was in his dad's arms as a baby in a large, half-page color shot. They were in a park that looked a little familiar. This was followed by several more shots of Simon as a baby, which were obviously taken in a studio. Simon was impressed that his parents had the motivation and gathered the resources to have formal pictures taken. *Must have cost a lot back then*, he thought. A few intriguing pictures followed these. In one, Luis was standing next to a woman Simon didn't recognize. She looked young and had straight shoulder length hair. Simon thought she looked a bit like Luis and assumed she was a relative he had never been introduced to. There were a few pictures taken just outside the bar where Luis worked. One featured all the employees of the bar in Red Sox shirts. One man held up a sign that read, "Crush the Reds," which Simon almost immediately figured out was taken around the time of the 1975 World Series. Simon didn't recognize anyone in the bar pictures besides his father.

The bar pictures were followed by a photo of Luis with the same woman who might have been a relative, standing in front of the family house. Both were smiling. In between their legs was a small, shaggy dog. "Looks like a nice scene," Simon thought. "Who the hell was she anyway?"

The last pictures in the album featured events and places Simon had some recollection of. Helen and Luis took Simon to a county fair when he was five, and the day was captured in many photos, all in color. Another photo was taken by Luis on Simon's first day at school as he prepared to board the bus. *I remember being scared out of my wits*, he thought.

The album brought Simon closer to his father. Even knowing a bit more about Helen's family was heartwarming. He quickly went through the other papers in the chest and found Helen's naturalization certificate from 1966, as well as an old, tattered, Irish passport inside in which was folded-up, a fragile birth certificate from 1943. It would be all that she would need for her application.

39. Dr. Mark Brenner

Harold Cobb's inquiry about the afterlife caused Simon to reflect more about what had actually happened. He assumed he had passed into a dream state, and that the sensation of floating, the apparition of his father, and the repeated near collision with a large building were all part of the dream. Simon had attended church with his mother and father as a young boy. Unusually, it was his Portuguese father who insisted this was necessary. His Irish mother stopped taking him after Luis died. Simon felt this was at least partly due to the need to socialize with people who would always remain unfamiliar, an uncomfortable duty for Helen. Helen had never expressed any obvious religious belief, nor any spirituality. She had on several occasions, however, mentioned "good Catholics" usually when expressing her disapproval for some potential debauchery that might manifest at a place like Bridgewater State. Simon grew up as a disinterested nullifidian—He was neither a true believer, nor an agnostic, nor an atheist. He just never got interested enough to care. Being Catholic was part of his identity, only because Helen told him so. In reality it meant nothing to him. But Harold did make Simon wonder if he had passed, if only briefly, into the afterlife, to be pulled back by the compassion of his colleague and the young student who helped her, as well as the many medical personnel who must have made heroic efforts thereafter.

There was also the question of the recurring numbers and musical notes which accompanied his disabling headaches. *Surely they couldn't be part of the afterlife?* he thought. *Were they just visual hallucinations, brought forth from some dark corner of the brain that throbbed in pain?* He looked forward to meeting with Dr. Brenner, with whom he hoped he could at least start to explore some of these important questions.

Brenner's secretary made excellent arrangements. He flew first class out of Norfolk to Detroit, where a well-dressed man holding a sign that read "Galves" whisked him off to a nice hotel in Ann Arbor. He was due to meet the good doctor the next morning at eight a.m. After a nice dinner at the hotel, he spent the remainder of the evening making notes which he felt might be helpful. Dr. Delarosa had already transmitted the medical details to Dr. Brenner. But he wrote down the circumstances of his accident, and then what he experienced immediately afterwards, as well as many details about his recovery. He described his progress in playing piano as well. He wrote down several questions he hoped Dr. Brenner could answer, including "What could be causing these terrible headaches?" and "What is my long-term prognosis?"

For Simon, the morning could not come soon enough. He took a cab to Dr. Brenner's office, located in an elegant modern building. He was told to wait in a small conference room, not unlike his room at Jarvis, and that Dr. Brenner would arrive shortly.

Dr. Brenner was nothing like what Simon had imagined. Dr. Delarosa described him as a bit unorthodox. Eccentric was perhaps a more apt description. He was a man in his seventies with a scruffy beard and shoulder length hair. He wore a mauve shirt, unbuttoned at the top to a greater degree than a man would normally unbutton a shirt to be comfortable. He wore jeans and tennis shoes. He looked like a hippy. Simon had scarcely ever met anyone remotely like him, let alone a physician and researcher.

Simon rose to shake the doctor's hand and sat back down. Dr. Brenner backed his chair up a bit and smiled. His demeanor was so strange, Simon wondered if coming to Ann Arbor had been a mistake.

"Welcome friend. How was your trip?" Dr. Brenner said.

"Nice. Good flight. Nice hotel. Thanks for all the arrangements."

"My pleasure. We like to treat people like you well." The doctor just sat there smiling. Simon wasn't sure if he was expected to say anything. He started to pull out his book of notes and questions. "What's that you've got there?" the doctor asked.

"I wrote down what I experienced after the lightning strike."

Dr. Brenner stroked his beard slowly, which as Simon would learn, he did often while contemplating something he had just heard.

"Plenty of time for that later. I'd like to get to know you a little first."

"What would you like to know?"

"I understand from Dr. Delarosa that you're a writer?"

"No, I'm a writing consultant. I help graduate students write clearly."

"A lot of physicians could use your help," Dr. Brenner chuckled. "Before the accident would you say you were healthy?" he asked as he leaned in closer to Simon.

"I would say yes, for sure. I had never been to the hospital."

"How about in the family? Any serious illnesses?"

"My father died when he was thirty-eight from what they believe was a heart attack."

"So sorry to hear that."

"Thank you doctor. My mother suffers from anxiety, some type of social phobia I would say. Other than that, nothing I'm aware of." Simon expected Dr. Brenner to make some notes. Instead, he seemed to just take it all in quietly, with a few strokes of the beard now and then.

"Okay. Do you consider yourself to be a learned man?" The question caught Simon off-guard.

"I believe I'm well educated," Simon said tentatively.

"That's not what I asked, Simon. I asked if you were *learned*. I mean, do you consider yourself to be curious about the world around you? Curious about things which are not always necessary for your own success or survival?" Simon shrugged his shoulders. He felt like Dr. Brenner was trying to trap him in some sort of riddle.

Dr. Brenner sighed and continued. "For example, tell me something on your trip here yesterday that made you curious. Maybe something you just had to look up on your phone or computer to satisfy your curiosity. Was there something like that? I don't mean something like what the hotel would be like. Or what I might be like. Those are things related to the moment that might make your stay more comfortable or alleviate any anxiety." Simon thought for a minute or so.

"Yes, I think there were several things. I wondered why people who don't normally drink in the mid-afternoon feel comfortable having alcohol aboard a plane. I wondered about the origins of the name, 'Ann Arbor.' I wondered why a large gas-guzzling limousine was necessary to bring me to town from the airport. I wondered why the young lady sitting next to me, who was obviously a college student, was sitting in first class."

"Very good, Simon!" Dr. Brenner leaned forward in his chair, quite animated. "On that last point, mommy's or daddy's airline points I would imagine. Now, did you find any answers?"

"Yes, I learned that Ann Arbor is named for the wives of the early founders as well as the stands of oak trees here."

"And that's something you will retain forever, correct?"

"It's something I'm not likely to forget."

"Very good, Simon. Now tell me about your piano playing."

40. Making the Darkness Conscious

"Sure," Simon began, "I had never played piano before. I had never taken a lesson. In fact, a couple of weeks before my accident I went to my first concert in Newell. But it was contemporary guitar. I really enjoyed it. A few days after being discharged from hospital I took a walk across the Newell campus and heard a woman playing piano. It sounded so beautiful, and I was hooked. I was drawn to the piano almost constantly. I started playing at the Newell Music Building, bought books, even bought a piano. I've come a long way."

"Would you say your progress has been remarkably quick?" Dr. Brenner asked as he stroked his beard a couple of times and then rested his chin on his right knuckles.

"Well, that's for others to judge I suppose. The woman I referred to, Jenna, and I are now in a relationship. She's a professor of music. She was so astounded by my playing after a couple of weeks she thought I wasn't being honest about my lack of musical background."

"I see. And how do you explain all this? Your remarkable obsession? Your ability to play so well in such a short time?"

"I don't have an explanation Dr. Brenner. I was hoping you would help me."

Dr. Brenner sighed, as if he was disappointed with that answer.

"You've demonstrated to me that you're a curious person. Do you also consider yourself creative?"

"I have an MFA. I don't think that necessarily makes me creative," Simon responded humbly.

"Yes, but did you obtain that degree to express yourself creatively through your writing?"

"Good question. I think to some degree, yes. I also got the degree to distinguish myself from other English graduates. I thought my career prospects would improve."

"Did they improve?"

"Modestly. I have a good job."

"But you correct other people's writing. You don't write anything on your own?" Simon felt a bit defensive about this question.

"Rarely," he responded quietly.

"That's very interesting. So, you've acknowledged that you're curious and at least somewhat creative, and yet that creativity has no regular mechanism through which it is expressed." Simon had never thought about his career trajectory in such terms. He just sat there puzzled, not sure if he agreed or disagreed.

"Are you familiar with Carl Jung?"

"The psychiatrist?"

"Yes, he was a famous Swiss psychiatrist and psychoanalyst. Could you read something Dr. Jung wrote?" Dr. Brenner handed Simon a piece of paper with a single sentence in bold letters. He read it out loud.

"'One does not become enlightened by imagining figures of light but by making the darkness conscious.'"

"What do you think that means?" Dr. Brenner sat at the edge of his chair, leaning towards Simon, seemingly hoping for a breakthrough in Simon's understanding.

Simon thought for some time. He feared whatever he came up with would be wrong according to Dr. Brenner.

"I suppose it means knowledge comes from banishing ignorance from the mind," he said noncommittally.

"That's certainly an interesting take on it. The next few days are going to be very interesting for you. Perhaps even a bit traumatic. It will involve a radical change in your thinking, Simon. I hope you're prepared for all that," Dr. Brenner said in a matter-of-fact way, as if he had told several of his other patients the same thing.

Simon thought the hippyesque doctor was exaggerating. He imagined only a battery of tests, some brain imaging, and some recommendations on how to control his headaches. If that's what he was in store for, he would have been perfectly satisfied. Instead, Dr. Brenner continued in his sphinxlike manner.

"There is the interesting case of the zebra finch, a type of small bird. Have you heard of it?" By this point Simon felt he was being tested in a way he didn't understand but was certain he was failing.

"I've never heard of the bird or any interesting case about it, doctor."

"That's okay. So, young zebra finches learn specific birdsongs from their fathers. They mimic what they've heard, much the way babies learn speech from their parents. So songs are learned right?"

"I'd say that's correct," Simon said tentatively.

"An interesting scientist in Texas has done an experiment where he's taken young zebra finches who've never heard any songs from other finches, and he has stimulated part of their brains electrically making them sing songs that are typical of zebra finches. Tell me, what do you think the implications are?" Dr. Brenner again leaned forward seemingly hoping for a breakthrough.

Simon once again thought he was expected to pass some sort of metaphysical test. "I really don't know Dr. Brenner. That songs are innately programmed in each finch's brain?"

"But a finch that doesn't undergo stimulation remains mute. It cannot sing." Dr. Brenner seemed like he was hoping for a more insightful response from Simon. "I'm not trying to quiz you. I just want you to think about the Texas experiment and the Carl Jung quote today. I want you to relax. Tomorrow you will meet a couple of other people like you." Simon assumed that the finch/Jung test had concluded and that he hadn't made the breakthrough Dr. Brenner was hoping for.

"Will I undergo any further testing?"

"We'll see about that."

"Dr. Brenner, what about my terrible headaches? Is there a cure for those?"

"I believe there is Simon. I believe the cure is within you. And you'll have to discover it yourself." Dr. Brenner smiled, a bit smugly, as if he had achieved something by leaving Simon so confused. "You seem quite tense to me. You are anxious about what's going to happen. It doesn't match what you expected—perhaps lots of exams and tests. Neither of us can really gain insight into what's going on unless you are very relaxed."

"I'm happy to relax. What should I do the rest of the day?"

"Anything you like. Explore the town. But do think about the Jung quote in particular. We can meet again early tomorrow morning. You'll also meet a couple of very interesting people tomorrow as I said." Dr. Brenner got up, shook Simon's hand and left.

41. RECONNECTIONS 1993

Helen's trip to Ireland was filled with uncertainty. She had arrived originally in Boston by ship in 1958. Neither she nor Simon had ever been on a plane. With a perceptible degree of apprehension, Simon drove her to Logan Airport where a couple of kind passengers provided her with guidance about how to check in. The greater uncertainty was about what would happen when she arrived in

Dublin. She had not been back to Ireland in thirty-five years. She had spoken to her family, including her mother, only once every couple of years, usually around Christmas. Her father passed away in 1986 but had been estranged from the family for some time prior to that, and there was no pressure to return to Ireland at that time.

The purpose of the trip wasn't very clear to Simon. He assumed Helen was trying to make amends prior to his grandmother's death. He was surprised she was motivated to do this for a mother she hadn't seen in so long. His grandmother had actually summoned Helen, and this was also surprising. The family in Ireland was large and why it was so important for one wayward daughter to return home was unclear.

Simon saw Helen all the way to the gate. She was clearly nervous and walked slowly on to the plane when the time came. Simon gave a short wave and she was off. Very early the next morning, there was a message on the home answering machine, "This is your uncle Charles. Just to let you know your mother arrived safely."

Helen would be gone for three weeks—the longest she had ever been away anywhere since she left Ireland. Simon in turn, would be without his mother for an extended period for the first time. At first, he felt liberated. There would be no guilt about being away from home. He could do as he pleased. There would be no solemn, tasteless dinners. Instead, he could prepare his own meals, or better yet, enjoy something better at a local restaurant. But as her first full day away ended, Simon began to experience the emptiness in his life. He wouldn't have a substitute teacher assignment for nearly a week, and work at the grocery store was quite limited as many college students were back home for the summer and were working full time. He resolved to keep the house in excellent shape, anticipating what Helen might have wanted done. His only other planned activity was a little reading and television. He lubricated a few sticky windows, trimmed a few hedges, and painted a small cabinet in the basement as its surface was peeling. All this was accomplished in a couple of hours. He started reading a copy of *The Shipping News* by Annie Proulx from the library. He was enjoying it but paused after twenty pages, and thought, "This is no way to spend a beautiful summer afternoon."

Simon hadn't forged any meaningful friendships in college. This was partly due to his introversion, and partly due to being a commuter student with a panic attack-prone mother. He did know a few people who lived in New Bedford who attended Bridgewater, but not well enough for informal socialization. He felt like he was in a tough situation. He had been liberated from his mother for three weeks, and yet had nothing to do. If he didn't do anything interesting, the time apart would have been wasted. He had worked with a fellow English major named Ian on a couple of group projects in college and knew Ian was living and working in New Bedford as a copy editor for a Cape Cod tourism magazine. He found Ian's parents' number in an old notebook and called early in the evening. He was given a different number by Ian's mother who told him her son was living on his own. He was uncomfortable about calling and rehearsed the framework for a basic conversation. He would ask Ian about life after college, his job, and eventually ask if he or anyone else was doing anything interesting and just felt like hanging out. It wouldn't be too hard Simon thought, because Ian was quiet and introverted like him.

"Simon Galves here."

"I know. My mom just called and told me she gave you my number."

"Hope I'm not bothering you."

"Not really. I'm just hanging out. My girlfriend and I are going out later."

"Oh, that's great. How is life after college?"

"It's okay. Finally got enough money for an apartment. Job sucks. Pay sucks. You?"

"I'm still living at home. Same job situation, though. Substitute teaching," Simon said.

"You still with that Angela girl?"

"No. We broke up a long time ago."

"Good. I thought she was really flaky. Well, it is nice to hear from you, but I'm surprised that you called." This last comment made Simon feel like he was disturbing Ian, and he immediately felt unwelcome.

"I was just seeing how you were doing, and thought maybe we could hang out sometime. That's all."

"Yeah, that would be okay. I'll let you know, all right?"

"Alright, Ian," he said as he finished the call. Simon felt awful. He thought about how he would have reacted if Ian had called him out of the blue. *I would suggest we go out for a beer, or watch a baseball game on TV, or something. What harm could that do?* he thought. A couple of hours later, he came up with another idea.

He knew one person who had always been warm and charming, not to mention very attractive—Mia Fernandes. He hadn't spoken to her since high school. He knew she attended U. Mass and might be home for the summer. At the very least, he couldn't imagine her being as dismissive as Ian.

Mia's mother answered the phone. "Wonderful to hear from you, Simon. You've graduated I take it?"

"Yes, I work in town."

"Terrific. Mia is actually here now. Hang on a sec."

"Gosh, it's been such a long time! It's so nice to hear from you," Mia said with the warmth Simon remembered.

"It's great to talk to you, Mia. How's college?"

"Going well. I took a bit of time off. Hope to graduate next year. Are you in town now?"

Simon sensed a clear opportunity to connect. "Yes, I am. We should get together. Maybe ice cream or something."

"That would be nice. I'll be around for the next week."

"Where are you going after that?"

"Oh, going to visit my boyfriend in Albany. We've been together three years. You'd like him a lot. He's a science fiction fan."

Simon's heart sunk. Of course, ice cream with Mia suddenly lost most of its appeal. "Oh, I'm sure I will. Well, I'll let you know when I'm free. Busy work schedule. If I don't see you before you leave, have a wonderful time."

"And you have a great summer, Simon."

Simon took a deep breath and lay down on the couch. *My mother is friendless because she's not friendly*, he thought. Yet trying to be friendly had gotten him nowhere. It was going to be a long three weeks.

42. A DAY IN ANN ARBOR

Simon did exactly what he was supposed to do during his first full day in Ann Arbor. He thought about, "Making the darkness conscious," over and over again. *Too bad Dr. Brenner speaks in riddles,* he thought. Simon began to think he was simply too concrete, too analytical to understand Jung's meaning. He started to feel the day was being wasted. He read a couple of student compositions. Then he searched desperately for a piano. A hotel clerk told him there was an Episcopal Church nearby which she herself attended, and that there were multiple pianos in a large common room in the basement. It was a Thursday and the main doors to the church were locked. A side door, however, was left ajar, likely inadvertently. In little time, he found himself in a large room with several well-maintained upright pianos. He started to play. First, "Clair de Lune," followed by Beethoven's Piano Sonata No. 8 in C Minor, which he had been rehearsing just prior to arriving, both on the piano and in his mind.

He got a call from Jenna. "Checking in to see if you're okay. They haven't zapped any brain cells with radiation I hope?"

"No actually. I don't think this Dr. Brenner wants to even do any scans."

"Really? So what is he doing for you?"

"He's eccentric. I believe he wants me to discover something about my own condition. He's really cryptic. Tomorrow I'm supposed to meet a few other people like me."

"Can he help you with the headaches?"

"I don't know. Maybe he wants me to discover my own cure." Simon chuckled. "Let me bounce something off of you. What does it mean to you if I say one becomes enlightened not by imagining figures of light but by making the darkness conscious?"

"Is that a riddle?"

"No, it's a quote by Carl Jung that I'm supposed to spend the day deciphering."

Jenna thought for a while. "I would say that it means one becomes enlightened by uncovering all the suffering in the world. That's probably what he meant by darkness—not by simply seeing the positive."

Jenna didn't benefit from the context of Simon's meeting with Dr. Brenner. He was pretty sure she was quite a way off.

"That's an interesting take on it. Not sure that's what Jung or Dr. Brenner meant."

"Hey, I gave it a shot. When are you coming home?"

"Saturday, unless I'm lobotomized."

"Struck by lightning and then lobotomized. Newell will not have been kind to you." At that point a voice called out from behind Simon.

"Excuse me sir, may I help you?"

"Oh hello," Simon responded. He said goodbye to Jenna and turned around to see an older man in a gray shirt and pants, typical clothes of a custodian. "I'm sorry, I was just looking for a place to play the piano."

"You don't look familiar. Are you a member of this church?"

"No I'm not. I'm from out of town, just here for a couple of days for some medical tests." Simon hoped that by mentioning medical tests the gentleman would be a bit sympathetic and forgive his trespassing.

"How did you get in?"

"There was a side door that was partly open. I just wanted to practice here for a while. Nothing else."

The gentleman softened his stance quite a bit. First he sighed, then he smiled. "Let's hear it," he said.

Simon played "Clair de Lune."

"That was beautiful," the custodian said. "Just make sure that door is shut when you leave. It will lock automatically. You're really not supposed to be here, but I'll overlook it."

"Thank you sir. That's very kind of you. I'd like to ask you a question. What does it mean to you if I said one becomes enlightened by making the darkness conscious?"

"Does that have something to do with music?"

"It might. I'm not sure. I'm trying to figure it out myself."

The custodian sat down on a nearby piano bench and began contemplating. "Maybe it means there are dark parts in our mind, and we become enlightened by opening them up, instead of chasing what we can actually see already. I don't know. Just my take on it. You have a very good day sir."

"You as well."

43. A JOB AT THE LIBRARY

Helen's return from her trip to Ireland in 1993 was uneventful. Simon was able to retrieve her from Logan at the expected time. She sat stone-faced in the front seat. As taciturn as she normally was, Simon expected to hear something about her trip, but she offered nothing, so Simon had to ask.

"How is your mother?"

"She's gone. Passed away Sunday."

"Terribly sorry to hear that."

"Yes, she had been ill for some time. I had no idea."

"Did you have much time to spend with her?"

"Some time. She was very frail and in hospital the past week or so, and unable to really talk. I did spend time with my family."

"That must have been some consolation for you. But I realize you've been away from them for so long, it must have been hard."

"It was very hard. They barely know me, and I barely know them. But my mother knew me well. And she forgave me."

"Forgave you for what? Leaving home?"

"Yes, you can call it leaving. I would call it more running away if anything." Simon had never heard his mother's departure from Ireland described in such terms. He wanted to learn more, but knowing she had just lost her mother, he didn't think it was a good time to press her.

"Are you happy to be back home?"

"Very much so. I don't want to go back there again," she said.

Simon wondered if some sort of conflict had erupted with her family. Or, perhaps, she simply didn't feel welcome, due to her long absence and her distant personality. Again, he chose not to inquire further. "What did you do these past three weeks?"

"I didn't do much. I worked several days. I kept the house in top shape too." After a few minutes she said, "Did that man come looking for me again?"

It took Simon a few moments to realize she was referring to Steve, whom he hadn't thought about for months. "No, no sign of

Steve. Thank goodness. I do worry about you running into people like that at the motels. I wish you would consider some other line of work."

"I tried the school. They didn't want me, remember?"

"I do remember. There may be something else you could do that you might like."

Rather than shrugging her shoulders or saying nothing, Helen responded, "Perhaps there is."

Simon appreciated her response. He took it to mean that she wasn't closed to his advice and likely that she didn't resent him for finding her the job in the school cafeteria.

Helen resumed her cleaning job. As she had been off for three weeks and had only two weeks paid vacation, she felt the need to work especially hard upon her return. Over the years, the household finances had settled into a well understood arrangement—Helen was responsible for the mortgage payment of roughly four-hundred dollars a month; Simon had been taking care of the rest, including leaving her cash for groceries on the kitchen table each week. Each was responsible for their own car and other expenses. Simon would have taken care of everything if he had a job which paid better. Then Helen could work only if and when she felt like it. Over the following weeks Simon thought about other potential opportunities for his mother.

"I've come up with another place for you to work, Mother. Some place you enjoy being, where you can work quite independently—the public library."

Helen provided one of her half smiles, which Simon took to mean strong approval. "Do they have any jobs?"

"I've seen people restocking books, checking people out. I think you're well-suited to that. I don't know if there are any openings. It's certainly a safe environment, and you always liked going to the library. So did I."

The idea was good enough that Helen decided to explore it right away. She went on her own and completed an application. Two weeks later she received a call for an interview. A week after that, she landed a job as a library clerk. The pay, as expected, was no higher than the cleaning job. But she could work in solitude much of the day. When she couldn't, the required interactions with others would be brief, quiet, and polite. Simon hoped that the job might gradually make her a bit more social as well. It was so perfect a job that one night at the dinner table shortly after she started working, Helen offered, "Thank you for recommending me the job at the library. I'm much happier there than in the motels."

Libraries naturally attract employees with an interest in books and reading. Helen wasn't one of those. Books often dominated the quiet conversations among the other clerks, and having read none of them, there was no pressure for Helen to participate. She seldom ate lunch and instead read her Dublin newspaper or a magazine. The clerks were all encouraged to check out books, mainly to provide patrons with meaningful recommendations based on their interests. Helen seldom interacted with patrons that way, instead referring them to other clerks. She generally steered clear of the library manager, a gentleman named Dennis Rossi, who was overall quite happy with her work. One day Mr. Rossi did inquire about her interests.

"I've noticed you don't check any books out."

"I'm not much of a reader."

"Some of our older magazines are available for circulation. You can check those out if you wish."

"Thank you. I'll consider that."

"Or videos. We have some of the latest movies, and some older classics too."

"Thanks for the suggestion. I do watch television, but I don't have a VCR."

"I just want you to be able to enjoy all that the library has to offer. We don't pay very much, but there is the great fringe benefit of being able to check out what you want, often before anyone else. I think that's a great thing about working here."

"I appreciate it, Dennis. I'll think about what I'd like to check out."

44. MUSIC THERAPY

Among Simon's prized possessions was a Sony Discman portable stereo he bought when he was in college. Helen owned an old record player and a few records by the Clancy Brothers which she never listened to. The portable stereo had a CD player and a radio. Simon had a few CDs which he sold to a secondhand shop shortly after graduating. The stereo found its place on the kitchen counter where Helen would sometimes use it to listen to National Public Radio. Mostly, the stereo gathered dust, as Simon himself had lost interest in it. Helen brought it up one evening.

"You don't have any CDs to play on it?"

"None. I sold the last one a couple of years back. I'm thinking about selling the stereo too. We don't use it much."

Helen looked concerned. "Actually, I would like to play CDs on it. I can check them out from the library. They've been encouraging me to check out books or movies there. I think I'd enjoy listening to music on the stereo."

Surprised that his mother expressed an interest in music, Simon encouraged her. "That's great. I bet they have a nice collection of music there. You could even take the stereo up to your room and listen up there instead of watching television."

Helen watched hours of mind-numbing TV programs in the evenings and Simon hoped some of this time could be allocated to something else.

"Yes, I could. It might help me relax too to listen to music."

Helen asked one of her colleagues if the library had CDs of Irish folk music or something else with which she was a bit familiar. No luck unfortunately. Instead there were only two categories: jazz and classical music. She returned home the next day with *Chopin 24 Preludes Op 28*. Simon placed the stereo in her bedroom and helped her load the CD. After dinner, the beautiful sound of Chopin's piano music could be heard quietly through the house.

Simon remained downstairs feeling that the music helped him relax as well. Within a few days, Helen adopted a new music routine. She would always check out only one CD at a time, listen to it repeatedly for a few days and then exchange it for another. Interestingly, she didn't choose popular works by Mozart, Beethoven or others, but more obscure titles. Simon thought perhaps these were easier to check out for her due to lower demand.

Within a few weeks, Simon started to sense that the classical music upstairs was therapeutic for Helen. She seemed less tense.

Her shoulders looked more relaxed. Her habitual stern look eased somewhat. She was still aloof and taciturn, but the change was unmistakable. Dr. Coates and his successor had her taking a complex regimen of psychotherapeutics for years, but, at least from Simon's vantage, it was a little evening classical music that had the effect she was seeking.

"Seems like you're really enjoying the music, Mother."

"Yes, I am. I'm making good use of your stereo."

"I would say you're actually looking much more relaxed. I know a new doctor has taken over from Dr. Coates, but perhaps you could discuss taking less of all your medications."

Helen looked a little embarrassed. She recalled the appointment Simon attended with Dr. Coates in which he carefully went over the multitude of pills Helen took daily. "I could do that, yes. Dr. Archibald seems very reasonable overall," Helen responded.

Emboldened as he grew older and Helen's vulnerabilities becoming more and more apparent, Simon went further. "I think that would be a very good idea, for you and Dr. Archibald to consider reducing or stopping some of your medications. It can't be good for you to be taking so much. You're still young after all. I can even come with you to the next appointment if you feel that would be helpful."

Again, Helen looked embarrassed. "I have an appointment in two weeks. I can manage it on my own. I'll ask him about medications. I appreciate the suggestion."

Helen's appointment came and went and she didn't reveal anything that transpired to Simon. But he did notice a significant difference. She seemed more energetic, not quite lively, but certainly not as somber as usual. One evening after dinner, while she was washing dishes, Simon heard her humming a tune, something he had never observed before. She also seemed to walk more briskly. Instead of retreating to her bedroom immediately after dinner, Helen stuck around in the kitchen for a while, often drinking tea. Simon sat with her reading the newspaper or a book. Silence pervaded the scene as usual, but Helen had become unmistakably more social. Simon figured that one or more of her many sedatives had been discontinued, alleviating some of her longstanding languor. Moreover, she listened to her music more purposefully, carefully reviewing the booklet inside each CD to read about what she was about to listen to, and sometimes playing tracks she enjoyed over and over again. Simon was delighted by the change in his mother. The job was keeping her relatively safe, and the music was bringing her joy.

45. ENLIGHTENED IN ANN ARBOR

Simon had no idea what to expect on his second day in Ann Arbor. A receptionist at Dr. Brenner's office led him to a well-lit conference room where he was expected to wait, seated at a table. A few minutes later a young woman in a wheelchair entered. Simon moved a chair out of the way to accommodate her.

"I'm Regina. Nice to meet you. I'm a patient of Dr. Brenner's."

"Simon Galves. Do you know what we'll be doing today?"

"It's always a bit uncertain with Dr. Brenner. I think sometimes he makes it up as he goes along. The basic idea is to tap into our own talent and passions more freely." This sounded very vague to Simon.

"I guess he won't be doing blood tests or scans then?"

"Not usually. Didn't you have some already?"

"I did, back in Newell, Virginia." Out of politeness Simon didn't ask what had happened to Regina. She revealed her story a couple of minutes later.

"I was in a car accident and had a bad concussion, and several fractures. I'm not paralyzed or anything. Just a healing broken ankle. I was a passenger. My mother was driving. She's actually doing quite well. Nearly recovered."

"That's very good to hear."

"How about you?"

"I was struck by lightning outside my office. I had a lot of trouble walking and concentrating at first. I also still have really bad headaches."

"And what darkness was illuminated?" Regina asked.

"Oh, you must have been assigned the Jung quote as well. I've become obsessed with playing piano. It's a real driver in my life now. How about you Regina?"

"I paint. Just exhibited my work in Chicago. Sold several pieces."

"Fantastic. How is Dr. Brenner helping you?"

Regina was about to respond when Dr. Brenner himself walked in. He was dressed in jeans and a T-shirt, looking more like a care-free tech worker than a physician.

He said, "Looks like you two have gotten acquainted."

Simon and Regina both nodded.

"Did you think about the Jung quote, Simon?"

"I did think about it. I even asked a few people about it. I'm not sure I've accomplished what you intended."

"So, tell me what you think. I gave you that assignment not to confuse you and certainly not to embarrass you. I've always feared that the meaning of what Jung intended is so radical that it's best to prepare my patients for what I believe has happened to them. Regina already knows what I believe." Regina nodded. "Regina, did you paint before your accident?"

"Never touched a brush."

"And I know, Simon, you had no experience with the piano before your accident. Tell me. Why do you think you're able to play so expertly after so short a time?"

"First, I don't know how expertly I play. I've made a lot of progress that's for sure, and in a short period of time." It was a comfortable response for a humble man.

"Are people astonished by your progress?"

"Some, yes."

"Do you account for it simply through your dedication? The amount of time you've spent playing?"

"I don't know how to account for it."

"How many hours would you estimate you've played piano since your accident?"

Simon thought for a moment. "Over the past two months I would guess I've played about 120 or 130 hours."

"So a couple of years of lessons for someone starting out. I'm guessing your playing is much more advanced than someone taking a lesson a week with some practice for two years."

"I suppose it is, Dr. Brenner. I really don't know what sort of progress I've made compared to others. Maybe it's just the intensity of it that's allowed me to play reasonably well."

"Interesting point, Simon. Let's talk about Regina. She never painted a thing before her car accident. And Regina, you really didn't learn to paint at all did you?"

"No. I just started painting scenes from around my home in Illinois. I didn't take classes."

"Can you put your story together with Regina's, Simon?"

Simon thought for a good minute, trying to come up with a response that would satisfy Dr. Brenner. His mention of a "radical" explanation was especially hard to reconcile with his initial potential explanation. He thought injury to a part of the brain leads to new obsessions, and fortunately both his and Regina's obsessions were creative and constructive. Dr. Brenner stared at Simon intently, as if he was trying to follow his thought pattern. It became clear that Simon wasn't going to be let out of this thought exercise. If he failed, he would be asked to try again.

He tried combining a sequence of ideas: illuminating darkness, piano, radical explanation, painting beautifully with no prior experience or training, his own unbelievable rapid progress. He finally quietly offered:

"You're saying I've always had the knowledge and ability to play the piano well. The lightning strike just brought it out."

Dr. Brenner smiled broadly, and turned to Regina, "Bingo. We have a winner!"

Simon sat still with a perplexed look. The implications of what at that point he considered simply Dr. Brenner's theory were too great to take in all at once. No one said anything until Simon spoke.

"But how, Dr. Brenner?"

"You remember the finches?" Dr. Brenner asked.

"Yes, but their songs are probably programmed into their brains, passed down through the generations. Their songs are probably very simple, not like playing the piano or Regina's gallery paintings," Simon said.

"Does it surprise you that human beings are more complicated than finches?" Simon didn't respond.

"You're saying that I was always programmed with the ability to play the piano?"

"I'm saying we are all programmed with ability, islands of

genius as Donald Treffert calls them, and that you accumulated the knowledge to play piano in some unconventional way without ever expressing it. The lightning strike brought it out. Aren't you glad I asked you to come up with this yourself?" The doctor looked pleased.

"Actually I am."

46. MATHIAS HENKE

A few minutes later on a large monitor in the conference room, Dr. Brenner started playing a video. In it, a tall, balding gentleman, elegantly dressed in a black three-piece suit stands next to a grand piano. Applause from a small crowd follows. The man speaks in German: *Dieses Stück habe ich nicht mehr nach meinem Unfall komponiert.*

"He said he composed this piece just after his accident," Dr. Brenner said to Simon, now totally absorbed in the video. "It's called 'Blitzinfonie.'" The gentleman sat down to play. The piece started slowly, softly, building gradually in intensity. The pianist appeared remarkably at ease, completely absorbed in the music, seeming to play for pure enjoyment rather than the audience. There were several movements. He played for nearly thirty minutes. Simon thought the "Blitzinfonie" was extremely complex, a bit difficult to follow, but also extremely beautiful. The pianist stood up, bowed to another small round of applause and the video ended.

"What did you think of Matthias Henke?" Dr. Brenner asked Simon.

Regina seemed less intrigued by the video, as if she had seen it before.

"I thought he was terrific. Great piano player. What does *Blitzinfonie* mean? The bombardment?"

"No, it means 'lightning symphony.'"

Simon sat still, waiting anxiously for Dr. Brenner's explanation.

"Matthias composed that symphony, two months after being struck by lightning while on a camping trip in Alberta, Canada."

"And he was not a pianist before?"

"Not at all." And as if on cue, there was a knock on the conference room door. The doctor smiled and said, "You can ask him about it yourself."

Matthias entered. He was dressed much like Dr. Brenner.

"I'm sorry I was running a little late. It's great to be here. Simon, welcome. I've heard a little about you."

"Nice to meet you, Matthias. I enjoyed the 'Blitzinfonie.' We just finished watching the video."

"Thank you. That was taken in Vienna at Mozart House last year." Matthias said, "It's terrific to meet another person like me."

"How long ago was your accident?" Simon asked.

"Fourteen years. I had no background in music. I am a botanist from Munich."

"Matthias, perhaps you could tell Simon a bit about your accident, and how you started playing. It's always good to share stories."

"I would enjoy hearing it again as well," Regina said.

"I was camping in Jasper National Park, Alberta, in June 2009. I was with my younger brother, and my brother-in-law. We were hiking. We're not expert hikers or anything. We just like the outdoors. We were hiking the Sulphur Skyline Trail. It's only a few hours, but we got started late that day. My brother was not feeling very well in the morning so we let him sleep. He started to feel better after we all ate something, so we were starting past twelve o'clock."

"That does sound quite late to start hiking," Simon said.

"Yes, we did not plan things well. We noticed not many people on the trail, thinking most people had already finished hiking for the day. The day was cool, and it got cooler because it got cloudy. The clouds got darker, too. We reached the end and started to turn back. It was around three o'clock. It started to rain. It was very unpleasant. A very cold rain. We had rain jackets, but they were completely useless. We were getting soaked. Then the thunder and lightning started. We knew it was a dangerous situation. We don't have such big storms like that in Germany. So much lightning. So we started to look for some shelter. Off the trail, about maybe three-hundred meters, we saw a very large rock with what we call *überhängender Fels*, another big rock on top. I said I would go there and see if the three of us could fit under it until the storm was over. Everything got much more intensive. I started walking toward the rock, and I am told by the other two that a strike hit the metal pole on the frame of my backpack. I don't remember this of course."

Simon listened intently. "Did you feel anything?"

"It's hard to know now what I felt and what I just imagined. It felt like floating in a cloud. I just kept going higher and higher. Then I would come back down, and then very fast, thrown up into the cloud again. It was very cold. Then I started to move very fast forward. It was really fast and frightening. I could see that I was about to hit the side of a big mountain. I would be smashed. But at the last second, I went much higher into the clouds. This kept happening over and over again. I don't know how long it lasted. My neck was burning. My back was burning. My head was aching. I woke up in hospital in Edmonton, they said four days later."

Simon was astonished by how similar Matthias' experience had been to his. He wanted to jump in and describe his own experience but waited patiently for Matthias to supply additional details.

"So, after the accident, they said they found me unconscious and carried me under the rock and waited for the storm to pass. Then my brother ran to a ranger station and called for help. A helicopter came to the ranger station and took me all the way to Edmonton to hospital. They kept me in a coma and ran some tests. When I woke up my wife was there. My young son was there too. I had burns on my neck and on my back, that the doctors said were doing fine. I tried walking but kept losing my balance. So they sent me to therapy. About three days later, we all flew back to Munich, and I continued my therapy there. Do you want me to keep going, Dr. Brenner?"

"Yes, I think so. I'm sure Simon would like to hear more."

"I cannot explain what happened afterwards Simon. My balance started to get better, but only slowly. My son does take piano lessons. We have a piano at home, and one night, in the middle of the night, I had a dream about playing piano. I was playing really well. Then, I heard, 'Papa, was machst du?' which means, 'Daddy, what are you doing?' I was not having a dream. I was sitting at the piano in my pajamas."

"That's incredible," Simon said.

Mathias continued, "My boy was standing next to me. I had been playing the piano like a professional without even knowing it.

Since that time, I cannot stop playing, learning, composing. I quit my job for a while. It is my life now. It's mostly how I make a living,"

47. A TRIP TO FREEPORT, 1994

The library job, the classical music CDs, and Dr. Archibald's willingness to taper the cocktail of medications to which Helen had become habituated, all combined not only to affect Helen's mood, but also her behavior overall. She said little to Simon about how she was getting on at the library, but one Saturday morning when he went there to check out a book, he revealed to a weekend manager named Irene that his mother worked there.

"Helen is just terrific! We love having her here. She's been so helpful."

The helpful part didn't surprise Simon as he knew his mother to be extremely diligent. The *we love having her here* was especially good to hear, especially after the hurtful comments he had received from the school cafeteria manager.

Helen was definitely more relaxed after work. She actually started to check out a few books and read at least parts of them. This became her activity after work and before dinner. She would stay in the living room, which is usually where Simon read. This, by itself, was a big change from the days when she would remind Simon of chores to be done and then retreat to her room immediately. There were also many more half smiles. She held her shoulders back in a more relaxed pose, while before, her posture was poor with shoulders curved inward as if to protect her chest. Helen had never engaged Simon in much conversation. He wasn't sure if she knew how. But after a couple of months at the library, he believed she was much more receptive to participating in conversations he started.

"I ran into a lady at the library who said you were doing a great job there," he said to her.

"Really? Who?"

"Irene."

"Irene is a very nice lady," Helen said as she half-smiled.

"What is your day like there, Mother?"

"Every day is different. Sometimes I start with restocking. Sometimes I work the check-out desk. Sometimes the reference desk." She listed these possibilities with some enthusiasm. Simon could tell she was proud to work at the library.

"Good. Is there a lunch break? You never really got a break when you cleaned motels."

"Yes, we have different breaks. Mine is usually from eleven thirty to twelve fifteen. We take our lunch in the lunchroom." Before her new job Helen had rarely eaten lunch.

Simon had noticed her preparing a sandwich each morning before work. Having lunch while sitting with others was a huge change for Helen. "Sounds wonderful, Mother. Sounds like you're making some friends."

Helen looked intensely at Simon with a confused look. "I don't know about making friends, but we do have lunch together. There is also a trip planned in a couple of weeks."

"What kind of trip?"

"It's a bus trip we are organizing among ourselves. A shopping trip to Freeport, Maine, and also to a beach up there."

"You should definitely go. It will be a lot of fun."

"I don't know. It's thirty dollars. Freeport is where all the fashion outlets are. People are going to buy clothes." Helen generally wore old, staid clothes, usually dresses but sometimes a blouse and slacks. Simon couldn't remember her ever buying clothes. "I could actually use some new clothes," Helen said with a serious look.

"Go for it, Mother. It's just for the day, and even if you don't buy anything, it'll be fun for you. I can give you some extra money if you need it."

"That's very generous, Simon. It's mostly women going, with their husbands or children, or even grandchildren," Helen said, and then looked downward.

It took a few seconds for Simon to figure out what she wanted. Then he said, "Would you like me to come, Mother? I could use some new clothes, too."

"Oh, only if you feel you have the time."

"I will have the time, and I'd be happy to come with you."

The day of the outing arrived, and Helen grew nervous. There were a number of solo travelers. Simon figured his mother wanted him to come, not because she would be the only one alone, but because she was apprehensive about how to behave the whole day and Simon could be helpful in that respect. She hadn't bought clothes in so long that he might be more knowledgeable about what would be a good value and where specifically she ought to shop. Certainly there were many ladies on the trip much more qualified than Simon about what would look good on Helen, but it wasn't likely she would feel comfortable asking any of them.

Helen said little on the trip, but the group was warm and cheerful, and made it clear that she was one of their own. She bought three dresses and a new handbag. Simon bought a pair of Khaki pants. They skipped the side trip to the beach, preferring to have lunch at a small sandwich shop in Freeport. A couple of ladies from the library dined in the same place and sat with them. Helen remained reserved but at one point, she started discussing a book she was reading which one of the ladies had finished.

Simon was delighted to learn that his mother had been reading and that she even engaged in such a conversation.

The bus returned to the New Bedford Library parking lot around five p.m. Warm goodbyes were said and the passengers looked forward to seeing each other at work during the week ahead, as well as promising to organize similar trips in the future. Despite being the only young adult on the trip, seeing his mother enjoy herself to a greater extent than he had witnessed before, made Simon very content.

"That was a wonderful day, Mother. I hope you enjoyed it as much as I did."

"Yes, very enjoyable. I'll ask them when they plan to do something like this again. Maybe in the fall."

48. Enzo at the Library

Enzo Carpetta was a widowed New Bedford real estate lawyer who spent many hours in the library. Specializing in representing poor and struggling tenants, homeowners, and small businesspeople facing eviction, foreclosure, or bankruptcy, his was a busy but not financially thriving enterprise. For some time, he shared an office with his older brother, a successful general practice attorney, but the limited space, commotion, and regular parade of shady characters through Phillip Carpetta's office led him to the decision to seek other premises. The library provided free, quiet space. He mostly met clients at their homes or offices, but even when that was not possible, he had the option of booking a private meeting room at the library.

So, Enzo was in the library nearly every day. He did one of three things: reviewed cases, prepared briefs and notices, or did historical research on laws and properties in New Bedford. He took notice of Helen long before she noticed him. He admired her wiry figure, artistic look, and assiduousness from afar. They exchanged half smiles on several occasions. Impeccably groomed, soft-spoken and somewhat shy, Enzo kept his distance until one day Helen was assigned to help him.

"I need some maps of Roberto Clemente Park. It deals with parking and whether a landlord can rent to a low-income client," he told Irene one day.

"We have lots of maps in the archives. Helen can help you."

Helen smiled and disappeared into the dusty archive rooms. She emerged about fifteen minutes later with fragile folded paper maps dating back twenty years.

"Thank you, Helen," Enzo said. Helen looked surprised that he had used her name. She nodded.

"You're welcome, sir."

"My name's Enzo Carpetta, by the way. It's very nice to meet you."

"Nice to meet you as well, Mr. Carpetta."

"Please call me Enzo. It's funny how you can see someone almost every day and not know their name, isn't it?"

"I suppose that's true." Helen really didn't know what Enzo was referring to. In the days that followed, more smiles and pleasantries were exchanged. On one occasion Helen was able to supply a book that Enzo needed that had been misfiled. Enzo used this as an opportunity to advance his interest.

"If you have a break, would you like to join me for coffee? Just down the street perhaps?"

Helen appeared shocked, unsure how to react. There was nothing crude about Enzo and nothing risky about a cup of coffee. She wasn't being propositioned. A respectable looking man simply wanted to spend some time with her. Eventually she said, "That's very nice of you. I don't usually have a break though, sorry."

Enzo sighed. "I understand," he said. "Thank you so much for finding this book for me. It will be very helpful." He turned around to return to the table at which he had been working.

"Wait a moment," Helen said. Enzo turned around.

"Yes, Helen?"

"It was my pleasure to find that book for you, Enzo." Enzo looked a bit perplexed that that's all she wanted to tell him. "I finish work at four. I could join you for coffee at that time if you're available," Helen said nervously.

Enzo beamed. "That's very nice. How about coffee and pastries then when you get done? You know where to find me," he said as he smiled broadly.

Helen nodded. As four p.m. approached, Enzo grew more excited and Helen more nervous. She finished filing away a few books just before four. Enzo watched her do this, trying to appear relaxed. He suddenly feared that she had changed her mind, as she had a conversation with Irene at precisely four, which he thought might involve additional work that would keep her late.

But no, she made her way to Enzo's table. "I'm ready."

Enzo and Helen walked slowly to Salvatore's, a nearby café that served coffee and Italian pastries. Helen's only comment was, "I've never been here before."

Enzo's natural shyness and Helen's aloofness made things difficult at first. They each ordered an espresso and cannoli. Helen made little eye contact. Enzo's wife had died nine years earlier from breast cancer and he had scarcely dated since. He had to dig deep to find conversational skills. "I detect an accent, Helen. Where are you from?"

"Dublin, Ireland. Been here most of my life, though." She gripped her cup and looked at the table.

"That's very interesting. I was born in Fall River and grew up there. But my parents were immigrants, too, from Calabria, Italy."

"That's very nice, Enzo. Irene told me that you do very good work for the community. That you help poor people." Helen smiled and added, "She said, 'He's not a greedy lawyer.'"

"That's very nice of her to say. It makes me feel good to help people," he said. "You must feel the same way. You've been very helpful to me these past few weeks."

"I'm just doing my job," Helen said, but her cheeks flushed.

"Do you like it? Your job?" he asked.

"Very much. Much better than my last job cleaning motels."

"Yes, that does sound better."

Their quiet conversation continued, full of lengthy pauses, with both Helen and Enzo trying to figure out what to say next. Nevertheless, Enzo appeared to enjoy himself. As for Helen, her reaction to Enzo was somewhere between tolerating him and enjoying his company.

49. Matthias, the Other Pianist

Simon sat quietly in the conference room in awe of Matthias. Not only did the German's story mirror his own, but he was clearly a much more skilled pianist who was prolifically creative and had turned his obsession into a meaningful livelihood.

"Do you get headaches, Matthias?" Simon asked.

"No, I don't get headaches. My head hurt after the accident for a while, but no headaches, now."

Dr. Brenner interjected. "Simon, can you describe your headaches?"

"Sure, throbbing in the back of my head. It becomes a pounding. It gets more intense with each passing minute."

Dr. Brenner interrupted. "Do you hear the pounding?"

"No, I don't hear any noise. It just feels like the back of my head is going to explode. Actually, it feels like someone is pounding on the back of my head trying to crack it open, getting frustrated, and hitting me harder and harder."

"Okay, go on."

"I've learned that lying down and closing my eyes makes the whole thing easier to endure. There is no way to function during these headaches so that's what I do. But it doesn't relieve the pain. It's just the only thing I feel like doing. The pain keeps getting worse when I lie down. After about half an hour, I start to see something—musical notes and sequences of numbers. They start out in the distance and then get closer and closer."

Matthias sat more erect and moved a bit closer to Simon, clearly captivated by what he was hearing. "What do the numbers and notes say?" he asked.

"At first, I cannot see them clearly, but then they get closer and closer. They close in on me even though my eyes are closed. But now that I have some experience with music I can read the notes. The numbers are just sequences of five or six digits—13572, 144336, like that. They make no sense to me." Simon paused.

"Do you ever try opening your eyes while these numbers appear?" Dr. Brenner asked.

"No, I have not. I have this instinctive fear that if I do open my eyes suddenly, the numbers may disappear, but that my headache will get suddenly much worse, that my head will explode. I have this fear that the headache will finish me off all of a sudden." He stopped.

Matthias said, "Go on. Get back to the numbers and notes."

"They don't come close in a gentle way. They close in on me, like they want to attack me. They get very large and menacing. It's frightening, so sometimes I put my arm over my eyes, but they keep coming. They seem to swerve away at the last second to avoid a collision, but it's still so frightening. All the while my head is pounding worse and worse."

"What happens next, Simon?" Dr. Brenner asked.

"There comes a point where it's just not possible to bear the situation anymore. The headache must either get better or I must die. There are a few distinct throbs on the back of my head that are worse than any before. I suddenly get nauseated, throw up, and the headache disappears quite quickly after that."

"Do you return to a normal state?" Dr. Brenner asked.

"Yes, but it takes a couple of hours before I'm able to function normally."

"What do you usually do after a headache?"

"Just what I had planned to do. Work, chores, play piano."

"So, playing piano isn't the immediate impulse after the headache subsides?"

"I would say no. If anything, the opposite. I feel like doing something that doesn't require so much concentration."

"What do you think, Matthias?" Dr. Brenner asked.

Matthias took a deep breath. "I did not have that experience, but what the notes mean is obvious. Simon, the numbers are fingerings, I believe they are where you are supposed to put your fingers when you play."

"What?" Simon looked astonished.

"Yes, that makes sense," Dr. Brenner said.

"Gentlemen, I understand fingerings since I've been learning to play, but do you mean 'supposed to when I play'? Supposed to play what?" Simon asked.

Regina, who had been listening quietly jumped in. "For some time after my accident I saw paint strokes in front of my eyes, usually just before falling asleep. They were telling me to do something."

"Simon, we discussed yesterday that you are a creative person, at least somewhat creative, correct?" Dr. Brenner asked.

"Yes, we discussed that. I had not thought of myself as that creative, but I suppose I am to some extent."

"So what have you been playing on the piano?"

"Debussy, Beethoven, Chopin, Mozart," Simon said.

"You are interpreting their works?" Matthias asked.

"I'm just learning about interpretation. I wouldn't say I'm good at interpreting. I just play the piece as written as best I can."

Matthias looked a bit puzzled by Simon's answer. "And how about your own pieces? How are you doing with those?"

"My own pieces? You mean compositions? I have none."

"There's your problem," Dr. Brenner said.

50. A HALTING COURTSHIP

In the days that followed their coffee and cannoli date, Enzo and Helen very gradually grew more comfortable with each other. He continued to spend at least half of each day in the library, leaving periodically to use a pay phone in the lobby. She continued with her work, smiling at times, looking ever more at ease as she passed by him. There were several more coffee dates, and on one occasion, lunch. But this was poorly planned, hurried and less enjoyable, mostly for Enzo, who had remembered at the last minute he had a client to meet at one p.m. The dates were all quite similar. Helen remained stolid. Enzo cautiously tried to engage her in conversation. She would offer the bare minimum. He was genuinely attracted to her. She was articulate, fit, and could be mistaken for a professor. Her much more modest background was hidden, both by her appearance and demeanor, and by her reluctance to discuss it. Enzo did probe carefully in an effort to get closer.

"I have just the one older brother, the lawyer. Both my parents have passed on."

"Both mine as well. My mother just a few months ago."

"Sorry to hear that, Helen. You have much family in Ireland?"

"Yes, four siblings, three brothers and a sister, all younger. I'm the only one here in the States."

"May I ask what brought you here?" Helen immediately felt uncomfortable, and Enzo could sense it.

After a long pause, Helen offered, "I came here to live with my cousin. But she moved to Chicago a couple of years after I arrived." Helen crossed her arms and moved her chair back a bit, perhaps unconsciously, but the message was pretty clear. More questions about her background and family in Ireland were not welcome.

"Tell me a bit about your son?"

"My son?"

"Yes, your son, Simon isn't it? Didn't you say he helped you get the job at the library?"

"Yes, Simon did. He's a very nice young man. A teacher. He lives with me."

"He's not itching to get out on his own? My two daughters have been on their own for a few years since leaving for college. They couldn't wait to be on their own, but they stay very close to me, especially since their mother died."

"Simon is very attached to New Bedford. We have a nice house and he helps take care of it well. So I don't think he's ready to go out on his own."

Enzo grew frustrated after weeks of faltering conversations. He was shy, but gregarious. Polite and respectful, yet curious. Helen's aloofness was hard to pierce, and he started to wonder if it was worth trying. It was he who always suggested they get together after work. He initiated all their conversations. He shared details about his life to make her feel closer to him. She reacted indifferently and didn't reciprocate. He persisted because he believed beneath her cold exterior, beneath what he perceived was profound sadness, was a gentle and kind soul with whom he could have a meaningful relationship. But the gentle and kind soul may have been too much work to uncover. One afternoon, when he had relatively little to do, during an unrushed coffee date, he shared his feelings about the situation frankly.

"We've been out together now many times, Helen. I need to ask you, do you enjoy spending time with me?"

Helen looked confused. In her mind, whether or not she enjoyed Enzo's company wasn't even a question she had considered carefully. She felt obliged to tell him the experience was acceptable.

"I am fine with spending time with you, Enzo," she responded.

"That's not exactly encouraging. I know you're 'fine' with it. We wouldn't be here if you weren't. I'm wondering if you like it?"

Helen suddenly looked fearful, and then took a deep breath before responding.

"I do enjoy spending time with you. But I'm not accustomed to it, to receiving the attention. It sometimes makes me nervous. You always seem very relaxed, but you and I are very different. I hope you can understand that."

Enzo looked a bit confused and rested his chin on his right hand.

"I don't think of myself as someone who makes people nervous Helen. But I will leave it up to you. Next time, if you'd like to go out and do something, you let me know. I won't trouble you with it before that."

Helen said nothing for a couple of minutes. Enzo was very respectable and having virtually no one apart from Simon in her life, his respectability was a good starting point for a meaningful relationship that might make her happier and less stressed. But inviting Enzo to coffee one afternoon required courage and skills that were simply not part of her social repertoire. If she put if off for days or weeks Enzo would give up and then many awkward moments would follow as she would continue to see him in the library.

Finally Helen said, "Have you been to the fashion outlets in Freeport, Maine?"

"No I haven't."

"It's a fun day trip they organize for the library staff. Would you like to accompany me on the next one? Simon and I had a very nice time when we went."

"I would love to. Thank you for the invitation."

51. EXPRESSING CREATIVITY

"My problem?" Simon asked Dr. Brenner, who smiled while leaning back on his chair. Matthias also smiled, as if he understood exactly what Dr. Brenner meant.

"Yes, what do you think the lightning strike did to parts of your brain?"

"According to what I've come to understood through my own thinking it through, it has illuminated the darkness. My hidden knowledge of piano has come to the surface and I'm able to play."

"I think that's true to a large extent Simon, but there is an important missing piece. It has also unleashed your creative instincts," Dr. Brenner said.

"I believe he's right," Matthias added. "It's not just about playing pieces like an expert, it's about the piano being a creative outlet for you."

"If it wasn't about being creative, I would just be painting replicas," Regina added. Her comment resonated with Simon, who felt that he had come to a new and higher level of understanding about what had happened to him.

"How is this related to the headaches, Dr. Brenner?"

"Of course I can't say with absolute certainty, and what I can offer is just conjecture which many of my colleagues would say sounded maybe philosophical, or maybe even foolish. But here's what I believe: You seem to think the headaches bring on the sequences of notes and numbers in your head. I think it's the other way around. Those sequences are expressions of creativity that you're not taking advantage of. There is some sort of electrical impulse running through your brain that brings them on. If they are not allowed to continue to activate other parts of your brain, your peripheral nervous system, your fingers, they cause only the pain that you feel—even if you experience a headache before you see the notes and numbers." Regina and Matthias nodded to indicate both their understanding and their agreement with what Dr. Brenner had subtly presented as a bit more than a theory and a bit less than a concrete scientific explanation.

"So what am I supposed to do?" Simon asked. "All I see are random bits of notes and numbers. I can read them, but they make no sense to me. Am I supposed to write them down and play them? I don't think that's possible because I have so much pain."

"I don't think you fully understand Simon," Dr. Brenner responded. "I just think you need to be more creative. It's all within you already. How would you describe your piano playing now?"

"I play many classical pieces. I would say I'm very mechanical about it. But I haven't been playing for very long. My teacher is trying to get me to be more relaxed and to interpret the pieces more creatively."

"I think you're on the right track. I don't know if you're an 'acquired savant,' someone who has acquired remarkable, prolific skills after a head injury, or just someone whose passion and creativity has been released. But there is natural progression in savants from mimicry, to improvisation, to full-fledged creativity. The mimicry would be just hearing a piece and playing it in the same way. Improvisation would be what you call interpretation with a few extra touches. The final step is you playing your own pieces."

"I don't know if I can do that," Simon responded.

"I can help you," Matthias said. "Let's try some things this afternoon."

Simon was encouraged to take a long break from the discussion to sit and reflect by himself about what Dr. Brenner, Matthias, and Regina had told him. Early in the afternoon Matthias summoned him from a quiet office area and the two made their way to a different nearby church which had a decent upright piano available in its main gathering area. The place was very serene.

Matthias stretched his fingers much the same way Simon had observed Jenna doing and then played the "Revolutionary Étude" Op. 12 No. 10. It sounded magnificent. He played it perfectly. Then

Matthias paused and began to play another piece. It started with slow soft tones, played gently with his left hand and gradually built up into something that sounded more excitable and dramatic. Then he played softly again on the lower register and ended with an almost imperceptibly faint sound.

"What do you think?"

"I think you're a great pianist. What was that second piece all about?"

"I don't know. What does it make you think of?"

Simon thought for a moment. "It sounded like someone making his or her way to some place quietly, secretly, maybe trying to catch someone by surprise. Then something dramatic happens. A conflict perhaps. It gets resolved and the person sneaks away quietly again. Does that make sense?"

"It makes perfect sense, my friend."

"It sounds modern. Is that one of your original compositions?"

"It could be." Simon was confused by the response.

"I guess I mean to say that I just came up with it now, at this very moment." Simon was stunned.

"But how?"

"I don't know how. I certainly didn't see any notes in front of me. I relaxed, and let the musical thoughts flow from my brain to my fingers. I cannot explain it."

"But Matthias, do you think you were being creative? To me being creative is still a conscious, deliberate process. It's not automatic or reflexive. You made it sound like you weren't even controlling what was happening."

"That's a good question. I think I'm being creative. I have a friend who is a wildlife photographer. I was thinking of what a nice piece this would be for him. He sneaks up close to animals, sometimes he's unable to surprise them, there is some commotion, and whatever happens he has to sneak away quietly. I think the piece I just played is about these thoughts I'm having."

"That's absolutely remarkable."

"Thank you. The difficult part is now playing it again, very slowly, writing parts of it down, and then playing it slowly several times to get everything right. But I could have it on paper probably in a couple of days."

"I would imagine that many pianists would take months or even years to do the same thing. You must be so prolific."

"Thank you, my friend. Your turn."

52. PLAYING EXTEMPORE

"What do you want me to do, Matthias?"

"Just go ahead and play."

"Play what?"

"Whatever you feel like playing. Just sit at the piano and play what comes into your head."

Simon hesitated but eventually switched places with Matthias, whose brilliant playing he found a bit intimidating. He sat there for more than a minute, waiting for something to come into his head.

"Relax. No pressure at all."

"It's not that. I still don't feel anything. I can play some pieces I worked on last week."

"No, this is about your own creativity remember?"

Simon closed his eyes, faintly hoping that notes would appear before him which would guide his hands to the right place. Nothing of the sort happened. But eventually his fingers started to touch the keyboard. He played a few faint notes at first with his right hand and a minor chord with his left. He kept his eyes closed. He started to sway a bit back and forth on the piano bench. Then came the real music.

A dramatic beginning of four loud minor chords, followed by an elegant melody that went across three registers. It reminded one of climbing stairs or going ever higher to some unknown place. At the top, more dramatic high, minor chords and a slightly different melody, softer, more serene. Finally, after about three minutes came the finale—loud, passionate, full of aggressive chords and notes, terminating with a soft, B flat minor chord. The piece was dramatic and in some ways elegant, but Simon didn't play with nearly the smoothness of Matthias, and his piece sounded much jerkier and more disorganized. He opened his eyes and turned around.

"What did you think?" Simon asked.

"I don't know. That was completely original?"

"Yes, just now. I made it up as I went along. First time I've ever done that before. Did it sound good to you?"

"It sounded interesting, but that's not the important thing. How did you feel playing it?"

"I felt really emotional if that makes sense. I was recalling how I felt shortly after being struck by lightning, how I felt rising into the clouds and then coming back down again. I felt like that experience guided my fingers. Does that make any sense?"

"Dr. Brenner will tell you there isn't any making sense or not making sense for people like you and me. I do understand what you're saying."

"Do you feel the same way when you play?"

"Yes I feel emotional but not the same way. I don't think about something that happened. I just feel some emotion—joy, sadness, anger, whatever, and that guides me like your experience guides you."

"I don't play as smoothly as you, Matthias."

"I've been playing for many years. You just started. The technique will improve. Did you enjoy what you just played?"

"Hmm… I worried about how it would sound to you. I feel much more relaxed now though. Feels like some stress has been relieved by playing my own piece. So overall I would say I enjoyed it a lot."

"Good. I would encourage you to keep doing the same thing. Be original every day. It doesn't mean you can't play Beethoven. I do. I'm German after all. But mix it in. You will find it much more rewarding."

"Dr. Brenner implied that I might also get some relief from my headaches if I do that."

"I don't know. I never got the type of headaches you have. Our condition is a mystery to many people. My doctors in Germany simply don't believe me at all. It's all a mystery. Even Dr. Brenner is a mystery isn't he?"

"He is certainly different. No scans, blood tests, nothing. Were you surprised by that?"

"A bit surprised. I did have all that in Germany and nothing showed up. I guess Dr. Brenner felt it was not worth doing any more. But you must say you were better off by coming here, right?"

"Yes I am. The lightning may have illuminated the darkness, but I suppose Dr. Brenner and you did too."

"Dr. Brenner is more interested in what happens to us in the long-term. He's been studying people like us for twenty years or more. Some people go on to do wonderful things."

"Some? What about the rest?"

"He doesn't talk about the rest too much. I think some people really struggle and have problems."

"You know what's funny, Matthias? I would say my whole life has been a struggle with problems, so that wouldn't be anything new for me."

"Is that right? Now at least you have a gift to help you with the future."

"I suppose I do. What else am I supposed to do here during my visit?" Simon stood up from the piano bench, stretched his arms and stood next to Matthias.

"My first visit was pretty relaxed. Not much to do. Dr. Brenner will meet with you again, give you some things to read, and ask you to keep some type of diary. A couple of times a year he will ask you to come back here for a couple of days. If he senses something is going wrong, I think he does do some testing. So far from what I can tell, you are doing quite well."

"That's reassuring to hear," Simon said.

"I think the main value is to know you're not alone. You are part of a small community. We all help each other find a good direction in life. After my accident, I felt closer to my wife and children. We spend much more time together. Of course, maybe that's because I nearly died, but I do think it also had to do with something that changed in my head. Has your life changed at all in some other way?"

"I think so. I am very touched by the kindness that's been shown to me since the accident. I live in a small college town and almost everyone has been so kind in so many different ways. I also have a girlfriend."

"Wonderful. Also a lightning strike victim? I only ask because that has happened according to Dr. Brenner." Simon looked surprised by the question.

"No. Fortunately she's not. She's my piano teacher and a music professor."

"You're a very lucky man then, Simon."

53. A Day in Maine for Helen and Enzo

"I'm going back up to Freeport next week, just so you know. I'll be away the whole day," Helen announced to Simon over dinner one evening.

"Wonderful, Mother. Would you like me to come again?"

"No, that's fine. I have a friend who'll be accompanying me."

Simon was so surprised to hear this he froze and said nothing for a long time. "A friend? Does she work at the library too?"

"No, it's a gentleman, and we'll be driving up in his car and join the group there. We plan to come back later after having dinner there."

There were multiple reasons for Simon to be both concerned and confused: Was this a respectable gentleman? What was his motivation to spend the day with Helen? After all, sleazy Steve had suggested a drive in the country. Helen hadn't mentioned this friend to Simon before. He decided to probe her, albeit carefully.

"Does this gentleman work in the library?"

"Interestingly he's there every day doing his work. He's a lawyer who helps with evictions and foreclosures."

Simon looked relieved and smiled. A respectable library patron as a friend was reassuring. "I'm happy for you, Mother."

"Thank you. He will be coming to pick me up on Saturday morning. His name is Enzo."

"I think you'll have a nice time. It's also nice that you'll be spending the day with your group from the library," Simon said.

The day arrived and Enzo rang the doorbell promptly at eight a.m. Helen was upstairs, so Simon opened the door.

"Good morning. Simon, is it?"

"Yes it is."

"I'm Enzo Carpetta, a friend of your mother's, here to pick her up for the trip to Freeport."

"It's a pleasure to meet you."

Enzo was casually dressed, and his friendly disposition and obvious politeness put Simon at ease.

There had never been any shouting or calling for people across rooms or up the stairs of the Galves house. It had simply never been that way. Simon ascended the stairs and knocked gently on Helen's door and told her Enzo was waiting. She came downstairs a minute later, wearing an attractive summer dress she had purchased in Freeport on the prior trip.

"Wonderful to see you, Helen. You look terrific."

"Thank you, Enzo."

"Okay, looks like we're all set. Simon, you're welcome to join us, if you like," Enzo said. The invitation made it clear to Simon that Enzo was nothing like sleazy Steve. Simon actually had little to do that day, but he hoped that whatever relationship his mother and Enzo had would be more likely to blossom if he didn't go.

"That's very kind of you, Enzo. Actually, I'm going to do some work around the house and some reading. I hope you both have a wonderful time."

Helen walked out to Enzo's car, not quite with enthusiasm, but more briskly than she usually walked. Seemingly shy and gentlemanly, Enzo was an ideal companion for Helen for a day trip.

They joined the other library employees in Freeport around eleven a.m. Enzo bought a new wallet. Helen bought a couple of dresses. She asked Enzo to weigh in on her choices, which he actually did to the best of his ability. They had a pizza lunch with the group. It was September and still warm, so everyone headed to Old Orchard Beach. Enzo and Helen took a walk there together. At some point Enzo asked to hold Helen's hand, which she offered with some hesitation. Her hand was cold and clammy, but after a few minutes warmed up as she became more comfortable. Near the end of the walk, Enzo kissed her, and she didn't resist.

The bus returned to New Bedford straight from Old Orchard with Helen's library colleagues. Enzo and Helen returned in his car to Freeport and had lobster rolls for dinner at the Jameson Tavern Restaurant. They were both quiet as usual, but for the first time Helen offered a few conversation starters, telling Enzo that it had been many years since she had had lobster and asking him what he thought about it.

Enzo was also more open and engaging than he had been. "I really had a nice day with you today. I hope you enjoyed it too."

"Yes, I thought it was very enjoyable. Thank you so much for bringing me up here."

"No need to thank me." There was no indication in their conversation that their relationship had fundamentally changed from a somewhat tepid, distant friendship to a newly romantic couple. Neither mentioned anything about Enzo's kiss.

They returned to Helen's home around eleven p.m., and Enzo made sure she got inside safely. Simon had been worried. He had expected his mother back earlier in the evening. She smiled a bit more broadly than usual when she saw him.

"Did you have a nice time, mother?"

"I certainly did. I had a wonderful time." Never one prone to exaggeration, the fact that Helen had used the word "wonderful" was a breakthrough moment.

"That's terrific to hear. Enzo seems like a very nice gentleman."

"He definitely is."

"Will you see him again?"

"I see him almost every day at work, and I hope we can spend some time together on the weekends, too." Helen smiled again.

Simon smiled back. His lonely mother had found a companion. He also felt liberated. Watching out for and worrying about his mother might be a bit less burdensome with Enzo in the picture. She, in turn, with a new person in her life, might pay a bit less attention to Simon's comings and goings and respect his independence. It had been a very fruitful weekend indeed.

54. Last Day in Ann Arbor

Simon spent a final loosely organized day in Ann Arbor. He met with Regina for lunch, whom he found very quiet and otherwise pleasant, but with whom he felt he had little in common. He was expected to meet with Dr. Brenner at three p.m. and waited patiently for him in the conference room. Dr. Brenner showed up at three forty-five, provoking a little anxiety since Simon's flight out of Detroit was at six.

"So sorry to keep you waiting Simon. I was supervising a fellows' clinic and things ran late."

"No problem. I appreciate you meeting with me again. A reminder that the car is picking me up in half an hour."

"Well, tell me overall what you thought about your visit?"

"I thought it was very interesting, very insightful. I feel I have a better understanding of what happened to me and how I have changed."

"That's all I could hope for."

"I need to ask, Dr. Brenner, why me coming to my own conclusions? It seems unorthodox. I have limited experience with doctors, but usually people seek answers from them."

"My feeling is that by you discovering your own truths, it has a much more powerful impact. If I told you what I thought was going on, I'm guessing you would be a bit more skeptical. I used to do that. You can imagine that with my style I've met quite a few doubters, many of whom sought a second opinion. So I try to provoke some innovative thinking and stand back. Make sense?"

"Yes it does."

"So tell me what you believe you have learned, and I'll let you go."

"The knowledge, the skill to play the piano has been with me for a long time. An electrical strike has activated some part of my brain that has brought it to the surface. The headaches I experience are the result of pressure from creativity I haven't been expressing. By being more creative I should expect some relief."

"Wow. Wasn't that worth the trip to Ann Arbor?"

"It certainly was. So what do you think I should do now?"

"You need to nurture your newfound talent. As knowledgeable and skillful as you are, and I'm no expert, I'm guessing you don't play like Matthias."

"Certainly not. He's brilliant."

"You need to connect more with the music, not obsessively all the time as you've been doing, but passionately, intensely. Does that make sense?"

"I think so. I've been playing many hours a day. Trying to learn as much as I can."

"I don't think that's the right approach. I think you should actually play less, and only when you feel a deep urge inside, not to learn, but to be creative. Creative emotion should drive your playing. Otherwise you'll just be a pianist who has learned a lot in a compressed time period. That would not be taking advantage of your gift."

"You really believe it's a gift, Dr. Brenner?"

"I do and I've studied a few dozen people like you. It's a gift with a downside though in many cases."

"You had hinted at that before. Can you explain?"

"I didn't do any scans because I don't believe they would show anything more than what they showed in Newell. However, and I don't mean to hold you up with more Socratic questioning, but do you believe it's possible to be struck by one-hundred million volts of electricity without some downside?"

"I've been told I'm very lucky to be alive for one thing."

"That is certainly true. And your brain has changed functionally, if not in terms of its anatomy. But it would be highly unusual if you escaped without any damage."

"You mean to my brain? Besides the burns I suffered?"

"Yes, Simon. I'm confident that your headaches will subside but know that some other negative consequences may show up. In my experience they almost always do."

"That's a bit discouraging. How do I prepare for that?"

"You can't, because no one can tell you what will happen. I want you to check in with me at least every month. We have an online portal where you can answer questions about how you're feeling and what's been going on. You can tell me all about your piano playing."

"I will do that. You've got me a bit worried. The difficulty I had walking, that doesn't reflect the type of damage you're referring to?"

"Sorry, Simon, no. In the days that follow a strike it's not unusual for coordination to take time to recover."

Dr. Brenner gave Simon copies of two books to read: The first was Daniel Treffert's *Islands of Genius*. Treffert describes fifty years of experience studying savants, including many who seem to know things they have never formally learned. The second book was Oliver Sacks' *Musicophilia*. In it are stories of an unusual affinity or aptitude for music among people who otherwise function poorly, or who have suffered a traumatic event. Sacks actually describes the story of a physician who was struck by lightning and develops a passion for playing the piano. Dr. Brenner knew Simon was a reader and would find both books helpful both in furthering his understanding of his condition and also to feel more connected to others like him. His closing caution about latent negative consequences left Simon feeling uneasy. He wondered why Matthias hadn't talked about his experience with latent effects and how they manifested in his life. Still, having had an overall meaningful trip to Ann Arbor, Simon made his way home where he spent many hours just reflecting on all that he had learned.

55. HILLS AND VALLEYS

"How did it go overall?" Jenna asked as she and Simon settled in for a relaxed dinner with drinks at the Ale House.

"It was really illuminating, and that word has a double meaning for my trip."

"What does he think about the headaches?"

"He thinks they won't happen anymore, because I've learned I need to unleash my creativity."

"Isn't that what you've been doing?"

"I guess not in the strictest sense. He thinks I should improvise and play my own compositions."

"That's extremely difficult, Simon, especially for someone who hasn't been playing very long."

"I actually started composing while I was there."

"Really? I'd love to hear it. My piano's back. You can play at my place. Stay the night."

"I'd love to."

Jenna owned a lovely Jura cappuccino maker which she put to good use when she and Simon returned to her place. As comfortable as he was with Jenna, and though she had heard him play many times, he suddenly felt a bit nervous about sharing his own composition with her. Jenna offered him a shot of brandy which seemed to do the trick as he sat on the piano bench in front of Jenna's beautiful Schimmel baby grand piano.

"I guess I've got to think for a bit," Simon said.

"Just play what you played up in Michigan."

"I guess that's a start."

Simon closed his eyes and leaned back for a moment and then started to play the same dramatic piece he had played for Matthias. Every note, rhythm and dynamic feature came back to him in exactly the same way, with so much clarity it surprised him. In fact, this second time, he played it with considerably less hesitation. Once he finished, he closed his eyes again and leaned back, before opening his eyes and turning around to gauge Jenna's reaction.

Her eyes were lit up.

"What did you think?" he asked.

"Not sure what to think. That was really beautiful."

"Are you serious? You enjoyed it?"

"I did, but more importantly it brought out a whole lot of emotion. What's it about?"

"I don't know. After I played it the first time I thought about it for a while. It's dramatic, full of ups and downs. It sounds like stress, anger, but then mixed with hope at different points. It's hard to explain."

"Maybe it's not about some event. Maybe it's about you."

Jenna's insight hit Simon poignantly. "Yeah I guess it's about me and my life. Full of ups and downs. Full of stress and anger. But I always have hope. I think you're right."

Simon bore a sad look. He had planned more experimentation with the piano but sat there quietly with his arms at his side.

Jenna said, "That's enough piano for today. Do you want more coffee or another drink or something?"

"No, I'm fine."

Jenna stood up and behind Simon and rubbed his shoulders. "I thought it was beautiful. Tell you what, let's go to bed, and tomorrow I'll help you write it down. I'm sorry if I made you feel sad. I didn't mean to."

"No, don't be sorry. You're spot on. And music is all sentimentality disguised as rationality and complexity."

"Who said that?"

"I did. I wrote it down a few months ago."

"That's almost as amazing as what you just played. You have an extraordinary gift. I think it's always been there. It's as if you were lucky to be struck by lightning."

"Thanks. I think I would like another shot of brandy if you'll join me."

"Yeah, let's do that for starters." Jenna had hinted at an interesting night of sex, a little booze, a little sleep, and a lot of quality conversation, but no more piano. They both fell firmly asleep around five a.m., stirring awake only after ten a.m.

"I can make some breakfast if you show me where things are," Simon said.

"That's pretty nice of you. You like waffles? I've got some mix and a waffle maker."

"Sounds like a plan." Simon prepared the food while Jenna made coffee. Simon kept thinking about his reaction to Jenna's suggestion that his piece was all about him. What troubled him was that she had such a clear notion of his life and his character. She had, in some ways, defined him. If she was right, he would not be able to escape the cycle of highs and lows, anger and stress—because that's who he was. He feared that dissecting the piece in detail in order to transcribe it onto notation paper would be even more distressing. But it was certainly a good idea to do it.

"So, we're going to use notation paper?" Simon asked Jenna.

"Yes, something wrong with that?"

"Hmm, I spent many hours online looking for piano related things. Seems like there's a lot of software programs that will just transcribe what you play without you or me having to write things down."

Jenna smiled, brushed up against Simon, stroked his hair gently and kissed him on the neck. "Have you used any of those programs?"

"No I haven't."

"They really aren't that great. They do a good job of capturing the notes, but not so great with the rhythm or the dynamics of a piece. Besides, I think by writing it down you will learn a lot. It's fine to use a program to help with notation once you know the direction you're heading in, but I would stay away from the programs that do all the work for you." Simon shrugged his shoulders, as if hoping Jenna was right about how much he would learn.

Jenna and Simon sat together at the piano, coffee cups in hand.

"Let's start with a title. What do you want to call it?"

"I don't know, definitely not 'the life of Simon Galves.'"

"Yeah I would suggest something a bit more mysterious. But I don't want to suggest names. It's your piece."

After thinking for a minute or so, Simon came up with "Hills and Valleys."

"I like it. Kind of like Newell, huh? Full of hills and valleys."

"Kind of. But I wasn't thinking about Newell. Actually, I was thinking about my life."

"Yes, I was thinking that, too."

Jenna and Simon spent about nine hours transcribing the Hills and Valleys from the newly illuminated parts of Simon's mind, to his fingers, to notation paper. It was a laborious process and there would be no way for Simon to do this on his own. Even his most basic attempts were full of errors. "You played that as a triplet, but you wrote down sixteenth notes here," "You need a fermata here, because you hang on to the F# for just a moment longer than expected," she told him. In the evening, Simon played it as written, which was difficult, because his instinctive play kept superseding what had been written down, no matter how accurate it was. After a few moments, he stopped looking at the paper completely.

"Okay, that's not working. I'll tell you what. I'll play it based on the sheet. You tell me if it sounds right," Jenna offered.

Jenna played "Hills and Valleys" exactly as they had written it, with the mastery of a talented musician, teacher, and scholar. Her touch was much smoother than Simon's, and the piece sounded much better in her hands.

"I thought that was just perfect, my dear," Simon said.

"Okay, I think we nailed it."

56. PA RAFFA'S AGAIN

Theirs was not a quick moving, passionate romance. Enzo was by no means aggressive. Well aware of Helen's anxiety and distance, he moved especially slowly. He always paused before saying anything to Helen, as if to rehearse it in his mind first. His smiles and gestures seemed planned rather than spontaneous. Though he was naturally shy and softspoken, even Enzo started to get frustrated. Their relationship had become nothing more than a series of quiet coffee dates with an occasional weekend outing for shopping or lunch. Enzo and Helen hadn't shared any real emotional or physical intimacy. On one coffee date when Helen seemed especially aloof, Enzo asked, "I'd like to know what you hope to get out of this whole thing?"

"What do you mean?" Helen asked in return with a very worried look.

"I mean what do you hope to get out of our relationship, Helen?" Helen looked even more anxious and didn't reply.

"I'm sorry. I didn't mean to make you anxious. Let's talk about it some other time." Enzo smiled reached across the small round table at which they were seated and held Helen's right hand. She looked immediately relieved.

Enzo simply hung in there. There were no more provocative questions.

One day in the library, when Helen was doing computer training at a separate facility, he met one of Helen's coworkers, Frances, a woman in her early seventies who had worked there for decades.

"I'm Frances. I work with Helen. I remember you from the Freeport trip. I hear nice things about you," Frances said quietly while Enzo was taking a break and walking around.

"That's very nice to hear. I've enjoyed getting to know her."

Frances smiled, "That can't be easy, Enzo."

"What do you mean?"

"I mean she seems like a tough person to get to know. I've been trying for some time." Enzo was a bit surprised by Frances's candor.

"Could we talk for a few minutes, somewhere a bit more private?"

"Of course." Frances led Enzo to her small office.

"Like you, I've been trying to get to know Helen for some time."

"May I ask why?" Frances asked in a motherly tone.

"I guess I just believe that under that scared, wispy exterior there's a sad but warm and caring woman. Maybe that's just wishful thinking. I don't really have a whole lot else going on socially. Both my daughters live far away. I have a couple of friends, but they've got young families. My older brother is a lawyer too, but much busier."

"I understand, and I hope things work out the way you want them to. Please do come out on our bus trips again." Both Frances and Enzo stood up, and though they had just met, Frances offered Enzo a hug, something he greatly appreciated.

Enzo came by the house, usually on Friday evenings or on Saturday mornings, in advance of a dinner or some other outing. He brought flowers sometimes, which Helen appreciated as she immediately transferred them to a vase on the kitchen table. Other times he brought a box of chocolates, which she stored in a cupboard. Neither she nor Simon had a sweet tooth, and the boxes soon accumulated into a pile which Simon took to the teacher's break room at a middle school where he was working. Enzo engaged Simon, something Simon truly appreciated. Not just small talk about work or the weather. Enzo seemed to have a genuine interest in Simon's life. Both men were articulate and masterful with both the spoken and written English language, and this by itself was a source of kinship and mutual admiration.

"Mother's upstairs and will be down shortly," Simon said one evening as he greeted Enzo and let him in.

"Good to see you, young man. We're going to a movie this evening, *Quiz Show*, do you know it?"

"I've heard of it. Something about cheating on a TV quiz show from the sixties."

"Yes. Your mother's choice."

"Oh, really?" Though she watched hours of television, Simon had never known his mother to be up to date with movies in theaters.

"Yes. She picked it. So, I can blame her if it's not entertaining," Enzo chuckled. Helen came downstairs, and he said, "You look lovely, Helen."

"Thank you, Enzo. You look dashing as always," Helen said with a smile that had gradually grown a little broader since she had met Enzo.

"Both of you have a wonderful evening," Simon said. He felt good about Enzo for a couple of reasons. Enzo was obviously respectable, and he worried less and less about his mother's well-being every time he met him. Beyond this, he was genuinely starting to like Enzo on a personal level. If they had a chance to talk at length, Simon believed he and Enzo would have much in common.

That opportunity came the following Friday evening when Helen announced to Simon, "I'd like to tell you that Enzo and I are taking you out to dinner this evening, and Enzo has made it clear he's not taking 'no' for an answer." Helen smiled and looked pleased with herself.

"That's really nice, Mother. Are you sure I won't be intruding?"

"Not at all. We'd both be delighted."

Enzo rang the doorbell a few minutes later bearing a bouquet of flowers. He had sensed that the chocolates were not being consumed and so flowers became his standard Friday night offering.

"I assume your mother has told you the plan for the evening?"

"She has."

"And we'll tie you up and drag you out if we have to. And don't even think for a moment about paying," Enzo said smiling.

"This is really generous of you, Enzo. I don't want to intrude on your evening though."

"Nonsense. Helen and I spend a lot of time together ourselves. She speaks so highly of you. It would be great to get to know you better."

Simon was shocked. It had been unimaginable that his mother would talk about him to anyone, let alone speak highly. Sensing Simon's surprise, Enzo continued.

"Oh yes. She talks about your kindness. In fact, Helen and I were thinking about Pa Raffa's tonight, because Helen enjoyed it so much when you took her there." Helen nodded and smiled as she leaned up against Enzo, an affectionate gesture Simon didn't expect either.

Not knowing how to react, Simon just said, "Pa Raffa's is excellent. I hope we can get a table."

"Don't worry, I called in advance," Enzo said.

What transpired was an evening that exceeded Simon's expectations. In addition to the usual Italian fare, about whose authenticity, Enzo, much closer to his roots than the majority of Italian Americans, made some lighthearted jokes, Enzo ordered a bottle of San Giovese. It helped everyone loosen up a bit, even Helen. She beamed as Simon and Enzo discussed his time at Bridgewater State. Enzo had attended Northeastern School of Law in Boston, and their time in Boston was another mutual point of discussion. Helen seemed content to watch Simon and Enzo get along so well, but added additional fuel when spontaneously she said, "Simon's a big science fiction fan."

"You're kidding. Really, Simon?"

"Well, at least when I was younger. I guess I still am. I like the classics. Philip K. Dick, Ray Bradbury."

"I've read them all young man. What's your favorite?"

"*Dandelion Wine* by Bradbury."

"Not science fiction but I've read it. Love it. I'm a fan of the classics too. Arthur C. Clarke, *Childhood's End* was particularly memorable."

"Wow. Tremendous," Simon replied.

With those positive vibes, an earnest bond between Simon and Enzo had been cemented. Delighted, Helen reached out and held Enzo's hand.

57. OAKLAND

Simon left Jenna's feeling good about what had been accomplished. After returning home he had the urge to do more work. *"Hills and Valleys" is not an interesting title at all*, he thought. He took out the notation sheets completed in Jenna's superb handwriting and started making small changes—A decrescendo here, an additional rest there. Then he re-transcribed the whole thing. He played it, not from memory but slowly following the sheet music. He thought it sounded a bit better. He retitled his piece "Flusso e Reflusso," Italian for ebb and flow which more aptly described the pattern of decline and regrowth that characterized his life at that point. He played it a dozen times before finally going to bed.

It had been only a short time since he had returned from Ann Arbor, but Simon did feel optimistic that his headaches may have disappeared forever. As he lay down, not only did he not have a headache, but his mind also felt very much at ease. He stretched while in bed, relaxing muscles throughout his body including those in his neck and the back of his head. He fell asleep promptly and woke up feeling quite refreshed. He had a full load of clients the next day and was eager to get to work.

Jenna called soon after he woke up. "You free for lunch, sunshine?" she asked.

"Sorry dear, booked through lunch. It's going to be a long day," Simon said.

"No problem. I came up with an idea."

"Better title than 'Hills and Valleys'? I came up with a new one."

"Oh, no. My mom is turning seventy-five next month. We're doing a family thing in Oakland. Pretty informal. Would you like to join us?" Simon had met Jenna's affable father Harold but the prospect of being surrounded by her entire family made him a bit nervous. He feared not everyone would take kindly to him. But given how much he liked and cared for Jenna, he knew saying no wasn't really an option.

"That sounds really interesting. You sure they want me to come?"

"Oh yes. It was my mom's idea. And my dad was gushing about you too."

"Oh okay. So it's not a surprise party then."

Jenna laughed. "No, the Cobbs don't do surprises well. Trust me."

"Well, I just hope I make a good impression."

"Just be yourself, Simon. Have you been to Oakland?"

"Nope. Never been to California at all. Stayed pretty much in New England till I came to Newell."

"I think you'll love it."

Simon and Jenna grew closer in the weeks that followed. They would have been inseparable if it wasn't for their busy professional lives. They found time, generally in the evenings, to relax over dinner or drinks. Simon stayed over at her place several times.

She visited his a few times as well, concluding that it was altogether too dismal. "When are you going to move out?" she asked.

Simon was noncommittal. "I have a lease. I'll think about it in a few months." In reality the dark, drab basement apartment had grown on Simon. He couldn't imagine a quieter upstairs neighbor than Anna. The price was certainly right, especially in a small city full of overpriced student housing and expensive new condos and town-houses. The tranquility was good for his reading and commenting on student compositions, and perfect for his piano playing. Besides, the thought of moving the piano to another location was unappealing enough to discourage him from thinking about moving.

Jenna and Simon landed in Oakland on a chilly but bright, sunny November afternoon. Harold greeted them at the airport with the warmth Simon remembered and drove them to the Lake Merritt neighborhood.

"Welcome to the glorious multicultural city of Oakland," Harold said.

It was easy to tell that Jenna loved her town and loved her neighborhood.

"That was Lakeview Elementary School. That's where I went to school. But they shut it down a few years ago. It's an administrative building now," Jenna said.

"That's a shame. Just not enough kids? That's happening now in New Bedford."

"Exactly. The neighborhood has changed a lot. A lot of older folks now. A lot more diverse."

"Looks like it. I guess just about anyone can blend in here. I love it."

Harold drove up Santa Clara Avenue to the family home on a small side street with a dead end. Houses in Oakland don't come cheap and the Cobb home was an impressively large stone and stucco light pastel green house with a small but immaculately maintained front yard. Jenna's mother rushed out the front door as the car pulled up. She was very much like Harold, modestly over-weight, warm and informal.

"You must be the famous Simon! Audrey Cobb, it's a pleasure," she said as she gave Simon a hug.

"Great to meet you too, Audrey. It's beautiful here. Beautiful house too. And happy birthday."

"Oh, thank you, Simon. It's no big deal, really. An excuse to see my little girl and to meet you. She's always easy to coax out here. Her brother, not so much."

"Well, boys are different for sure," Simon said.

"You can say that again," Audrey said, and they laughed.

It took only a few minutes for Simon to feel completely at ease. Naturally quiet, he feared that the lack of spontaneity in his conversation and long pauses might not be appreciated or worse, misinterpreted, as discomfort with Jenna's gregarious African American family. Instead, Audrey seemed to know what to expect from Simon and she took an instant liking to him. The planned birthday party and reunion seemed destined to remain small and informal. Jenna's brother Carl, for example, still wasn't sure if he would make it from Los Angeles. Audrey's sister and brother-in-law from Seattle would attend, and that would be about it.

That evening, Jenna and Simon decided to take a walk down Santa Clara Avenue toward the former Lakeview Elementary, where she wanted to show him where she played hopscotch and jumped rope as a little girl. It was mostly for her own benefit, therapeutic nostalgia one could call it—longing for a simpler time, usually in childhood to help relieve some of the stresses of a busy contemporary life. They passed by the Lake Park United Methodist Church.

Jenna pointed at the building and said, "It's mostly a Chinese church. That's where I learned to play piano."

"Really? Lots of great memories there I bet."

"Yes, I had a great teacher. Mr. Chiu. His eyes would light up every time I finally figured things out. Every kid should have someone like that when they learn." Jenna and Simon paused for a few moments in front of the church. They could hear a watering hose being used on the side. A few seconds later a casually dressed woman came out front.

"Jenna?" the woman said. "Wow, welcome home."

"Diana, it's terrific to see you!" Jenna recognized her old friend immediately. She turned to introduce Simon. "Simon Galves, meet Diana Pang. She and I grew up together in the neighborhood." Simon smiled and shook Diana's hand.

"A pleasure, Simon," Diana said. "You two here just for a few days?"

"Yes, mom's seventy-fifth birthday. Just a small celebration."

"You should come and play this Sunday after church. Everyone will love it."

"A concert? Maybe. What do you think, Simon?" Jenna asked.

"I think you should go for it."

"I have a slightly better idea. How about we hear some 'Flusso e Reflusso' this Sunday?" Jenna asked.

"Me? Perform? In front of all those people?"

Diana laughed. "It'll be a lot of Chinese kids with their grandparents. Trust me, it won't be a high-pressure crowd. We'd love to have you play Simon."

"Don't worry sunshine. You can practice until then. If you don't feel ready, you can back out. No big deal," Jenna said.

"Well ladies, I guess I can't refuse."

58. First Performance

Audrey's birthday took place Saturday and was low-key and uneventful. The Sunday concert at the church came together just as Diana had indicated it would. After church services ended around noon, roughly two dozen people stuck around, mostly Chinese grandparents and young grandchildren. Some attended simply as they were waiting for rides back home, and so left early. Some people filtered in and out. The youngest children wandered all over the place. Diana and Jenna sat up front. Despite the informality of the crowd, Simon still felt nervous. He warmed up with a few scales and waited for some sign from Diana that he ought to start "Flusso e Reflusso."

"I'd give it till twelve fifteen, Simon, there's still a few people milling about who might join us."

A few minutes later Diana stood up to announce, "Thank you all so much for sticking around to hear this afternoon's music. I'd like to welcome a special guest, Mr. Simon Galves, who has come all the way from Virginia to be with us this afternoon. Simon is relatively new to the piano and will be playing an original composition." She looked to Simon for the name, who whispered it. "'Flusso e Reflusso,' Please welcome Simon."

After a smattering of applause, Simon stretched his fingers

a few times and played his first original composition. Its drama, melancholic tones, followed by a hopeful melody were all executed perfectly. Simon quickly forgot the audience. Instead, he immersed himself completely in the music. His eyes were closed much of the time. He played passionately and emotionally. What the audience thought of "Flusso e Reflusso" simply didn't matter. He felt very relaxed as he ended, not because he had finished his first public performance, but because playing the piece was mellowing in and of itself.

A smatter of applause followed from an audience that wasn't all that sure how to judge what it had heard. Diana, however, offered high praise. "That was absolutely beautiful, Simon. You came up with that?"

"I did, but Jenna really helped me a lot. To make it more refined and to get it down on paper."

"Well, you two make a great team then."

"I'm really proud of you, sunshine," Jenna said. He had not only given his first performance for an audience, but had also been a good sport, doing his best to entertain a few families on a Sunday afternoon.

The pair made their way back to Newell the next morning, arriving late in the afternoon.

"Stay with me tonight, Simon," Jenna said.

"Yeah, I'd like that. Let me swing by my place and get some fresh clothes."

"You do that and I'll make some spaghetti and open a bottle of red wine."

Simon returned to Jenna's reflecting on how well the trip had gone and how much he had enjoyed meeting her family.

"My mom just texted. They absolutely loved you, Simon."

"That's great to hear. I loved them, too. Great family. Would be great to see them again sometime. I'm so glad everything went smoothly."

"Yes. So when are you coming out with your next brilliant composition?"

"Good question," Simon said, smiling. "I think I need to catch up on work first for the next couple of weeks."

Jenna suddenly had a confused look on her face. "What? You think I should come up with something new right away?"

"No, your hand. It's twitching. Can't you tell?"

Simon, who had been seated on a dining chair, suddenly fell off to the side onto the floor, striking his head. His pupils rolled back into his head and both his arms began shaking violently, followed by both of his legs, one of which caught another chair, knocking it over.

"Simon! Simon! Can you hear me?"

Horrified, Jenna was caught between staying with Simon and getting up to call 911. As an educated woman, she knew he was having a seizure. She stayed with him with her right hand on his chest. The convulsions stopped about thirty seconds later. He said nothing for another minute.

"What happened?"

"You had a seizure. A big one." Jenna called for the ambulance.

Dr. Brenner's warning came back to Simon immediately. He was unlikely to escape a lightning strike only with a newfound ability to play the piano. There had to be a price, and he was starting to pay it. He started to feel quite well, but Jenna insisted he stay on the ground on his side until help arrived.

59. Hospital Again

Simon was taken to Newell Mercy and gradually became more alert so that he felt quite back to normal when he arrived.

Dr. Delarosa met him and Jenna in Simon's hospital room.

"You're quickly becoming my favorite patient, Simon," Dr. Delarosa said as she smiled.

"Trust me, that was never my plan," Simon said. "Dr. Delarosa, this is my girlfriend, Jenna."

"Nice to meet you, Jenna. I understand you witnessed the seizure?"

"I did. It started when I noticed his left hand quivering. We were just sitting at the dining table. Then he started really convulsing—his arms, legs. He fell backward onto the floor. His head hit the floor. He started making grunting sounds. What was really scary was his eyes. I was terrified. It lasted nearly a minute."

"Thank you for all those details. It definitely started with quivering in his left hand? You're sure about that?"

"Yes, I am."

"I recall her mentioning that too. I was just sitting and didn't notice my hand quivering," Simon added.

"Unfortunately, this could be bad news," Dr. Delarosa said, her tone having changed quickly from reassuring and upbeat to quite somber. "You had what started as something called a focal seizure. It later affected your whole body. My concern is that there is something structural in your brain that caused it."

"But you did the scan, and it was normal."

"Yes, but things can show up later on. That's why we often repeat scans, especially if a new symptom comes up."

"I had a very good visit with Dr. Brenner. You were right, he was pretty unorthodox. He did mention that it would be rare to escape a lightning strike without some kind of negative effect."

"He's right," Dr. Delarosa said. "And sometimes it takes months or even years to show up. I don't want to sound too discouraging. I know how much you've gone through."

"So what happens next?"

"We've got you on some seizure control medications. We'll do another MRI tomorrow morning. I'll come see you myself tomorrow to discuss it. Let me know in the meantime if you have any questions."

Jenna nodded and Dr. Delarosa left.

Simon took a deep breath. "Funny isn't it, Jenna? We had a wonderful weekend in California, and then this happens."

"Let's be hopeful. Maybe nothing will show up on the MRI. Maybe it was a one-time thing."

"Maybe," Simon said. He thought for a minute then said, "I have a question for you. Something we've not talked about yet."

"Go ahead, shoot."

"Do you believe in God, Jenna?"

She knitted her brow and said, "I do. Why do you ask?"

"I want to get your take on how you believe God works."

"You mean the old cliché, 'in mysterious ways' sort of thing?" Jenna asked.

"Not exactly. Do you believe God has a plan for all of us?"

"Yes, I think he does. I think God intended me to become a music professor, for example."

"And that's worked out wonderfully for you. Here's what I think. I'm not a hundred percent sure I believe in God. Frankly I never thought about it much before my accident. If there is a God I don't think he has a plan for me. I think I've been coming up with my own plan, and God keeps foiling it because he doesn't like it—strikes me with lightning, knocks me down all the time in other ways, as if to say, 'I may not have figured out what to do with you yet, but I don't like the direction you're heading in now.'"

It took her a minute to digest that idea, but finally, Jenna said, "Wow, that's a really curious take on God. You don't think God loves you?"

"If he does, it must be some kind of 'tough love,' or maybe he doesn't love me."

"I love you, Simon," Jenna said quietly as her eyes welled up. "Seeing you have that seizure, it made me so frightened. So sad about possibly losing you." Jenna started to sob.

"Come here," Simon said, gesturing for her to lean over on to the bed, carefully avoiding the IV pole.

"I love you too, Jenna," Simon whispered as he kissed her on the lips. "Whatever else has happened since I've moved to Newell, you've made it all worthwhile." Jenna and Simon embraced in a long hug.

"Are you going to call your mother?"

"I don't know about that. She wasn't all that worried about me being struck by lightning, so I don't think she'll be too concerned now."

"If you were my son I would want to know. I'd be concerned. What could it hurt to call her and let her know what you're going through?"

"The hurt comes from how she might react. I feel like I know your parents now. They are warm, generous, loving people. They would do anything for you and your younger brother. My mom's not like that at all. It doesn't come naturally to her. If I call her and tell her the lightning strike might have caused serious damage, she might not know how to react. She might ask me what she could do, which is just another way of asking, why are you calling to tell me? It's very hurtful to be on the receiving end of that kind of indifference." He waited for her to let his words sink in.

"That is hard to understand. My parents would fly out here

right away and be at my side if I was in your position. No wonder you feel like no one's looking out for you sometimes."

He nodded. "True. I've always felt I had to look after myself. As I got older, I felt I had to look after my mother. I know that she's never going to reciprocate. I think she does love me, but she doesn't feel that motherly instinct in her heart. She doesn't really feel warmly toward anyone. And to be honest, you reap what you sow. She's pretty much alone."

"That's very sad to hear, Simon. You would think she'd be proud of her son, a great writing consultant and budding concert pianist." Jenna squeezed his arm and smiled.

"I'm not sure she even knows I'm a writing consultant, let alone a budding pianist—that's how indifferent she has been. All that having been said, you've sort of convinced me. I'll give her a call soon. I've already prepared myself for what her reaction might be."

60. A CALL TO HELEN

"Good morning. So, I have news, both good and bad," Dr. Delarosa said to Simon who was eating his hospital breakfast.

"I'm fine with hearing the bad news first."

"On the MRI, you have an enlargement of the perivascular spaces, those are areas around blood vessels in the brain. It's clear evidence of injury to your brain, though I can't say what the long-term effects might be."

"Have you seen this before?" Simon asked.

"Oh yes, in many patients who've had a stroke, which you did not. That's why I'm not sure what the implications will be."

"And the good news?"

"The EEG you had this morning doesn't show anything consistent with epilepsy. You may not have additional seizures."

"But because of the brain damage, I might have *something*, correct?"

"I wish I had an answer for you. Only time will tell. I still think you're an exceptionally lucky person. Take it easy. No driving for three months, and stay close to someone who can look out for you."

"I've heard that a lot," Simon replied.

Simon, as he had half-promised, decided to call his mother after Dr. Delarosa left.

"Mother, it's Simon."

"Yes, are you recovered now?" she asked, immediately.

"Actually, I had another setback," and he explained about the seizure. "The doctor is hoping it won't happen again, but there is brain damage on my scan from this morning."

There was a long pause. Simon and Helen could easily have participated in some sort of video call, but he feared she might feel uncomfortable seeing him in dire circumstances, as she might not know how to react. "I'm sorry to hear about the damage, Simon. I hope you make a full recovery." Helen's tone once again suggested she wanted to end the conversation.

Still somewhat distraught after hearing the mixed news from Dr. Delarosa, Simon grew angry and frustrated. "Well, mother, I sure am sorry I disturbed you this morning."

Helen sensed Simon's tone. "You're not disturbing me at all, Simon. I'm just relaxing at home. I'm just not sure what I can do to help."

"I'm not expecting any help from you, Mother. I just thought as my mother you would want to know how I'm doing. I was expecting a little curiosity about what's been going on in my life."

Helen's tone became defensive. "To be honest, I'm not great with phones. But if you'd like to talk more often I'm certainly willing to do that."

"You make it sound like you're doing me a favor," Simon said raising his voice.

Another long pause. "What do you want from me, Simon?"

"A little curiosity, perhaps. I suppose compassion is a bit too much to ask for."

"Please don't judge me that way, Simon. You don't know all that I've been through."

"Because you don't tell me anything. May I ask, do you even know where I live?"

"Virginia."

"Where in Virginia?"

"I'm sorry, Simon, I've forgotten."

"Forgotten? Or never paid enough attention to remember in the first place. Also, I have a girlfriend. I don't suppose you'd want to know anything about her?"

"You're very angry and you're in hospital. I'm sure your girlfriend is lovely. It may be best for us to end our conversation. I'd like to chat another time. I'm sorry if I made you angry."

This last admission made Simon a bit guilty for raising his voice and making Helen defensive. "You haven't made me angry. I'm just frustrated with your indifference, not just now, but for all these years. Yes, we can chat another time, but I will wait for you to call me. That way I will know you're genuinely interested in my life. Does that sound reasonable?"

Helen hesitated. She had never called Simon. "When should I call you?"

"When you feel the need to connect with me. When you feel it in your heart." Simon imagined his response would make Helen uncomfortable.

"I will call, and we can talk about your recovery, and your girlfriend, as well as your new job," Helen said.

"You don't need an agenda, Mother. You just need to care."

"Okay. Good day, Simon. I hope you'll be out of the hospital soon and make a full recovery," Helen said tersely, the multiple hints about her lack of compassion apparently taking her from uncomfortable and defensive to a little angry herself.

"Good day, Mother."

It had been a tense, emotional call. Simon called Jenna immediately afterward seeking consolation both for the news from Dr. Delarosa and from the conversation with Helen.

"Maybe the damage won't lead to anything. It's important to be optimistic," Jenna said.

"You're the optimistic one. I'm the unlucky one. How many other people do you know who've been struck by lightning?"

"You could ask that question of millions of other people and the answer will always be zero. Yes, unlucky in one sense, but it uncovered your gift."

"A gift that may not be useful in the long run if I've got a damaged brain."

"Please don't be so down, Simon. I'll be on my way over as soon as you're discharged. Let's have lunch somewhere nice. By the way, you did call your mother right? How did it go?"

"I did and it went as I expected it to. She was cold, indifferent. I got angry about that. She got defensive when I got angry. I asked her to call me next time, which she agreed to do. She's never done that before. Who knows, I may never hear from her again."

"I'm so sorry, Simon. Consider yourself adopted by my mom and dad. They both asked about you this morning."

"That's very kind of them. I'm going to try to stay positive. Lunch sounds wonderful. Let's get some work done. Let's play piano. And let's have a nice night at your place."

"I like the way you think. I think your brain is working just fine."

61. DANNY'S SEAFOOD

Over the course of a couple of months, Helen's and Enzo's relationship became increasingly predictable. She would work weekdays in the library. He would be there most days, at least for a while. They would go out for coffee late in the afternoon. On the weekends, they would have some sort of outing. Enzo was regularly surprised by how little exploring of the region Helen had done in the many years she had lived in New Bedford. They went to Boston one Saturday and visited the New England Aquarium. Helen had never before been to an aquarium. On a chilly October Sunday, they visited Provincetown, in Cape Cod, less than two hours from New Bedford, another place she had never previously been. She had never had Thai food. She had never gone bowling, something she actually wound up enjoying a fair bit with Enzo, who had only bowled a few times before. Enzo always drove and always dropped Helen off, making a point to come inside for a few minutes to speak with Simon if he was there. Helen may not have been overtly cheerful, but Simon could tell she was much happier and that she both trusted and respected Enzo.

"Next weekend we've got tickets to the Boston Pops. John Williams conducting. It'll be great," Enzo said to Simon.

"That sounds terrific, Enzo. I think you'll have a wonderful time, Mother."

"I'm sure we both will," Helen said. Enzo kissed Helen goodnight, a fairly long passionate kiss with his right arm wrapped around her waist while they stood on the front porch. Simon remained inside, looking away, for fear of embarrassing his mother. He was truly happy for her. His only fear was that her odd personality and aloofness might eventually turn Enzo off. It was encouraging that they were clearly sharing some degree of physical intimacy.

In early November, Enzo's older daughter Katie came to visit from Texas. Enzo suggested that she, Enzo, Helen, and Simon all have a nice dinner to get better acquainted. Simon looked forward to it. If Katie was anything like her father, he was sure they would get along well. They all met at Danny's Seafood, in the north end of New Bedford.

Katie was a petite, bubbly, twenty-one year old who looked a bit like her father. Her warm personality was obvious to anyone who met her. The evening was generally enjoyable. Simon engaged Katie a lot about her college experience and her future plans (still undecided). Enzo spoke a bit about clients who had had a hard time with landlords. Simon shared a few interesting experiences with rowdy middle school students. There were plenty of tasteful jokes. But Helen was largely silent. Katie asked her a few questions about her work in the library. She answered tersely. Nevertheless, Helen wore a relaxed look and a smile most of the time. She was comfortable and happy to be part of the group. Around nine p.m., Helen commented that it was getting late. It spurred Enzo to wrap things up and the two separate parties headed home.

Enzo drove the short distance to his home with Katie. "I had fun, Dad," she said as leaned her head on Enzo's shoulder. He turned and kissed her forehead.

"It was a fun evening I thought too," Enzo said.

"Simon is such a nice guy," Katie said.

"He is definitely," Enzo replied. "What are your thoughts about Helen?" Enzo asked, a bit tentatively.

Katie sighed. "I don't know, Daddy. Is it serious with you two?"

"I would say it's pretty serious, sweetheart."

"And you want my honest opinion?"

"As always."

"She's awfully quiet isn't she?"

"She is very quiet. She's been through a lot. It takes a while for her to open up."

"But I would say it takes you a while to open up, Dad, but you do. We were there for three hours, and she barely said a word. I hope she's not like that all the time." Enzo didn't respond. "I just want you to be happy. I want you to be with someone who cares about you. Who looks out for you. Someone you can laugh with." Katie was careful not to say anything too critical about Helen.

"I know you do, dear," Enzo paused. "Helen doesn't laugh." He looked down, coming to a realization that his young daughter had made a few good points.

"I love you, Daddy," Katie said as she hugged Enzo when they arrived back at his place.

He hugged her head to his chest after they got out of the car.

"Helen doesn't laugh? That doesn't sound good at all," Katie said.

"She's got a lot of baggage. She doesn't share much with me about it."

"Are you sure you want to get caught up in all that? You've been through a lot too. You need a life partner, not someone to take care of. You know what I mean?" Katie asked.

Enzo sighed and held his daughter tight. After a minute he offered, "Yes, I suppose I know what you mean, dear. I think, though, she must have a big heart. Look what a wonderful young man she raised."

Katie hugged her father more tightly but said nothing.

62. THE BREAKUP

Enzo reached a critical point roughly a month later. He contracted influenza—nothing life threatening, but severe enough to keep him confined at home resting and self-medicating with tea and lozenges. He and Helen were supposed to go out to lunch on a Saturday. He called the house early that morning.

"Good morning, Simon, how are you?"

"I'm well, Enzo. You sound absolutely terrible. Did you come down with something?"

"Influenza according to my doctor. Nothing to be done really. Just need to rest and get over it. Is Helen home?"

"Unfortunately, no. There is some sort of book return amnesty program at the library this morning and she is helping out. She'll be back around eleven. I know you are planning lunch with her."

"On that note, unfortunately, I'm too unwell to make the lunch. I also don't want to get her sick. Need to find the energy this morning to drop off some papers for clients."

"I understand completely. What do you need to drop off?"

"Oh, some things for clients to sign. Three clients. It will take me about an hour, but I think that's all I'll be able to do today."

"I can't help you recover any faster Enzo, but I certainly can drop off some papers for you, if that's okay. Just dropping off, right? I don't need to explain anything to the clients?"

Enzo paused. Simon's generosity was unexpected and touching. "That's correct, but you're a young guy. You probably have better things to do on a Saturday."

"I can spare an hour. Don't think twice about it. I'll swing by your place in a little bit. Would that be all right?"

"This is really generous of you, young man. I will have to find a way to repay you."

"You've been kind to my mother. That's important to me. No need for anything else." Enzo didn't respond to that.

Simon completed the errand as promised. In reality, it took far less than an hour. Two of the clients lived close together. Helen was home when he returned.

"Enzo called around nine, Mother. He won't be able to go out to lunch today."

"Is that so? What happened?"

"He's come down with the flu."

"He must be quite ill, then."

"He sounds terrible. Will spend the weekend just resting."

"Okay, thanks for letting me know," Helen said, and she went upstairs with a new CD she had checked out.

Helen didn't call Enzo that weekend, and he didn't appear in the library until the following Friday, when he felt fully recovered. He didn't trouble Simon with any additional errands, instead relying on his brother and a couple of kind people who worked in his brother's office. There had been no word from Helen the entire week, and Katie's insights into Helen's peculiarities and what Enzo needed continued to resonate with him to the point that he was angry.

"Coffee this afternoon, Helen?" Enzo asked her on Friday rather abruptly.

"That would be fine, Enzo."

"I know it would be fine. I suppose I'm asking if you would enjoy having coffee with me this afternoon, Helen."

Helen had never before experienced such a harsh tone from Enzo. "Yes, I would enjoy it, Enzo. I always enjoy having coffee with you."

Coffee at Salvatore's began with the usual silence, broken after a few minutes by Enzo.

"Did you have a nice week, Helen?"

"I did."

"As you've certainly heard, I was laid up with the flu the entire week. Really only started working today."

"Yes, Simon told me. You're fully recovered now?"

"Yes, pretty much. A few lingering body aches but no big deal."

"That's good to hear."

Enzo looked vexed. "Helen, I think I was expecting a little more."

"What do you mean?"

"It's nice of you to ask if I've fully recovered, but I was hoping you would have at least called me sometime during the week to find out how I was doing."

Helen said nothing.

"Your son was actually quite concerned and very helpful as well. A lady who is about to retire from my brother Philip's office actually even volunteered to help me with some paperwork. A phone call to check in would have been nice."

Helen sat silently, unsure what she was being accused of, and also why a phone call from her during the week was so important to Enzo.

Enzo pressed, "Why didn't you call me, Helen? Especially after I had to cancel our lunch."

Helen looked down. "I don't have a good answer to that, Enzo. I should have called. I'm sorry."

"It's not a question of being sorry, Helen. It's about feeling something. Feeling some concern for me. I thought you'd be more interested in my well-being."

Helen said nothing.

Enzo was obviously angry, and Helen suddenly looked vulnerable and afraid. He decided not to discuss the specific issue but to talk about their relationship more broadly.

"I think we're looking for different things. My wife died at 42, as you know, leaving me with two young daughters. I've relied on the kindness of my brother, sister-in-law, my friends for support. I was hoping to find a woman to share my life with. I enjoy spending time with you, Helen, but now I feel that perhaps we should go our separate ways."

Helen sat silently with a shocked look on her face. The first real man in her life since Luis died, a very good man, was unhappy enough with her to suggest ending their relationship. Then she thought about how awkward it would be to see Enzo in the library often.

"You have nothing to say to that, Helen?"

"I'm sorry, Enzo. These things don't come naturally to me. It has to do with what I've been through. I know it's hard for you to understand."

"You've hinted at what you've been through, but you've never told me."

"It's hard to talk about, Enzo. I'm sorry."

Enzo took a deep breath. "Well, I would enjoy being cordial with you in the library. I don't want things to be awkward, but I'm not interested in carrying on as we have." He hoped for a response. Helen said nothing. "Good day, Helen," Enzo said, and he got up and left.

63. Frustrated Composer

"Enlarged perivascular spaces huh?" Jenna said as she lay on the couch enjoying a glass of Chardonnay, her back pressed up against Simon's chest.

"That's what it showed. And no one can tell me what the long-term outcome will be. I think I should try to be as productive as possible."

"What do you mean?"

"I think I should compose more pieces, as many as I possibly can, in case this thing goes away."

"This thing?"

"This talent, this obsession, whatever it is that drives me to play the piano."

"If there really has been darkness that's been uncovered, Simon, why would it go away? Why would the darkness be covered again?"

"Maybe it won't. But I don't know that. Better take advantage of it now."

"I will help you translate what comes from your mind to your hands to paper."

"I can't do it without you, Jenna. These will be joint works."

"Let's not get ahead of ourselves. Do you want to perform in public again?"

"I don't know. Maybe. I must say the church in Oakland was hardly a stressful event."

"There are many music festivals including a very good one here in the spring. It will give you a goal to work toward."

"I'll think about it."

Simon spent the next few days playing obsessively, almost all original compositions. He didn't share his work with Jenna as she was quite busy with work. All his pieces had a similar theme. They started softly, melancholically. At some point there was drama, many notes played *mezzo forte*. This was followed by something more peaceful, some sort of resolution. In Simon's mind, this well-established "Galves" pattern yielded compositions which were quite distinct from each other. The style was contemporary, and Simon didn't realize it at the time, but no one else at the time was playing anything like him. He wasn't emulating a style nor following in anyone's footsteps. He didn't have enough experience to do that. Instead Simon's music consisted of capsules of emotion and his own life.

Within three days, Simon had composed seven pieces, each

an average of fifteen minutes long. He numbered them because he wanted Jenna's input about titles. It would have been a heavy burden to expect Jenna to sit with him patiently helping him translate his pieces to paper. He downloaded a demo software program to transcribe his playing but found that Jenna's concern about inaccuracies was correct. So instead he bought some notation paper himself and did his best. Many subtleties in his playing were not captured, but he believed he had written down enough as a framework that Jenna could help him refine. There were nearly two-hundred notation pages in all.

On a Thursday evening when Jenna had prepared a fish dinner at her place, Simon revealed to her a thick, nearly replete book of notation paper.

"Holy smokes! You did all this? When did you do all this?"

"Whenever I could. Early morning. At night. In the middle of the night."

"What about work? You must be exhausted."

"I am." Jenna opened the book in the middle and carefully studied a couple of pages.

"This is really impressive, my dear. But it still needs work."

"Oh, I know. The dynamics and stuff like that."

"Even the rhythm and time signature. You use common time most of the time. Hard to imagine that that would be best for all your pieces."

"I realized that after a bit. So you think this is salvageable?"

Jenna paused. "Salvageable? Yes, of course. But I'm afraid you're trying to create a lifetime's body of work in a few days. I'm not a composer, but I believe no matter what gift you have, that's just not possible. How did you feel when you composed all these pieces?"

"Really tired," Simon said as he chuckled.

"Did you feel inspired?"

"The music came naturally. Not sure what you mean."

"I know it came naturally. But was your music inspired by emotion, like 'Flusso e Reflusso'?"

"No, not the same way as 'Flusso e Reflusso.'"

Let's see what we've got. Jenna made her way to her piano, opened up a random page with "#4" scribbled on top as a temporary title, and started to play it. It was the middle of the melancholic pattern which characterized all of Simon's pieces. She stopped after a couple of minutes, turned to Simon and smiled.

"May I be honest with you?"

"Of course."

"I love you to death my dear. But this sounds a lot like 'Flusso e Reflusso.'"

Despite their mutual affection, and her highly tempered feedback, Simon felt a little hurt. It was as if the huge investment in time and effort over the week had been wasted. He looked visibly sad.

"I think you're right. I guess I was trying to be prolific before those perivascular spaces get too big. Who knows what will happen then."

"I know, Simon," Jenna said as she stood up behind him and put her arms around his shoulders. "I don't think being a composer works that way. Inspiration comes and goes, sometimes when it's least expected. 'Flusso e Reflusso' is a nicely inspired capsule of your life. You need inspiration like that. We could spend a lot of time refining what you have here, but you need to ask yourself, will people be really interested in listening to it?"

"I think you're right. They would be bored."

"I wouldn't necessarily go that far," she said, tempering her original comment. "But they may not find all the pieces equally moving. Do you understand what I mean?"

"I think so."

"I would wait until you find something inspiring again. If it happens, wonderful. If not, you've got a beautiful composition already."

Simon felt defeated at first, but he knew Jenna was right. He felt better after a few moments. At least he had a kind, erudite, wonderful girlfriend who could steer him in the right direction.

"You know. You inspire me. Maybe I could compose 'Piano Sonata for Jenna.'"

"Don't you dare! I'm not worthy," Jenna said, chuckling.

"Maybe I could be struck by lightning again, uncover a bit more darkness."

"True, but then you might be inspired to take up the cello or become a poet, and forget about the piano, so, not a great plan."

"The fish was excellent, sweetheart. Your cooking is inspiring."

64. DROPPING

Rather than waiting for it, Simon searched for inspiration. He walked through meadows and forests full of falling leaves. He drove to Virginia Beach and watched waves crash along the shore. He sat in near darkness in front of his piano, a candle lit on top of it, hoping to recreate a setting Beethoven may have found inspiring. And he tried daily to make new music, but each time, his pieces sounded like variations of "Flusso e Reflusso." He started to feel a bit differently than he had prior to his seizure, and that caused him stress. To prevent another seizure, Dr. Delarosa medicated him with two anticonvulsants, one of which made him tired, especially in the evenings. The change was gradual and Jenna noticed it before Simon did. He fell asleep on her couch on several occasions before eight p.m. She covered him with a blanket, and she needed to shake him quite vigorously to wake him up for work in the morning.

The most troubling change was a gradual return of the coordination difficulties Simon had experienced shortly after his accident. He began to walk more slowly and cautiously. Running was out of the question since it would require a too rapid coordination of his brain and feet. Even more troubling was a new tendency he developed to drop things—pens, dishes, books. He would hold a coffee cup quite firmly, for example, and quite suddenly, the muscles in his hand would relax and the cup would fall to the floor. This sort of thing happened every couple of days.

He didn't tell Jenna. He hoped his coordination difficulties would spontaneously resolve. If she knew the full extent of them, she would insist he seek additional help from Dr. Delarosa, who would likely only confirm that his problems represented part of an inevitable decline. But Jenna was shrewd. She could sense not only that Simon was moving slower but also that he was in a somber mood much of the time. Certainly part of it was his inability to produce another truly original composition but she knew that wasn't all.

"You ever think about taking some time off of work?"

"Why would I do that?"

"Just to rest, for a week or so. You seem very tired to me."

"It's the medication. It wears me out, but I need to take it."

"I know. How's the walking going?"

"I'm a bit slow, but I think I'm getting better," Simon said in an effort to allay Jenna's concern.

"I don't see you getting better, and I see you every day," Jenna said with a worried look on her face.

"You're right. Getting my strength back will take some time."

"Do you have a check-in with Dr. Delarosa?"

"Next week."

"Make sure you tell her what's going on. I also think you speak more slowly, and your voice is softer."

Simon had noticed that some of his student clients mentioned that they were having trouble hearing him both on the phone and in person. He sounded softer to himself, but the pace and cadence of his speech he thought were normal.

"She's not going to be able to do much for me. She might do another scan which will show those perivascular spaces getting bigger. It's all part of a worsening picture," Simon said despondently.

"But maybe there's something that can be done to slow down the process. You never know." Jenna's observations were painful to hear about. What he perceived as relatively subtle changes that he could keep hidden and which might go away, were obvious enough to Jenna not only to notice but to cause concern. He held her tight and tried to reassure her that he would be okay.

In the weeks that followed, Simon decided he would fight his neurological decline with a self-conceived program. He had no idea what might work, and his plan had no medical foundation. He decided he would exercise vigorously. He went to the main gym at Newell early each morning to lift weights and ride a stationary bicycle. This invigorated him prior to work. After work he would rush home and play piano, choosing complex and difficult classical pieces which he believed would help him maintain his technical skill and coordination. Then he and Jenna would connect and he committed himself to seeing the evening through without collapsing in fatigue at her place or his. He pushed and pushed and pushed. His morning exercises became more strenuous, his piano playing more intense.

After a couple of weeks, he was quite certain that things were improving. He was stronger and more energetic. Dr. Delarosa's main concern was keeping him seizure free. Simon told her about the slowness and the difficulty with coordination as well as sudden dropping of objects. She completed a thorough neurological examination and told him things were "stable. I don't have any obvious explanation for the symptoms you're describing, Simon."

"I've been exercising like a fiend every morning. I hope that will prevent me from declining."

"Exercise is important in many ways. Yes, it certainly can't hurt. I encourage you to keep exercising. Just don't overdo it."

Things were certainly looking up for a time. On the eve of Jenna's birthday, Simon arrived at her place with a bouquet of flowers. He had planned a nice dinner for the following night. He rang her bell and she greeted him with a broad smile. Then suddenly, Simon collapsed in Jenna's doorway, nearly knocking her down in the process.

65. A Brother's Help

Enzo's sudden departure from Salvatore's left Helen looking despondent. She had said hardly anything. Reaching out to Enzo while he was ill would have been the right thing to do, but she wouldn't have known what to say. Despite being a strong, independent man, Enzo would have appreciated the courtesy and compassion that comes with a simple call. Even leaving a message on his answering machine such as "Hoping your recovery is going well" might have been enough for Enzo to continue the relationship. Helen could also have assisted Simon with the errand he did for Enzo, but this was so easy for Simon to complete, he didn't bother mentioning it to Helen that day. She sat in the coffee shop for some time looking pensive. Her failure to check in on Enzo was just a symptom of a bigger problem—her inability to connect with him as deeply as he wanted. Nothing she could do about that.

It was Enzo who suffered more. Angry at first, of course, then worried that his anger had damaged even his cordial relationship with Helen, and then the loneliness set in. As stoic as she was, he missed her company. She was willing to spend time with him. A half smile, a comment that the coffee "was agreeable" was enough to keep a lonely, widowed, shy, humble man engaged. It was a nice complement to phone calls from his girls, dinner with his brother and sister-in-law, and occasional drinks with his "buddies" from Fall River. He had invested a lot of persistent emotional energy in the wiry library clerk, and after months, she had not reciprocated. He had been hopeful but not smitten. He believed Helen had been neither. Helen carried on in her usual way at work, smiling politely when she passed Enzo. Sometimes she was charged with providing him with assistance, which she did professionally, as if he was any other library patron.

It became, at some point, unbearable for poor Enzo. He sought out a good workspace in a different library branch, one which actually better met his needs as it was closer to his home and where he wouldn't run into Helen. After rejecting two successive dinner invitations to his brother's place, it was his brother, Philip, who decided to help him out.

"I think you can do better than the librarian," Philip said when Enzo stopped by at his request.

"Well, I feel completely alone again, so I'm not sure," Enzo replied.

"I probably shouldn't tell you this, but Katie stopped by when she was here with some souvenirs she bought for us. She mentioned that she wasn't too impressed."

"Oh did she?"

"We drew it out of her. I asked her specifically what she thought about Helen. She said she's very quiet, aloof, and wasn't sure if she was right for you," Philip said.

"That's basically what she told me too," Enzo replied.

"I obviously can't judge a woman I've never met, but I do know you don't need to get involved with rescuing someone like that, brother. You've got a big heart and need someone more like you." Enzo had always looked up to his older brother and always took his counsel seriously. He nodded in agreement.

"Anyway, great gal, used to work in our office named Erin. She's gone back to school to study nursing. Been divorced five years. I talked to her. She's expecting your call." Philip had always been very proactive in looking out for his brother so his boldness in setting Enzo up wasn't unusual. Besides, Enzo appreciated it. Philip had excellent taste in women.

"Thank you, brother, I'll call her tonight."

"No pressure, Enzo. Call her, go out to dinner, see if you like each other. If not, no big deal. That's basically what I told her."

Enzo did wind up having a very nice time with Erin, a vivacious, affectionate forty-five year old who seemed to have a genuine interest in him. "I've had a wonderful evening," Enzo said at the end of the night. Then the shy, softspoken man from Fall River put his arms around Erin and kissed her on the lips.

Erin smiled and asked, "So what are you up to tomorrow?"

Simon noticed Enzo's absence from Helen's life almost immediately. The absence of a habitual weekend outing was especially noticeable. Instead, Helen spent Saturdays in her room watching television or listening to music. At first, Simon didn't feel comfortable asking her what had happened, hoping that Enzo was perhaps away on business for some time, or that he was otherwise pre-occupied. When after more than a week Helen revealed nothing, he decided to probe her gently about it.

"I noticed you and Enzo didn't go out Saturday. Was he busy, Mother?"

"I don't know if he was busy, Simon. He has decided to end our relationship, at least the way it was."

Simon's heart sank. "That's very disappointing to hear. I was truly happy that you had found someone like him. I also liked Enzo a lot."

"He thought very highly of you, too."

Simon didn't dare ask Helen directly about what had happened. That would have made her extremely uncomfortable. But he assumed that it was most likely her fault. Enzo may have tired of her cold demeanor. Instead, Simon tried to be circumspect, asking Helen a few questions through which he might learn more.

"It's nice to hear he thought highly of me. I think he is truly a nice gentleman. As I said, it's disappointing to hear that you've broken up."

"It was his decision."

"Was that an abrupt decision?"

"I think he had made the decision before we had coffee last week."

"I see. Last week seemed like an ordinary week, didn't it?" Simon had forgotten briefly that Enzo had been ill, and even that he had helped him out with delivering papers.

"It was ordinary, except that Enzo was ill." Helen paused, then continued very quietly. "He was disappointed that I didn't call him when he was ill."

With Helen's admission, everything fell into place for Simon. Helen and Enzo had carried out a relationship for several months, and when he had become too ill to go to lunch, something Simon had made her aware of, she didn't bother to express any concern, even as a social obligation.

"Why didn't you call him, Mother? Actually, you could have done something nice for him. Brought him some soup. Offered to run some errands for him."

"I don't have a good answer about why I didn't call him."

"I guess you were not all that interested in Enzo, then. It would have been reasonable to call him." Simon had unconsciously adopted a bit of a chastising tone. He decided to wait for some reaction from his mother.

"I agree with you. Enzo is a very nice gentleman. I was fortunate to be able to spend time with him. I should have reached out to him when he was ill," Helen said with a tinge of sadness in her voice.

"Well is it final then? Perhaps an apology by you might help. Just a suggestion."

"I fear he's made up his mind for good, Simon."

66. PROGNOSIS UNKNOWN

"I'm okay, I'm okay, please don't fuss about it! See, I'm up!" Simon said, leaning against the doorframe.

"What the hell happened, Simon? You just fell like that. You didn't trip or anything." Jenna exclaimed, her eyes intensely focused on Simon.

"I'm okay Jenna, seriously I am."

Tears streaked down Jenna's cheeks. "How are you okay? You went down like a ton of bricks. Has that ever happened before?"

"No, it hasn't. My legs just gave out from under me all of a sudden."

"Should I call Dr. Delarosa? Should I call 911?"

"I just want to rest for a few minutes, please. I'm just going to lie on the couch."

"I'm afraid you're going to fall again, sweetheart."

"I'm fine. Maybe it was a fluke."

"Were you dizzy?"

"No, I felt fine. Just that my legs gave out, just like that. I just want to rest. I'll call Dr. Delarosa in the morning."

Simon felt reasonably well but was afraid to move in case he fell again. He lay on the couch. Jenna lay next to him. They spent a cramped night there in a firm embrace. Jenna urged Simon to call his doctor as soon as her office opened.

"I fell suddenly last night."

"How did you feel just before the fall?"

"I felt absolutely fine. My legs just gave out. No dizziness. I didn't trip or anything."

"I am concerned, Simon. I can squeeze you in this afternoon. Can you make it?"

"I certainly will," Simon said, as Jenna, overhearing the conversation, nodded.

Simon canceled his appointments for the day and made his way to the doctor's office hesitatingly, but with no further falls. She asked him again about any symptoms which preceded his fall and then examined him thoroughly. When she finished, she said, "Nothing really changed on your exam."

"So what do you think happened to me?"

"I'll be honest and tell you that I don't know yet. Making diagnoses in neurology can sometimes be extremely difficult. We will have to wait and see how your symptoms evolve. With any luck, they may not return."

"So, there's no test you can do? No more scans?"

"I don't think they will be useful at this time. Perhaps in a couple of months."

"What am I supposed to do? I'm worried I might fall again. I fell into Jenna's doorway, and she was there to help me. What if this happens on the street or somewhere else?"

"I don't have any great advice for you, Simon. One thing you can do is to text Jenna each time you leave your apartment, and then again when you arrive at your destination. If she doesn't hear from you, she can call you to find out what happened."

"I suppose that's reasonable. I just hope I remember to text her when I get where I'm going. Should I carry a cane?"

"I don't think a cane will prevent you from falling based on what you told me. Wear comfortable shoes and clothes. Carry some identification with Jenna's phone number. Keep her up to date with your whereabouts. But do carry on as usual. I don't want you to be a prisoner in your apartment, afraid to go anywhere."

"Could the fall be related to the seizure medications?"

"No, I think it's a separate phenomenon. It's encouraging that you haven't had a seizure which could be even more dangerous than falling."

"Have you seen this before? People falling suddenly?"

"Yes, I have. There are progressive neurological conditions which might cause someone to fall suddenly. Progressive supranuclear palsy is one, abbreviated PSP. It's quite rare."

"I don't like the word 'progressive' in it. I take it that can be quite serious?"

"Yes it can. But it takes a long time to make a diagnosis. Despite what happened, I want you to stay active and positive. You've had just one fall. I still believe you are an extremely fortunate man to have escaped a lightning strike with as little damage as you did. You're also lucky to have someone like Jenna looking out for you."

Simon left Dr. Delarosa's office feeling a bit disappointed and dejected. Disappointed because she didn't have any clear answers for him. While her advice to solicit Jenna's help to keep an eye on him was sound, it would have no effect on preventing him from falling. He felt dejected because he believed the fall represented another evolving and likely worsening consequence of the lightning strike. He imagined himself falling off a piano bench, or simply being unable to play because his fingers stopped responding to his mind. Worse still, Dr. Delarosa gave him no clear path to fight any potential decline. Could there be some form of exercise, some diet, some exotic therapy which might keep him healthy? She mentioned nothing, he thought, because there is nothing.

He met Jenna that evening at his place and shared the news.

"I'm happy to hear she didn't find any new damage."

"She didn't exactly say that. She only said that it may take some time to make a diagnosis."

"But you may not fall again, right?"

"Certainly possible. She told me to stay positive."

"Good. I will help you stay positive. I think that's the best thing I can do. Even more than helping you compose your pieces."

"Thank you, sweetheart. Speaking of pieces. Still no inspiration. I feel like there's more urgency now."

"Inspiration comes at unexpected times and in unexpected ways. I'm not a composer, but that's what I've heard many times."

67. A FINAL CONVERSATION

In the weeks that followed his breakup with Helen, Enzo cemented his relationship with Erin. He became so comfortable with his new situation in fact, that he stopped by the main library one day to speak with Helen. He believed that his abrupt departure from Salvatore's had been rude, and that whatever Helen had or had not done, he should not have reacted the way he did.

He found Helen carrying out her usual business. Enzo thought Helen looked especially dour, but it was near the end of her day and fatigue may have accounted for her disposition rather than any regret about what happened with him. He approached her directly.

"Got a few minutes to talk?"

"Yes. I'm nearly done with work."

"Good, let's meet over there," Enzo said as he pointed to his previously habitual table which happened to be unoccupied. By not inviting her out for coffee Enzo was sending Helen a strong message—This was a cordial, almost business-like visit rather than an invitation to reconciliation of some sort.

"How have you been, Helen?"

"I'm okay. No better nor worse than usual."

"I want to apologize to you for walking out the way I did. I was very frustrated and angry, and I shouldn't have done that. I am really sorry."

Helen didn't know exactly what to say. After a long pause she said, "That's fine. I understand."

"I also want to say that I enjoyed the time we spent together. Especially going up to Maine. That was a wonderful day."

"I enjoyed it too, Enzo." They both sat silently for quite some time. Enzo himself seemed a little confused about the whole purpose of his visit. Helen was simply waiting for some cue from Enzo about what she ought to say or do.

"May I speak frankly, Helen?"

"Of course."

"I don't understand you well. You seem so closed off. Unemotional at times. It was really no big deal that you didn't call me when I was ill. Sometimes people forget or other things intervene. That's understandable. But what made me upset was that it was a sign that you simply didn't care."

Helen grew immediately nervous. She crossed her arms in front of her chest, unconscious body language that indicated she was uncomfortable with where Enzo was going. She said nothing until Enzo pushed her.

"Did you not care about me, Helen?"

"I did care, and I still do. It isn't that. It really isn't."

"So what is it then?"

"What's what?"

"Why are you so closed off? Why did you shut me out the way you did? I thought there was a soft heart underneath that tough exterior. That's why I persisted, but I could never get through."

"I am really uncomfortable talking like this, Enzo. It's becoming very upsetting." Helen's voice crackled. She looked like she was about to cry, something Enzo had never seen her do, but then quickly regained her composure.

"I don't mean to upset you. I'm just really curious about you that's all. It would help me, I suppose, if I understood you better. You've got a wonderful son. You've got a quaint house. You have a nice job. Yet, you seem incredibly lonely and sad. Am I wrong about that?"

Helen grew increasingly uncomfortable, at one point, almost standing up to indicate that the conversation was over. "You don't know me well enough to say all that, Enzo," she said defensively.

"I'm asking, that's all. I'm sorry if I made you uncomfortable. I came here to apologize, and to say that I still consider you to be a friend. I will be in this library from time to time, and I don't want things to be awkward."

"I appreciate that," she said.

Having barely penetrated her cold exterior, Enzo left Helen feeling suddenly vulnerable. She kept her arms crossed tight."

"Enzo, I appreciate you coming to talk to me today. I also want to say that I am open to continue to spend time with you." For a few brief moments, Enzo considered her suggestion. But there were the many strained conversations he had had with Helen, the inscrutable enigma of her personality, and a troubled past about which he knew almost nothing. There was also warm, engaging Erin, a much better investment for his time.

"I am happy talking to you from time to time here in the library. I should tell you I've met someone else."

Helen's reaction was surprise. She didn't anticipate Enzo moving on so quickly. "I am happy for you," she said.

Enzo left after shaking Helen's hand—deliberately indicating that the romantic possibilities were over. Helen sat there looking downward with an obviously disappointed look. If she had trouble connecting with someone as gentle and kind as Enzo, she was certainly unlikely to find a meaningful relationship with another man, even if she had no plans to actively seek one.

The breakup was especially impactful when another trip to Freeport was organized. Simon remained disappointed with his mother, feeling that she had squandered a good opportunity with a good man. He told her he did not want to accompany her and that by going alone she might be more inclined to make new friendships. Helen signed up as a solo traveler at first, but then there was the potential awkward question, "Where's Enzo?" from her work colleagues. She also didn't feel comfortable on her own engaging in the lighthearted banter that had dominated the prior trips. She feared her reticence would come across as peculiar. So she backed out a day before the trip and received a full refund.

68. HELEN'S SAD NEWS

In the weeks that followed Dr. Delarosa's reassessment, Simon didn't fall again. He didn't have another headache. He walked perfectly well. He didn't have a seizure. But he found no inspiration. Instead of playing fanatically with enormous discipline, Simon played only when he felt especially relaxed and calm. If Jenna was busy with work in the evenings, he would light a candle, stick it on top of his shoddy piano, relax his fingers and play whatever came to mind. He was trying to recreate a dark, romantic setting that might be inspiring. Alas, all he came up with were more variations on "Flusso e Reflusso."

Nevertheless, as the year came to a close, Simon felt more hopeful. He followed Dr. Delarosa's advice about keeping Jenna aware of his comings and goings, but with each passing day, he felt more and more confident that another fall or something similar was unlikely. He told Jenna several times that he didn't believe the careful tracking was necessary, but she insisted he continue. "It takes only a few seconds, and it gives me peace of mind too."

So he continued. "Going to grocery store then gas station. Should be at your place by 6:30" was the type of text she received, and which brought her immediate reassurance. Her relationship with Simon had moved from friendship to romance, to something even deeper in a relatively short period of time. She was nurturing by nature and poor wounded Simon was a perfect recipient of her tender, maternalistic instincts. Being unfamiliar with that type of attention, Simon naturally resisted, frequently telling her he was fine and able to look after himself. Jenna had a meeting in Charlottesville for a couple of days and insisted that one of her colleagues could serve as a backup for Simon's text check-ins. He refused steadfastly. "If I fall, it will be somewhere in Newell, not out in the country. I'll be able to get help, don't worry," he told Jenna.

As for Simon, he in turn felt a natural instinct to protect Jenna. She was vulnerable in different ways. Far from home, long ago abandoned by her much older lover, and with relatively few people in her social network in Newell, Jenna told Simon frequently that she felt safe and secure whenever he spent the night at her place. She was among the few Black female faculty members at Newell. She felt her colleagues were mostly welcoming, but at times quite patronizing. Jenna was often described as "a great friend," especially by white female colleagues she barely knew, who proudly introduced her to others, as if to say, "Look at my commitment to diversity!" "Let's find out what Jenna thinks," she would hear often, even when the matter at hand was either of no concern to her or completely outside her field of knowledge.

Men at Newell treated Jenna with what she perceived as more genuine professional respect, but she also received a different kind of attention. Exceptionally pretty, soft-spoken, and well-dressed, Jenna was constantly resisting her male colleagues' efforts to flirt with her. She seldom experienced any outright harassment, the issue having received a lot of attention at the college, but the flirtations were annoying, and almost certainly inspired by the fact that she had been involved for so many years with the high-profile professor Albert Foster. At age 73, he was still on the faculty at Newell and known to boast about his exploits with young Jenna.

Simon was completely different. To him, Jenna was initially a beautiful pianist, then someone who would tolerate his company, then a friend, and then something more. Neither her race nor her past was of much interest to him. He loved her and that's all that mattered.

As the fall semester came to a close, Jenna and Simon realized that they hadn't made any plans for the Christmas break.

"Do you want to do something special?" Simon asked.

"You know I can't resist going home to see Mom and Dad. My brother will make an appearance I'm sure. Do you want to join us?"

"That's really generous, sweetheart. I'd love to."

"Great. I guess we should have thought about all this sooner. Tickets will be more expensive."

"I know. I've had a lot of other things on my mind," Simon said.

The next day Jenna and Simon booked tickets to San Francisco from Norfolk, with a stop in Chicago. They would leave December

23rd and return the 28th. Jenna called her mother to tell her the news, and she was ecstatic. "You know, I think of Simon as part of the family now. He's stuck with us, like it or not."

"I'm so glad you like him, Mom."

Little eventful took place in the following weeks. Simon was very busy with work, as demand for his services took the predictable end-of-semester upturn. Jenna too became much busier. Simon gave up on composing his own pieces, concluding that without the right inspiration, he was unlikely to produce anything worthwhile. Instead, he immersed himself in Chopin and Beethoven, pleased that his prodigious dedication and skill remained intact, despite being sidetracked by his own efforts to be especially creative. On December 21st, Simon received the most unexpected call he could imagine.

"Good morning, Simon. How are you?"

"I'm well, Mother. Merry Christmas."

"Merry Christmas to you too. I hope everything is okay. I wasn't expecting a call from you."

"I realize that. But if there's ever a time for me to call, it's now." Helen's voice sounded faint and especially sad.

"What's wrong, Mother?"

"It's my health, Simon. It's gone downhill."

"I'm very sorry to hear that," Simon said, waiting patiently for details.

"I actually don't think I have that much time left," she whispered.

Simon was shocked speechless for a few moments. "What's going on?"

Helen's voice started to crack. It sounded like she was sobbing. "I will tell you everything. Could you please come visit me?"

"Of course I can."

"I am in a hospice facility here in New Bedford."

"Oh dear. I will come as soon as I can."

"Thank you, Simon."

"Expect me there late tonight or tomorrow at the latest. I can't drive long distances, so will be taking the bus up there."

Simon called Jenna immediately and told her his mother was in a dire situation.

"Just go, Simon. Don't worry about me or the trip to California. Take care of your mother. My family will completely understand."

"Thank you, Jenna. I'm going to leave later this afternoon."

69. BACK TO NEW BEDFORD

Simon was overcome with many grim thoughts as he packed a suitcase and prepared to make the lengthy trip north to New Bedford by bus. He knew hospice meant a terminal illness, the end stage of what must have been a drawn-out process. *Why didn't she tell me before?* he thought. *I could have done something to help, perhaps.* The other constant grim thought was about his long-strained relationship with his mother. She had always been cold, frequently demanding, seemingly unsympathetic. Yet there were times when she wasn't so bad, and Simon felt some sort of breakthrough was possible. If only he had worked harder to help her connect with people, he thought, she wouldn't be so isolated. There was also his baseline anger which surged from time to time when he felt like Helen wasn't fulfilling her most basic duties as a mother. As he passed Richmond he thought, *I'm headed to see the woman who wished me a pleasant weekend after I was struck by lightning.* A host of contradictory emotions hit him in rapid succession: He cursed when he recalled the many times Helen had been indifferent to him. He sighed when he thought about the sad, isolated life she had lived. At one point he actually cried, when he thought about how she was probably suffering a great deal, and that despite her peculiarities, he did love her a great deal.

He had two bus transfers in Washington, DC, and New York. The sun had gone down by the time he got to New York and Simon knew he would arrive in New Bedford very late. His plan was to take an Uber to the house first, to try and get a good night's rest and then to meet his mother at Southcoast Hospice.

He arrived at three a.m. in a light rain. The street was silent except for the buzz of the streetlamps. Before he entered the house, Simon took a long look at his street. Nothing had really changed, which at some unconscious level, was reassuring for him. Inside, the house looked well-maintained and not dusty. Helen couldn't have been in hospice too long, he thought.

He went upstairs to his room and put his suitcase down on the bed. Helen's bedroom door was ajar, and he went inside to take a look around. The bed was made, and everything seemed intact. There was no evidence that anyone terribly ill had lived there. Simon stripped down to his underwear to sleep and lay flat on his back and stared up at the ceiling. As a young boy he counted the ridges in the plaster on the ceiling, work his father had done before he was born. As unfortunate as the circumstances which brought him back to New Bedford were, Simon felt at peace in his own bedroom, where he had spent so much time alone pondering his isolation, his future, and the mental cage his mother put him in as a young boy. At that moment, Newell felt like a surreal interlude. He had been struck by lightning, become a pianist, and fallen in love all within a single year. How could that possibly be real for someone whose life had been so dull until that point?

Simon slept only a little, tossing and turning as he did. He was simply too worried about Helen. In the morning, he made himself a cup of coffee, using the same coffee maker Helen had used for thirty years. He turned on the Sony Discman radio which Helen had brought back downstairs many years earlier. He felt queasy, though, and couldn't finish his coffee. It was eight a.m. Helen was probably up, and it was time to see her. He called for a taxi.

Simon was expecting a hospice building that was old, dark, and dingy. Instead, the hospice was bright and modern. A cheerful young man greeted him at the reception area. He first called Helen and then sent Simon upstairs to her room.

Simon knocked politely and, in a feeble voice, Helen asked him to enter. She smiled when she saw him, perhaps the broadest smile Simon had ever seen from her. She certainly looked unwell. Always pale, she looked paler than usual. Always very thin, she looked emaciated. Always well-groomed, her hair stuck out in several directions at once. She was dressed in a cotton nightgown. Overcome at seeing Helen in such a state, Simon took a few deep breaths and struggled to hold back tears.

"Sit down, Simon," Helen said feebly.

"I got here last night, Mother, but it would have been too late to come here," Simon said.

"I understand."

Simon reached out and held Helen's emaciated left hand.

"Thank you so much for making the trip," she said.

"Why didn't you tell me you were ill?"

"I suppose I didn't want you to worry. Why would an old woman need to burden you with her problems?" Helen asked, her voice hoarse.

"But you're my mother. I'm supposed to be burdened with your problems."

"That's very kind of you."

"May I ask, what is it that you have?"

"Metastatic ovarian cancer."

"And how long do they think you have left?"

"They don't know precisely of course. Only God knows that. But the doctor tells me anywhere from one and three months. Not long in any case. I do appreciate your visit."

"I'm happy to stay as long as you like."

"Please don't do that. You've got a rich life to get back to. I want you to enjoy it."

"Thank you for saying that. I've had a very eventful year as you know. I believe I've told you I met someone. It's very serious."

"I'm pleased to hear that." Simon pulled out his phone and showed Helen a picture of him standing with Jenna in front of Lake Merritt in Oakland. Helen glanced at the picture for not more than two seconds.

"She looks lovely. Reminds me of a friend of mine originally from Jamaica who wound up working with me in Dublin in unfortunate circumstances. It's a long story."

Simon had no idea what Helen was talking about. "May I get you something? Something to eat perhaps?"

"No thank you. They try to feed me well here, but I have no appetite. Could you see if you could find some hot tea somewhere. It soothes my throat."

"Of course, Mother."

70. FORGIVENESS

Simon went downstairs to a small coffee shop and returned with a paper cup of hot tea which he set down on a tray next to Helen's bed. She took a few small sips and then lay back against her pillow.

"Take your coat off. I hope you're not in a rush," Helen said as she cracked a half smile.

"Not at all, Mother. I just forgot to take it off."

"I'm not good at showing it, but I do love you," Helen said in her feeble voice.

Simon lost it at that point. His eyes welled up and the tears flowed. "I know, Mother. I know you've loved me. I've always loved you, too," he managed to say after regaining his composure.

"I know that too, Simon. You looked out for me so much. Even found me two jobs. I am proud of you," Helen said, her faint, hoarse tone hard to hear.

"I am happy you're saying that now, Mother."

"I want you to forgive me, Simon. Forgive me for loving you but not showing it."

"I forgive you, Mother. I hope you can forgive me, too, for being so angry with you from time to time. For putting my needs ahead of yours. For not being able to make you happy," Simon said. He reached out and rested his hand on Helen's shoulder.

"Make me happy? I hope I've not burdened you with that, Simon. If you knew what I've been through you would also know that making me truly happy is not possible."

"Why not possible, Mother?" Simon sat back, resting his chin on the tips of his fingers.

"It has to do with my family."

"Tell me about your family, Mother."

"Oh, not worth hearing about at this point. Let's just enjoy some time together."

At that point, Helen tilted her head back against her pillow and closed her eyes. Simon didn't press her. He was content to sit still and felt overwhelmed by the combination of sadness and love for his mother. Helen said nothing.

Simon sat quietly in his chair while Helen fell asleep. He wasn't sure what to do. He had brought nothing to read, so after about twenty minutes, he headed downstairs to the bright, clean cafeteria. A few elderly people were there as well as a woman who looked to be in her thirties with two young boys. Simon bought a cup of coffee and sat in a sunny corner to drink it. One of the boys, who looked to be about three, had a wind-up toy car which whizzed across the floor, eventually stopping when it hit Simon's foot, and the little fellow came running after it. Simon smiled.

The little boy's mother came over. "I'm so sorry he bothered you," she said.

"No bother at all," Simon responded.

"Are you visiting family?" the young lady asked.

"Yes, my mother. She's very ill. Ovarian cancer. How about you? One of your parents?"

"No. It's my husband."

Simon opened his mouth wide, then said, "I'm so sorry to hear that. My name's Simon."

"Jessica, nice to meet you. Yes, pancreatic cancer. He's forty-one."

"That must be so hard, Jessica. Again, I'm so sorry."

"Thank you. I've gone through all the emotions. Really nothing left to say or do. He's too weak to even come down here," Jessica said, the sadness obvious in her voice. "I want the boys to spend as much time with him as possible, so maybe they'll remember him when they're older."

"I understand. I'm sure he appreciates that too."

"Yes, he does. I'm sure your mother appreciates you being here."

Engrossed in poor Jessica's situation, Simon was caught a bit off guard by the focus on him. "I believe so," he said tentatively.

"Well, we're going to finish our breakfast. It was nice meeting you." Jessica picked up her three-year-old and his toy and returned to the table where her older son was sitting.

The encounter left Simon thinking. Helen had asked him to come visit her in hospice. Of course, it's a son's obligation to visit his dying mother, but was there any real emotion behind it? Did she really want him there despite telling him she loved him? Or did the hospice staff regularly encourage her to reach out and contact him? After all, he knew nothing of her cancer diagnosis until his visit. There must have been many discussions with doctors about treatments and prognosis in the prior months.

Simon headed back upstairs to find Helen fast asleep. He sat quietly, reading a few news stories on his phone, unsure of how long he would stay. About an hour later, Helen smacked her lips and opened her eyes.

"Did you have a nice sleep, Mother?"

"I think so. How long was I asleep?"

"A bit over an hour."

"My mouth is really dry. Would you mind getting me a glass of water?"

Simon did this immediately.

Helen seemed more alert after her nap and Simon sat patiently waiting for her to say something. She turned to him and smiled for a moment and said nothing.

To break the silence, Simon said, "Jenna is a pianist. I've taken up the piano. I really enjoy it. It's become a big part of my life."

"That's wonderful, Simon. Jenna is the young lady in the picture?"

"Yes."

"I'm very happy for you, Simon," Helen said flatly. She finished the entire glass of water and lay her head back down. By this point, Simon decided he wasn't going to stay much longer. He was happy to be by his mother's side, and she was as welcoming as she could be, but sitting for hours waiting for small moments of interaction between naps didn't seem worthwhile. Instead, he could check up on the house, make sure bills were paid, and keep Jenna up to date. He could return the next day to say goodbye and head back to Newell and call periodically to check up on Helen thereafter.

Helen closed her eyes again.

"I think I'll get going, Mother. I'll stop by tomorrow. The house is in good shape."

Helen took a few shallow breaths, and then tilted her head up, opened her eyes and looked straight at Simon.

"Look at you. You came out all Portuguese. You ever wonder about that?" she said with an unusually broad smile.

Expecting a simple "thank you" or "good-bye," Simon was caught off guard by the strange comment. "What do you mean?" he asked.

Helen smirked a bit and then reached out with her feeble right hand, which Simon held for a few brief moments. Then she lay her head back down again and Simon left.

The next morning, he came by a couple of hours before his bus was scheduled to leave. Helen was fast asleep. He waited about thirty minutes hoping she would wake up. Instead of disturbing her, he gently stroked her hair, kissed her on the forehead and made his way back to Newell.

71. HELEN'S END

Simon spent three days in Newell completely alone. There were no client appointments over the winter break, and Jenna was still in Oakland. Even his landlady Anna seemed to have gone somewhere. The town was eerily quiet. The solitude suited him, since he needed time to think about his trip to New Bedford, and the stillness of his drab but familiar basement apartment was ideal. He talked to Jenna the day after he arrived. She asked him to visit her place to water the plants.

Curiously, Simon had no desire to play the piano. He worried about his mother. He wondered when the inevitable would happen, and how he might react. He called her one morning. A polite nurse named Maria who had been looking after her told her Helen was sleeping comfortably. Maria also assured Simon that she would let him know when Helen's time was close.

Jenna returned from Oakland and could sense Simon's somber, stressed mood. He wanted to be with her, but he didn't want to talk. Instead, he spent a few hours at her place where they had lunch. Jenna wondered what she could do to help him at such a difficult time.

His only response, "I've got to work through this on my own."

As the spring semester began in January there was no news from New Bedford. Simon threw himself into his work, taking on a considerable load. He met Anuja one day at Jarvis. She could sense something was wrong. After some effort, Anuja pried out Helen's situation from Simon.

"Please just go look after your mother, Simon. What are you doing here anyway? You should be up there."

Simon adamantly refused. Both Anuja and Brian had graciously accommodated his absence during the time of his accident. It would be too much to accept their generosity again. Besides, he told Anuja, work was a useful distraction from the stress he experienced when he thought about his mother. Simon kept trying to reach his mother. Her cell phone was always turned off. He was able to reach Maria on several occasions, but his mother was always sleeping.

"How does she look to you, Maria?" he asked one morning around nine a.m. when Helen ought to have been awake.

"I think her time will come soon, Simon" Maria said in a kind, motherly way.

To get his mind off his mother, Simon forced himself to play the piano. He played a few classical pieces and "Flusso e Reflusso" several times, but this was all unsatisfying. He needed inspiration. He sat on a cold park bench for an hour and watched pigeons and passers-by hoping the experience would trigger something. He spent a day with Jenna at chilly, windy, Virginia Beach hoping the empty beach and crashing waves would illuminate something. Nothing. He was still stuck with "Flusso e Reflusso."

The dreaded call came on January 23rd around nine p.m. It was Maria.

"Good evening, Simon. I'm sorry to tell you that I don't think it will be much longer now. Her breathing is becoming shallow and she's barely conscious. Are you able to come here?"

"As soon as I can."

Simon at first decided to fly to Boston. He packed up his bag again and called Jenna to let her know he was headed north.

"I am coming with you, and we can drive up."

"Jenna, no. It's not going to be a pleasant experience. No need for you to experience that."

"I am coming so that I can be there for you. I don't care about the unpleasant experience." There was no changing Jenna's mind. Instead, she drove most of the night with brief respites when Simon drove and they made it all the way to New Bedford by seven-thirty a.m. They stopped quickly at Helen's house to drop off their things, and despite their exhaustion, went immediately to the hospice. Nurse Maria was not on duty. In her place was a young man who was finishing up the night shift.

"My name's Trevor. I've been looking after your mother for several nights now."

Helen appeared to be sleeping comfortably. Simon leaned over and kissed her forehead.

"She wakes up from time to time, in a bit of a panic, as if she can't breathe. It's happened a few times, and to be honest, I didn't think she would come out of it, but she did. She doesn't sleep for more than an hour at a time," Trevor said.

Simon stayed at Helen's side. Jenna went to buy coffee and some muffins. Around nine a.m., Helen opened up her eyes. She smiled one of her broadest smiles when she saw Simon. She said something, but her voice was so feeble he couldn't hear.

"I love you, Mother."

Helen mouthed, "I love you, too."

Helen put her head back and turned to the right, the most energetic movement she had made in a few days according to Trevor. She saw Jenna for the first time and smiled. She reached out with her hand, which Jenna gently held. She wanted to say something to Jenna, but again, her words were too faint to hear. Jenna leaned down to her and Helen whispered in her ear. Jenna just smiled and stood back.

Jenna whispered to Simon. "I don't know what she said."

Having known Helen for so long and with so much gushing emotion, it was easier for Simon to decipher Helen's message. "She said, 'Take good care of my boy.'"

At ten twenty-one a.m., Helen suddenly started to panic, and her breathing became very shallow. Trevor attached some oxygen prongs to her nose, but Helen found the energy to pull them off. She looked terrified. Simon held her left hand and Jenna her right. She squeezed with considerable force for such a frail woman. The shallow breathing became deeper and less frequent. By ten twenty-four a.m., Helen was gone.

72. AUNT COLLEEN

As one might expect the hospice was highly experienced in all matters related to the deceased. Later that morning, a designated staff member called each of Helen's four younger siblings in Ireland to disclose the news. Helen had an insurance policy with a death benefit which was tapped for the funeral costs. Her bank accounts, credit cards, and all related matters were taken care of. Simon was basically responsible for the house, which Helen had left to him. A hospice staff member helped to organize the funeral.

Simon felt numb. He hadn't grieved his father's death because he was too young to understand what was happening. Jenna did her best to help him. He didn't want gushy expressions of sympathy. He needed someone to be near him, to share coffee, and to respect his silence.

The funeral took place three days later. Simon's uncles and aunt sent flowers and some cards from Ireland. None of them called him. There were just eight attendees including Jenna and Simon—four elderly women Simon didn't recognize but assumed were colleagues who worked with Helen at the library, and a neighbor with whom Helen wasn't especially close and her neighbor's husband. That was the full extent of the social circle of a seventy-six-year-old woman who had lived in New Bedford since she was a teenager. Despite his years attending church as a boy, Simon was unfamiliar with Catholic funeral traditions. He supplied a priest with a few happy details of Helen's life. The priest delivered a simple homily embellishing some of these details. "She was a great lover of libraries and books," he said. Helen was lowered into the ground not next to, but fairly close to Luis' gravesite.

"Simon?" one of the elderly women using a cane called out.

"Yes. Thank you for coming."

"I'm your mother's cousin, Colleen. I live in Medford."

"Thanks for coming all this way," Simon replied.

Jenna was at Simon's side, and he introduced her. "My son

dropped me off here for a few hours. I thought it might be nice for us to chat a bit before he comes back."

"Sure," Simon said, and Jenna nodded. Colleen was the first member of Helen's family Simon had ever met.

"Why don't we go to a nice, warm coffee shop?" Jenna suggested.

"That sounds nice, dear. Nice to get out of the cold," Colleen responded with a broad smile.

Colleen didn't look at all like Helen. She was much shorter, hunched over and somewhat stout. It took some time for her to get into Simon's small car. Jenna drove them to a coffee shop nearby where Simon ordered coffee and biscotti for everyone. Colleen settled into a chair, resting her cane against the side of their table.

"You're the first relative of mother's I've met. I've heard mother talking on the phone a few times to people in Ireland but have never met anyone."

"I'm really glad we got a chance to finally meet, even if it's under these tough circumstances," Colleen said, with a barely discernible Irish accent, much less noticeable than Helen's.

"Did Helen ever mention me?" Colleen asked.

"A few times. I don't recall her visiting you."

"No, she hasn't come to visit me in a long time."

Jenna sat quietly, and Simon held her hand in his under the table.

"Of course, this is actually my first time in New Bedford," Colleen said.

"That's too bad. We would have liked to have you come down for a visit," Simon replied.

"That's very kind of you, Simon. May I ask, do you know how your mother wound up in New Bedford? Did she ever tell you?"

"She ran away, correct? That's what she implied. I don't really know much else. She said many times that she had a difficult family situation and a tough life back in Ireland."

"I see. Well, let me start by saying that the few times I've talked to your mother over the years, she's spoken very highly of you. She always said you were very kind. I can tell that already."

"Thank you, Colleen," Simon responded.

"I'm pretty sure this young lady has a big heart, too," Colleen said as she smiled at Jenna.

Jenna smiled back and pushed closer to Simon leaning against him.

"Would you like to learn your mother's story?" Colleen asked.

"Of course," Simon said, "I would very much like to learn what I can."

Colleen looked over at Jenna, as if seeking her permission to proceed.

"It's fine for Jenna to hear whatever you have to tell me, Colleen," Simon said.

"Okay. Your mother comes from a typical Irish family, five children in all, she being the oldest as you may know already. Her father, James, my mother's brother, owned a small bakery, really just a storefront with an oven in the back, very small. I remember thinking how big everything seemed when I first came to America. I left for America when your mother was thirteen and I was eighteen. I came here to study nursing, but got sidetracked eventually," Colleen said as she smiled.

Jenna noticed her coffee cup was empty and refilled hers as well as Simon's.

"So I didn't witness what happened to Helen firsthand, but she told me in great deal, in bits and pieces, when she showed up at my door a couple of years later."

"Well, she ran away, correct?" Simon asked.

"Yes, she did. My uncle James, Helen's father, brought another man into the bread business about a year after I left. A man named Ray. Uncle James introduced him to the family as *Uncle* Ray. I knew him a little because he was some type of delivery man and stopped by our house once or twice. Helen told me Ray was quite nice at first. He would play football with my younger cousins, but mostly he wanted to spend time with Helen." Jenna put her hand slowly up to her mouth, anticipating that what would come next would be difficult to hear.

"May I ask, how old was Ray at that time?" asked Simon.

"I'm not sure. I think he was a man roughly the same age as my uncle or my mother. I would guess around forty. And your mother was fourteen."

Colleen paused for a long moment, and looked carefully at Simon and Jenna, again as if seeking permission to continue.

73. HELEN'S STORY

"Please go on," Simon urged her.

"Ray told her that he wanted to turn Helen into a 'fine lady.' One day he came to the house with a birthday present, even though her fourteenth birthday had already passed. He dropped it off and left before she opened it. It was a very posh frock from an expensive shop in Dublin. It was nicer than anything she had at the time.

"Helen's mother told her she couldn't keep it. Her father agreed and said that Uncle Ray surely couldn't afford such a thing and that he was being irresponsibly generous. Helen told me she got very upset about this. A nice man had given me a nice gift, why should her mother or father have anything to say about it? Eventually she agreed that after wearing it once or twice, she would give it back to Uncle Ray. If he couldn't return it to the shop, he could sell it somewhere else."

Simon and Jenna listened intently, hanging on Colleen's every word.

"One day, Ray came by Helen's house looking for her father who had gone out to run errands with her mother. Helen was at home babysitting her siblings. Ray asked how she liked the frock. She told him she thought it was beautiful but couldn't keep it and gave it back to him, carefully packed in the box in which it came.

"Ray told her that was disappointing, and asked if she could just wear it once for him. You have to remember that your mother was just fourteen, and naïve. By the time she showed up at my door in Boston she knew how stupid she had been. I might have responded that I didn't want to do that and simply handed him the box, but your mother obliged Ray and changed into the frock. He told her she looked beautiful, said things like 'fits so snug back here' while he patted her bum."

"He sounds awful," Simon said.

"Oh, it got much worse. Ray insisted she keep the frock, that it would be their secret, and that she should come to his place from time to time where she could wear it. This all made my poor cousin very uncomfortable, but Ray was a grown man and her father's business partner. So, she agreed."

Jenna and Simon dreaded what they would hear next. Colleen paused to let them take it all in. "Please continue," Simon said.

"Helen told me that Ray would stop by the house all the time to talk business with my uncle. He and Helen had some sort of hand signal according to her to mean that she ought to come over soon afterwards with the frock. He insisted on this quite often, sometimes three or four times a week. Helen told me it was always the same. She was to change into the frock in front of him. He would tell her she looked like a princess, and then he would fondle her, and he did much more on many occasions. She didn't tell me all the details because every time she started to, it made her cry."

"What a disgusting, perverted man," Simon said. Jenna nodded, and hugged Simon tightly, knowing the pain of losing his mother was made worse by learning about what she had gone through.

"Well, a few months later she became pregnant, and you know how skinny she is. It was hard to hide for very long. She told Ray about it, and he went into a rage. He told her the baby couldn't be his—that she must have fooled around with a boy at school. She did her best to hide it from her mum and dad, but her mum picked up on it soon enough. She told her mum the baby was Ray's. Her mother was skeptical as Ray had always presented himself as a quiet, thoughtful, respectful man. Then Helen made the mistake of telling her father, my uncle James. He was incensed, told her Ray wouldn't do anything like that. Then he beat her badly and threw her out of the house."

"That's awful," Jenna said. She had been content to sit quietly and listen until that point.

"Then what happened?" Simon asked.

"She stayed with friends for a couple of days. Eventually she returned home while her father was working. Her mother told her she couldn't stay there, and that she and her father had made the decision to send her to a Magdalene laundry. Have you heard of those?"

Simon and Jenna both shook their heads no.

"They are vile places run by nuns where supposedly 'wayward' girls are sent to be reformed. In reality, the girls are worked to the bone and the nuns live comfortably at their expense. After a couple of months there she wrote to me in America. I was the only one she could turn to. She asked for help to bribe her way out. I ignored her first letter. Then she wrote again soon after the baby was born—a baby girl, whom she named Charlotte. The nuns whisked the baby away immediately. You have to understand, I didn't have much money myself, but I borrowed some and saved some, and eventually sent her one hundred dollars."

"That was very kind of you Colleen," Simon said.

"Thank you. Only she didn't use the money to bribe her way out. She just escaped somehow, ran away and bought steerage passage to New York. She showed up at my door. I didn't want to take her in at first. She never told me it was her plan to come to America. She had no papers and no job, but one of the passengers gave her money to come to Boston from New York."

"Your mother sounds like she was very resourceful, Simon," Jenna commented.

"Yes, she was a strange mix," Colleen added. "Resourceful sometimes, odd and naïve at other times. Anyway, I got her enrolled in high school and she worked part-time in a bar. I think we just got tired of each other after a while—as much my fault as hers. When she had saved enough money she took off and came down to New Bedford. I wasn't sorry to see her go. I moved to Chicago for a few years soon after."

"That's when she met my dad," Simon said with some certainty.

"Yes. She started working in a bar. I used to hear fairly often from her in those days. She used to call from the pay phone letting me know she was doing okay. She was so young, and I worried about her. I did send her some money from time to time for the first couple of months, but after a while, she told me she no longer needed it."

"It sounds like she would have been completely lost without you, Colleen. You were very kind," Simon said.

"Thank you. I think your dad was quite kind to her, too. They started their relationship not long after she got there. He promised to look out for her always. After a few months, he insisted she quit her job. There were lots of unsavory characters there in the bar who would harass her, and he asked her to look after you full time."

Simon bore a confused look and sat silently for a moment. "After a couple of months? She quit after a few months? You mean, after a few years right? After I was born?"

Jenna nodded to indicate some clarity was needed. Both Simon and Jenna assumed that Colleen, who was eighty-two, had simply misspoke.

Colleen took a long, deep breath. "Simon… she wasn't your mother."

Simon looked more confused. Jenna hugged him tightly. They both waited anxiously to hear what Colleen had to say next. She just smiled and gave them both some time to take it all in.

"What do you mean? Who else would she be?"

"She first met you when you were three years old, Simon."

Simon looked down and sighed.

"A few minutes ago, I thought I might have a half-sister named Charlotte somewhere in Ireland that I could try to find. Are you certain?"

"I'm absolutely certain, Simon. I'm so sorry. Your father was a widower trying to raise a young child on his own. I think Helen filled a need for him and for you."

Simon turned to Jenna. "I guess I've been an orphan for most of my life, then."

Jenna, as shocked as Simon, said nothing, just held him tightly.

"What happened to my mother?" Simon asked in a faint voice which was all he could muster at that point.

"Well, I don't know all the details Simon. I actually never met your father. I talked to Helen on the phone a few times in the early years and we even met once when she came to Boston for the weekend, so I can only go by what she knew and what she told me. My understanding is that your actual mother died not long after giving birth to you. Some kind of terrible complication. I do know that her name was Patricia, and that she is buried not far from your father."

A long silence followed. All three seemed perfectly comfortable with it. Simon began to think about all the implications. The cold, distant woman whose capacity for affection seemed so limited was not who he thought she was.

Colleen broke the silence. "Now, let's make it clear. Your

father and Helen were married about a year after she came to New Bedford. And you were officially adopted. So, she was your mother." These facts did nothing to quell the intense emotions of sadness and confusion Simon felt.

More silence. The coffee was gone. "May I ask, Colleen, what made you tell me all this now?"

"I came to visit Helen a few weeks ago. She asked me to tell you after she passed."

"Why?"

"I don't have an answer to that. She was ill and frail and asked me to do something. I didn't feel like probing her. Maybe she just didn't know how to tell you herself. You know how closed off she was."

Simon nodded.

After a few more silent minutes, Simon and Jenna drove Colleen back to the cemetery where her son was waiting in the parking lot. They both gave her a gentle hug and promises to remain in touch, and she was off.

Jenna and Simon found the grave of Patricia Anna Galves, 1952—1972 right next to Luis's grave. The headstone was simple and small, quite a bit smaller than Luis's with her name and dates only. Simon knelt on the cold, moist ground and touched it, unsure of what or how he might feel. Then he broke down, sobbing uncontrollably, frantically trying to wipe away tears with his coat sleeve. Jenna knelt next to him and rested her head on his shoulder. Seeing the man she loved in so much pain brought tears to her eyes as well. It was Simon who regained his composure first.

"I don't know why this hurts so much, Jenna."

"Oh, Simon, it's supposed to hurt. You've lost three parents, and two just now." Jenna's observation wasn't intended to be clever, but Simon smiled and kissed her.

74. HOUSE MATTERS

A cold rain began, so Simon and Jenna didn't linger long at the cemetery. They headed back to Helen's house and sat on the drab couch in the living room, the same one Simon had grown up with, the one on which his father died in his sleep.

"Tell me what you're feeling," Jenna said.

Simon sighed and took a moment to provide a thoughtful, earnest answer. "Maybe it makes sense."

"What do you mean?"

"She was so cold so much of the time. I used to come across other people's mothers, not often, because I didn't have a lot of friends growing up, but they were nothing like that. Take your mother. She told me I was part of your family just after meeting her."

"I've been lucky to have a mother and a father that are warm like that. Why do you say it makes sense?"

"I wasn't her kid, Jenna. There wasn't that kind of bond, and she wasn't the kind of person who could create it, or even pretend that it was there."

"I understand. It must have been very hard on you. And I also understand why she wouldn't have told you while you were growing up. What little boy wants to know that his real mother and father are dead."

"I get that."

"You know she might have been a bit resentful too. She had to give away her own baby girl. Then she came from Ireland, got involved with this guy, married him, and he died and left her to raise a little boy who wasn't hers."

Simon wrapped an arm around Jenna. "Yeah, there were some angry moments from her for sure."

Simon's numbness faded throughout the day, and he gradually became more talkative. A stressful month of anxiously waiting for Helen's death had come to an end, and he did feel that a burden had been lifted. He even started reviewing client manuscripts that evening for fear of falling behind. Jenna wasn't exactly sure how to be supportive as Simon tried to re-engage with normal life. She came up with an idea just before they settled into bed that evening.

"When do you want to head back?"

"We could go late tomorrow. I need to see a lawyer about the title to the house and maybe a real estate agent, but we could go after that."

"You're going to sell it right away?"

"Yes, what would I do with it?"

"I know, but don't you have great memories of growing up here?"

"I have memories, not sure how great they are."

"I don't know, Simon. You shouldn't let go of your past so easily if you have a choice. Do you like coming back to New Bedford?"

"It's nostalgic for me. So is this house. Maybe you're right. It means a lot to me."

"You should hang on to it for a while. You can even rent it out. I have an idea. Why don't you take me to all the places you enjoyed going as a boy? Your school, wherever. Sort of like I did with you in Oakland."

"You would enjoy that?"

"I would. And I think it would be good for you. It will help you to think of your life here and your mother fondly."

The next day Jenna and Simon did exactly that. They were a bit rushed because Simon still wanted to leave for Newell that evening. They went to his old high school and to the public library. Simon pointed out the table by a window where Mia used to sit. They went to the grocery store where he worked. They had lunch at Pa Raffa's. They would even have driven up to Bridgewater State, but they didn't have time.

"I have the house papers. This shouldn't be complicated, but we need to find a lawyer."

75. A CALL TO ENZO

Nostalgia was the theme for the day and Simon decided early on to visit Carpetta Law in downtown New Bedford.

"I need some help with a title transfer for my mother's house. She recently passed away," he said to a young woman who greeted him in a reception area.

"Sorry to hear about your mother. We can help you with that."

"Is Mr. Carpetta here?"

"I beg your pardon?"

"Mr. Carpetta. Is he in today?"

"Sir, Mr. Carpetta passed away in 2015. He does have a brother who handles real estate matters for the firm sometimes, but he is largely retired."

Simon apologized for his confusion. He had forgotten that Carpetta Law was actually Philip Carpetta's firm.

"May I speak with Enzo Carpetta then?" The young lady was surprised that Simon knew Philip's brother's name.

"You can. He doesn't come to the office, but he is reachable by phone."

Simon called Enzo immediately. His voice sounded hoarse.

"Mr. Carpetta. Simon Galves. Do you remember me by any chance?"

"How about you give me a few more clues so I don't embarrass myself," Enzo said.

"I'm Helen Galves' son. The lady from the library."

"Of course. The science fiction fan. How are you, young man?"

"Not so young. My mother passed away a few days ago."

"Oh, so sorry, Simon. I had no idea. I have nice memories of the time I spent with her."

"Thank you for saying that, Enzo. I'm calling about a related business matter. Just a transfer of the house title. Are you able to take care of that?"

"Well, I'm an old man who has trouble getting around. I will call the office, and someone will take care of it right away for you. Also, I will make sure they won't charge you a dime."

"I'm willing to pay."

"You are not paying. You are the son of an old friend. I would feel guilty charging. May I ask, what happened to Helen?"

"Cancer of the ovaries."

"That's terrible, Simon. I'm so sorry for you. May I ask you another perhaps more personal question?"

"Of course. I had trouble connecting with your mother and I ended the relationship. We were only together a short time. Did she mention me afterwards?"

Simon didn't expect such a question after so many years. He provided a diplomatic response. "I wasn't around her that much as I got older. I know she thought very highly of you. Spoke highly of you. Thought you were a real gentleman."

"Thank you, Simon. I wish I could help you today myself, but it will literally take me a couple of hours to get into the office to do something that will take twenty minutes."

"I understand, Enzo," Simon responded.

Simon settled his business quickly. After carefully considering Jenna's advice, Simon decided he would rent out rather than sell the house. Melinda, a young lawyer at Carpetta Law, not only completed the title transfer but connected Simon to a reliable property management company which would take care of everything, including finding a suitable tenant in a few months once the house was emptied. As per Enzo's instructions, she refused to accept a penny.

Simon and Jenna spent most of the day at the house. There were still many unresolved matters, including selling Helen's furniture and other items, which weren't worth much. Simon knew he would have to return at least once to take care of things. "I just want to spend a little time here, since things will never be the same again," Simon told Jenna. She not only respected his wishes but completed a few basic tasks such as turning down the thermostat, tidying up, and making sure all the windows were locked.

At some point Simon wandered into Helen's room. It has always been her very private refuge. Even as a child, her door was often closed, and Simon would knock politely before asking if he could come in. She kept it very tidy, and it remained so even as she entered hospice. On her nightstand was an old purse which she hadn't used for some time and a pair of reading glasses. Next to the glasses was a folded piece of paper on top of an envelope. Given how immaculate Helen's bedroom was, the paper seemed a bit out of place and Simon was immediately curious.

The envelope had edges which had turned brown. It was addressed to Helen and in the upper left was a stamped address for "Attorney Enzo Carpetta." The folded paper was a letter in elegant handwriting in blue ink. Simon thought for a few moments about whether to read it or not—though his mother was gone, he would be violating Enzo's privacy. From a strictly legal standpoint, of course, the house and its contents belonged to him. He took the letter downstairs.

"A letter from Enzo to my mother. Found it on her nightstand," he told Jenna.

"From when?"

"It's dated February 4, 1996. A few months after they broke up, I believe."

"Are you going to read it?" Jenna asked.

"I was going to ask you if I should. Enzo is still alive. He still wonders what Mother thought about him."

"From what I've learned about him from you, he seems like a wonderful man, Simon," Jenna said.

"He is."

"I think you should read it. She left it on the nightstand. She must have known you'd find it. She wanted her cousin to tell you her story. Maybe she left the letter on purpose for you to learn something about her and Enzo."

Simon nodded. He and Jenna read the letter together:

Dear Helen:

    I have apologized once for leaving abruptly but allow me to do so again. Let me also apologize for making you uncomfortable last month. I didn't mean to pry into your past. You have mentioned that you had a tough time before you came to America. Though I don't know your story, I am deeply sympathetic. I know it is easier for me to express my feelings in this letter, and perhaps also for you to hear about them on paper.

    As you know, my wife Nina died when the girls were still little. She had been the love of my life. We met while I was in law school, and she was studying accounting. You remind me of her in so many ways. Nina was quiet, reserved, and it took a lot for me to get close to her. In the end it was a matter of perseverance. She told me quite a few times that she wasn't sure what to do with my attention—that she didn't think she deserved it, and that she feared I would go on to find someone better. All this made her seem very vulnerable to me, and that drew me even closer. We became inseparable and marriage and our two daughters came along in short order. But I didn't write this letter to tell you how much I loved Nina, nor about the sorrow I felt watching her suffer

216

and die—My girls would curl up with me in bed and the three of us would cry together. This letter is about you—how much you're like someone I loved so deeply. If I could fall in love again, I think it could be with you.

I was angry, Helen, because you hurt me. You didn't seem concerned when I needed you to be concerned. But the anger has subsided. I had been quite smitten with Erin but no longer. We still enjoy each other's company as friends. It's you I want, and I want a second chance.

Affectionately,
Enzo

"Holy smokes!" Jenna exclaimed as she finished reading a few seconds before Simon.

"I had no idea he wanted her back. She said nothing about this. She seemed really sad after the breakup," Simon said.

"Why wouldn't she respond to the letter, Simon?"

Simon shook his head. "I suppose a letter is one thing. She would still have to connect with him emotionally. Maybe she felt she couldn't do that. I really don't know." Simon returned the letter to its envelope. He looked through the nightstand drawer for additional letters. There were none.

Simon and Jenna left New Bedford around six p.m., planning to spend a night in New Jersey before arriving in Newell the following afternoon. Simon was still subdued and looked fatigued, so Jenna did all the driving. Newell was cold and wet as it often is in January.

"What now, my dear?" Jenna asked.

"I'm really tired. Aren't you?"

"Yes indeed."

"I'm going to drop you off at your place, and then I am going to get some rest. We can connect tomorrow okay?"

"That's fine. I'm going to have an early night myself."

76. A Night at the Piano

Simon found his apartment once again strangely comforting. He took a hot shower, ate a sandwich he had bought at a rest stop on the way back, and was in bed by seven thirty p.m. Instead of falling asleep, he lay on his back staring up at the ceiling, for a time trying to determine if there were any interesting patterns in the ceiling tiles. He heard footsteps upstairs, which was unusual since Anna was so quiet. He thought about whether he would ever mention to her that his mother had died if he had the chance, but decided, *That woman has no interest in my grief.*

Jenna texted around eight p.m.: "Are you okay?" to which he replied, "Fine, going to bed, love you, see you tomorrow."

He woke up quite suddenly around three a.m. His scalp tingled, followed by some tingling in his hands as well. He dreaded having another seizure, but the tingling gradually subsided. He felt very alert and sat up. Simon assumed as he had gone to bed so early he had already obtained a decent amount of sleep, but mumbled to himself, "What am I supposed to do at this time of night?"

He got up and sat at his desk for several minutes. He had eight manuscripts to review for the week and began reading the first. Something didn't feel quite right. He was getting through it as usual. It was dismally written, and the flaws were obvious and easy to point out. He was drawn to the piano for the first time in a couple of weeks. He resisted the urge to play, determined to provide feedback on the entire manuscript before doing anything else. "If I'm up at three in the morning, I should do something productive rather than messing around on the piano," he mumbled. Once he had made his comments and suggested edits along with a couple of reading assignments for the young woman whose paper on disappearing forest habitats he had just reviewed, Simon prepared a cup of coffee. He sat on his piano bench and lit the candle he hoped would bring inspiration before he had left for his trip to New Bedford.

Simon began to play, spontaneously, passionately, mellifluously on and on. He wasn't sure where the music came from. A part of his mind and his fingers felt disconnected from the rest of him. At some point he felt like an audience member in his own concert. He was even able to think about other things, such as the manuscript he had just reviewed, while he was playing. The phenomenon would have been frightening if it were not so enjoyable. He threw himself into the music with broad hand gestures, swaying close to and away from the piano with each crescendo and decrescendo. He finally stopped playing after an entire hour. He sat back and closed his eyes. He felt very relaxed and absolutely delighted that he had come up with something new.

"I don't know what that was, but I think it sounded pretty good," he thought to himself. He tried to analyze the music that had just come out of him. It was contemporary music, full of tones which were at times melancholy, at times suspenseful, and at times hopeful, though never quite cheerful. There were clear transitions in the music Simon himself didn't really understand. At times the melancholic tones ended abruptly, and the next part sounded like a sprightly gallop. He had never played any piece that lengthy or complex. He showered, had another cup of coffee, and drove the short distance to Jarvis to meet his first client at nine a.m.

Jenna called him while he was on his way. "Good morning, my dear. How do you feel?" she asked.

"Pretty good. Slept well but only part of the night. How are you?"

"I slept pretty well, the whole night," Jenna said.

"I woke up in the middle of the night and started playing again. Something totally original. I think it's pretty good."

"Wonderful. I can't wait to hear it. You doing okay besides that?"

"I guess. Mother's been on my mind a lot as you might imagine. Just processing all she went through and all that she and I went through together."

"That's only natural, Simon. You miss her, even if you didn't spend much time together."

"I wish we had more time together," Simon said, sadly.

77. NOCTURNES FOR HELEN

Despite his alertness in the morning, all the nighttime playing made for a tough day at Jarvis for Simon. He felt like he could fall asleep at any time. One of his clients, Carl, an engineering graduate student even commented, "You look really tired, Mr. Galves. We can stop and meet some other time if you would rather." Simon ploughed ahead. Both his mother and his music were on his mind constantly. He wrapped up around four p.m. and headed home. The plan was to meet Jenna around six. He lay on the couch, planning, optimistically, to get a little rest by shutting his eyes for a few minutes. His phone rang sometime later.

"Are you okay? It's after seven. I thought you were coming over."

"I'm so sorry sweetheart. I fell asleep on the couch."

"I was worried you had a fall or something."

"No, no, just a bit exhausted."

"Tell you what. I'll pick up dinner somewhere and come to your place. Sound good?"

"Okay, sure." Simon had always prided himself on being punctual and reliable, so it was discouraging that he had succumbed to fatigue. Jenna drove over a few minutes later.

"I got us calzones. Sound good?"

"Sure. Come on in."

"You do look tired. I'm glad you didn't make it over to my place."

"I'm fine. Just a long day, plus the piano last night."

"About that. After we eat you can tell me what you came up with."

Around nine, Simon sat at the piano while Jenna sat on a chair next to him. He started his lengthy and complex composition. His execution was flawless. He played it exactly the same way he did before. Jenna expected a pause or a break at certain points. Instead Simon played the entire thing, finally ending with a deep, dark minor chord, closing his eyes, leaning back, and resting his hands on his legs.

"Wow. That's all I can say. That was so beautiful, even on this old piano."

"Thank you."

"So much better than 'Flusso e Reflusso.' How did you come up with all that?" Jenna asked.

"I don't think I really came up with it. It just came out of me last night. It wasn't a deliberate process."

"You're not struggling to find inspiration any longer that's for sure."

"I suppose I'm not."

"What do you think brought all this out of you?"

"After you called, I thought about the answer, the source of inspiration. No question, it was my mother."

"That makes perfect sense. Obviously, she's been on your mind a lot. But how did she inspire you to create that?"

"I haven't figured it all out yet, but I think the piece is about her, her life, my relationship to her, and her end as well. I've not just been thinking about how much I miss her. I've been thinking of how she lived and how she died. I've got some wine in the kitchen. Care to join me?"

"Of course. We should transcribe it, give it a name. You should play it at the Newell Music Festival in May." Simon didn't say anything in response. "What? Not a good idea?" Jenna asked.

"I don't know Jenna. It's so private. So emotional for me. I played it because it helped me cope with all the emotions I'm experiencing. Not sure how I feel about sharing it."

"I understand. But we should at least transcribe it. That way it won't be forgotten. What a wonderful way to preserve the memory of your mother."

"That much, I think we can do."

Determined to mitigate his fatigue and complete his work efficiently, Simon limited his playing for the days that followed to his new composition. Still quiet and somber but less tired, he made it to the weekend when he and Jenna planned the laborious process of transcribing what he had played. As before, Jenna's vast experience and talent as well as her great ear were indispensable. Many composition books were filled, tossed out, and refilled. By Monday morning, the work was done to both Jenna's and Simon's satisfaction. They had divided the piece into four parts.

"You need a name, Simon."

"I guess Helen's song?"

"It's not really a song. It's much more than that. It's dark, it's rough, it's hopeful all at different points. The four parts are so different from each other. Calling it a song doesn't do it justice."

Simon had spent no time to that point on a title. Weary from all the work, despite all the creative juices that had flowed since his mother's passing, he came up with nothing.

"'Nocturnes for Helen,' that's what I think," Jenna said.

"I've seen the term before. I've even played a few nocturnes. What are they exactly?"

"Basically, a musical composition that is inspired by the night. I think it's appropriate. You came up with them at night. We transcribed most of the music at night. Night implies darkness, and there was plenty of that in Helen's life from what we've learned."

"Oh yeah, I like it. Better than Helen's song for sure. I wonder if I'll ever find that kind of inspiration again."

"If you don't, no matter. You've created something beautiful. I really wish you would share it. Maybe start small. Share it with Anuja and her family. Maybe my parents by video chat. See if it moves them. I certainly felt like I understood your mother a lot better after hearing it."

"I'll think about it," Simon responded.

EPILOGUE

Early spring was uneventful for Simon and Jenna. There were no seizures nor any falls. He felt in most ways quite normal. The acute period of grieving gave way to thinking of Helen fondly, especially when he played "Nocturnes for Helen," which he did at least three or four times a week. Jenna played the "Nocturnes" as well, with a bit more flair and precision. But of course, every piece of music sounded better in her hands.

Jenna eventually coaxed reluctant Simon to perform at the Newell Music Festival. He wasn't a featured performer. He performed the "Nocturnes" to a crowd of roughly fifteen in the Music Building during a time reserved for faculty and staff performances. By this point he had added a number of new touches to the "Nocturnes," a bit more drama and less subtlety. He also made a conscious effort to convey the emotion of the piece through his hand gestures and the sway of his body. The reaction was muted, but Simon wasn't troubled. Who knew what the small audience was expecting after all? It would be Simon's last performance for some time.

Once his lease expired, Simon said goodbye to his dingy basement apartment and to Anna, who was genuinely sorry to see such an upstanding tenant leave. He moved in with Jenna, which had always sort of been the plan in the back of both of their minds. They settled into a nice, predictable, serene life in Newell. Simon gradually lost his fear of yet-to-manifest consequences of his accident. Dr. Delarosa evaluated him carefully a number of times in collaboration with a well-respected physical therapist in town. Simon's walking and overall mobility were declared nearly normal. He had no fear of falling and even felt comfortable taking a hike with Jenna along the Appalachian Trail one weekend. He did, however, develop a powerful phobia to thunderstorms which frequently bombarded Newell in late spring and summer. He would stay somewhere safely indoors, as far away from any potential electrical conductors, until a storm passed.

Dr. Delarosa told Simon he was unlikely to experience further seizures though she insisted he continue the anti-seizure medications for at least one year. A follow-up scan of his brain didn't reveal any new changes. This was a huge relief for Simon and Jenna, who felt they could go on to plan a healthy life together.

That fall Jenna and Simon were engaged. As it was the first year of the pandemic, the wedding, to be held in hard-hit Oakland, had to be postponed to a still-to-be-decided future date. Neither Simon nor Jenna was too troubled. Their bond was strong. Among the shuttered shops and masked faces of Newell, Simon looked for inspiration, determined to add something new to his limited repertoire. In November, he went to New Bedford and wandered familiar streets. With permission from his tenant, he spent a couple of hours in his old house, all in search of some new inspiration from something old and comforting. Nothing came to him.

In Newell, Simon would spend an hour each day completely alone somewhere pleasant and tranquil like the steps of the Music Building or a small park near his old apartment. He would sit and contemplate the many contours of his life to that point—the death of his father, his sequestered childhood, his poverty, his mother's solemn character, his loneliness, and later the rapid illumination of the darkness of his mind and the opening of his heart. After the hour was up, Simon would return quickly to the present, think about Jenna, and unlike in his earlier years, look forward to the years ahead.

About the Author

Goutham Rao is a practicing family physician, researcher in cardiovascular prevention, endowed professor of medicine at Case Western Reserve University, and author of more than a hundred publications, including six books. He has taught writing skills to physicians and other health care professionals for more than twenty years. Within a large health care system, Dr. Rao is responsible for promoting wellness and preventing burnout among physicians. During the height of the pandemic, he personally found creative writing therapeutic and started and leads a group called "Words for Wellness," which brings together health care professionals to discover the value of writing as both a creative outlet and a means to promote wellness. Dr. Rao grew up in Halifax, Nova Scotia, and lives outside Cleveland.

www.ingramcontent.com/pod-product-compliance
Lightning Source LLC
Chambersburg PA
CBHW011348010726
47493CB00011B/3002